BOOKS IN THE NARROWAY TRILOGY

RHIANNON WILLIAMS

BOOK THREE *of* THE NARROWAY TRILOGY

Ottilie Colter
AND THE
Withering World

Hardie Grant

EGMONT

Ottilie Colter and the Withering World
first published in 2020 by
Hardie Grant Egmont
Ground Floor, Building 1, 658 Church Street
Richmond, Victoria 3121, Australia
www.hardiegrantegmont.com

 A catalogue record for this
book is available from the
National Library of Australia

Text copyright © 2020 Rhiannon Williams
Design copyright © 2020 Hardie Grant Egmont
Cover illustration by Maike Plenzke
Cover design by Jess Cruickshank

Printed in Australia by Griffin Press, part of Ovato, an Accredited
ISO AS/NZS 14001 Environmental Management System printer.

1 3 5 7 9 10 8 6 4 2

The paper this book is printed on is certified against the
Forest Stewardship Council® Standards. Griffin Press holds
FSC® chain of custody certification SGS-COC-005088. FSC®
promotes environmentally responsible, socially beneficial and
economically viable management of the world's forests.

*For family
& the furry things.*

1

The Oyster Thief

Seven years ago ...

Scoot heard the crunch and tap of steel-tipped boots. He scaled the wall and curled into a crevice just as two men appeared below. The Wikric Watch were searching the slum tunnels.

'Come out, little girl. We're not going to hurt you.'

Scoot knew who they were looking for. Only minutes ago, he'd seen a mischievous shadow slip through a gap in the tunnel wall.

'Pearls are for princesses, my dear — not *mud mites*. Just hand them over and you can be on your way.'

The watchmen would reach the girl's hiding spot at any moment. They might march right by, but just in case, Scoot grabbed his slingshot and flung a stone in the opposite direction. It tinkled as it bounced. They paused to consider the sound before gripping their swords and hurrying away.

Grinning, Scoot leapt to the ground. Considering he'd helped the thief, he decided to argue for a pearl or two for himself.

He was just inching through the gap in the wall when he heard voices from within.

'Not to worry, they've moved on.'

Scoot peered through into an alcove. At first it was too dark to see, but then a veiled, greenish light appeared. A man with a pointed black beard had drawn something from inside his blue coat. It was a tinted glass jar with, Scoot assumed, glow sticks inside. He had seen them before, peddled by merchants from the Brakkerswamp further up the river. In his other hand, the man gripped a cane. From what Scoot could see, he wasn't putting any real weight on it. Merely decorative then. That said only one thing – money.

Facing him, shoulders squared, was a girl with dark blonde hair. A small wooden chest sat at her feet and a net bag hung from her shoulder, containing what looked like a fat wheel of cheese. She narrowed her eyes. 'What do you want?'

'To tell you about a job,' said the man.

'Why?'

'Because, you're young, and' – he tapped the wooden chest with his cane – 'on the run.'

'I am not. It's just some cheese and oysters. They'll stop chasing soon.'

'Pearls,' said the man.

'Oysters – ranky old sea bugs.' She opened the chest and plucked out a dark shell, sticking out her tongue as she did so.

The man shifted his glow sticks, splashing light across an ancient painting on the wall. Faded marking caught Scoot's eye. It was an old painting: a girl with long hair holding something to her lips. Her stance was familiar, like the old piper who played by the river dock at dusk.

The man was examining the oysters. 'From the pearl farms in Sunken Sweep, are they not?'

Scoot had heard about oysters from Sunken Sweep. The merchants said there were mystics in the south that could sense which ones had pearls and which ones didn't before you opened them.

With spidery fingers and a sharp silver knife, the man pried the shells apart and scraped at the flesh. The girl uttered a squeak of surprise. It was hard for Scoot to see, but he imagined a tiny full moon resting in a slug-like nest.

'Not to worry. There's a job. You'll have to go far away, but room and board are provided. It's hard work, Isla, but better, I can assure you, than what awaits you if you're caught.'

The girl stepped closer and demanded, 'How do you know my name?'

'It's your decision, of course, but I urge you to consider it. The recruiters will be in the Malefic Markets until sundown – just look for the man with the duck-feather cap.'

'Skip,' said the girl. 'My name is Skip, actually.'

This name, the man clearly had not known. 'Skip?'

'From Skipper. My family name.'

'Indeed?' With a small smile, he swivelled to depart.

Scoot had to move. He slid out of the gap and up the wall, scrambling back into the crevice. Waiting, he wondered at what he had heard. A job? A job someone his age could do? Should he go too? A bed was tempting. Food, even more so. But Scoot had learned early on never to trust anyone who offered to take you away.

By the time he risked returning, there was no sign of the girl or the wheel of cheese. There was, however, the chest of oysters. She had clearly decided she did not need them.

Scoot whipped out a snail fork. Suspecting it would be an excellent tool for picking locks, he had snatched it

from a lady's picnic basket. He considered it a favour —
now she would have an excuse not to eat snails.

Scoot pried open each oyster and filled his pockets
with pearls. There were enough to keep him fed for a
long, long time. He could even barter himself a nice
place to sleep.

He had already forgotten her name, but Scoot silently
thanked the thief and the man with the cane. This was
going to be a very good year.

2

Nightmare

Something heavy dropped onto Ottilie's bed.

Pictures whirled. Shoulder blades pressing up, making white fur roll. Black fangs dripping. Two knives spinning in her own small hands.

The room barely had time to form before she rolled onto the floor, scrambling for the blade she kept beneath the bed.

A familiar laugh cracked in the dark.

Blinking, Ottilie dropped the knife, crawled back onto the bed and shoved Gully off the other side. 'You are the *worst*!'

Her brother was still laughing.

She squinted at the shuttered windows — there was no light shining through the cracks.

'What are you doing here in the middle of the night?' Shock subsiding, Ottilie realised just how tired she was, and sore, too – she was stiff from a nasty fall in yesterday's hunt and the hard floor had done nothing to help it. But she was used to it. It was one of the more minor hazards of monster hunting. Ottilie and her friends were Narroway huntsmen. Dredretches, the brutal beasts they battled, threatened far worse than bruising and tight muscles.

'Stop laughing!' But she didn't really want him to. She couldn't remember the last time she had heard Gully laugh like that. Sinking some glow sticks into the jar of water by her bed, she watched him clutching his ribs with his thumbless left hand.

'It's nearly dawn.' He climbed onto the bed. 'I've got a hunt, but I wanted to say happy birthday first.'

He was right. It was the twenty-second day of summer. Back in the Brakkerswamp, Old Moss and Mr Parch, the elderly squatters who slept in the tunnel outside her hollow, had always celebrated her birthday on exactly this day.

But she had forgotten, and it was no wonder. There were too many miserable things soaking up her thoughts. What did turning fourteen really matter when her friends were in danger – even more danger than usual? Scoot was frozen in stone and Bill was missing, held captive by the witch, Whistler. She was lurking in some shadowy corner of the Narroway, no doubt readying for another attack. A birthday was such an ordinary thing, out of place at a dreadful time like this.

Gully pinned her with a hug. 'You never remember!'

'Lucky you always do,' she wheezed, peeling him off so she could breathe. 'Who are you hunting with?' She tried to keep her voice casual. It had become a habitual question. She liked to know – to be sure he was with people who would look out for him.

When Ottilie first arrived from the Usklers, she had thought the Narroway was dangerous. She could never have imagined it would get so much worse. The Narroway was like an arm connecting the Usklers to the ruined, dredretch-infested Laklands – and it, too, was plagued with monsters. The Hunt once believed the dredretches spilled over from the Laklands, but Whistler had revealed that wasn't the case.

She had fooled them. Whistler had summoned the Narroway dredretches herself, covertly raising an army and waiting for her moment to strike.

The Laklands were the perfect cover. No-one had searched for a culprit, a cause for the infestation in the Narroway, and Whistler had been able to pose as the Hunt's head bone singer without a lick of suspicion. It was all part of her vengeful scheme to punish their king, Varrio Sol, for some unknown crime.

Over a month ago, Whistler had made her first move. She unleashed her army upon the Hunt's westmost station – Fort Richter. She'd been in hiding since that defeat, but they knew she wasn't gone. It was only a matter of time before she made her next move, and whenever Gully had a shift beyond the boundary walls Ottilie felt more anxious than ever that he would not return.

Gully screwed up his face, trying to remember who he was rostered with. 'Fawn and Horst – I think.'

'That's all?' Ottilie frowned. She'd have preferred a larger group.

'And Ned.'

Her shoulders settled. Of course Ned would be there. They weren't fledglings anymore. They were second-tier huntsmen now, with no need for guardians to guide the way. Even so, the former guardian and fledge were almost always grouped together for hunts and patrols. Ottilie had a feeling that it was Ned's doing. Being a fourth-tier elite, he could make requests like that.

The bells tolled and Gully jumped. 'I have to go get ready!' He lunged across the bed and pressed his forehead to hers. 'Happy birthday,' he whispered, before hurrying out the door.

Ottilie fished the glow sticks from the jar and flopped back onto her pillow. A pale rectangle now framed the darkened shutters. She would be hunting later and wondered what the weather had in store for her. If it rained she might get a rest. Dredretches sought shelter in the rain. It was too pure, too clean for them.

She considered having a look outside, but couldn't face propping up her bones. She was just about to slip beneath the covers and enjoy what time she had left in her safe little haven when someone knocked on the door. It was probably her friend Preddy. Leo, her former guardian, never bothered to knock. Neither did Scoot. She scrunched her eyes shut. Thoughts like that always shook her – it was like forgetting to duck beneath a familiar branch.

Ottilie rolled out of bed, wincing as she put weight on her stiff leg. 'It's unlocked,' she croaked, crossing the room.

The door opened. Surprise heated her face and she managed what she hoped was not a nervous smile at the sight of Ned in her doorway.

'Gully's gone to get dressed.' She kept her voice low so as not to wake any sleeping second-tiers in the rooms nearby. Her eyes flicked to Scoot's empty bedchamber, just beside hers. There had been talk of Preddy moving in, but he hadn't been able to bring himself to do it. Scoot would have joked that it was because Preddy didn't want to give up his fancy room on the elites' floor, but Ottilie knew that wasn't the case. Preddy wanted to keep it for Scoot.

She twisted out of her thoughts. Ned was looking confused.

'You're not looking for Gully?' she said. 'I thought that's why you …'

He smiled. 'I came to see you.'

She didn't know what to make of it. Ned was pale and heavy-eyed, but that was a common look nowadays. They were all trapped in this calm before the inevitable storm. It was a nightmare with no sign of dawn to burn it back, and it marked them all with curved shoulders, weary faces and injuries. Their wounds, bruises and blood, once badges of honour that told tales of high scores, were now evidence of escapes – and promises of worse to come.

'I ran into Gully. That's how I knew you were awake,' said Ned. 'I just wanted to say happy birthday.'

Ottilie felt a strange bobbing and tipping, as if her heart were floating on water. She thought she should say something. *Thank you* seemed the obvious choice, but the words got lost somewhere as Ned stepped towards her and pressed a swift kiss to her cheek.

Her eyes slipped closed and then opened again as he stepped back. She didn't know what to do or say.

Reaching for something, anything, to break the silence, her gaze caught the lowest of the three burns along his forearm. The wound was swollen and bruised around the edges. It surely should have been healed by now. Without thinking, Ottilie took his hand and held his arm to the lantern light, all awkwardness forgotten.

'*Ned* …'

His hand twitched in her grip, but he didn't pull away. 'It's all right,' he said. 'I've had it checked in the infirmary. The patchies say the branding iron might have been laced with something. They're keeping an eye on it.'

'Does it hurt?'

His eyes darted to the side. 'Sometimes.'

'You don't look very well.'

'Trouble sleeping.'

Ottilie imagined most people were having difficulty sleeping since the battle at Richter. Whistler's silence was making it worse. She couldn't help but worry that the witch was staying away because she was planning something even more devastating than her attack on their western fort.

There was nothing anyone could do about it. They had been seeking her; the witching shifts that had been introduced to hunt down Gracie Moravec all those months ago were now refocused on the hunt for Whistler. But she had vanished. It felt hopeless. Ottilie was sure they would not find Whistler until she wanted to be found.

'I'm having a lot of dreams,' Ned added.

Something in his face made her ask, 'What kind of dreams?'

He pulled his arm free. 'Doesn't matter.' There was an edge to his voice. Face softening, he said, 'Happy birthday,' offered a tired smile, and headed down the corridor.

The burns were Whistler's doing. That's what Ned had told them. On the day Whistler revealed herself, Gracie and her wylers had attacked Ned, Gully and Scoot. Gracie dragged Ned to the canyon caves and Whistler had been there, waiting. Bill had been led in and out. Ned couldn't remember a whole lot after that, or perhaps he just didn't care to talk about it. Ottilie and Leo had rescued him before they joined the battle at Richter. She could still see him slumped against the ruined well, barely able to stand.

The thought of it made Ottilie's blood boil, and the fact that Bill was still Whistler's captive turned her stomach. She'd wanted to go back for him – she'd planned to search the canyon caves, but her friend Maeve had insisted on scouting first. Maeve was a fiorn – she could take on the form of an owl, which made her a far stealthier scout than Ottilie. The caves were abandoned, she said. Whistler and Gracie were nowhere to be found.

What did Whistler want with Bill? He was a goedl, a rare and ancient creature with a world of knowledge swimming in his skull; what would Whistler use him for? What was she planning for them all?

3

The Devil-Slayers

Navigating the morning mist was like passing through a world of memory. Time seemed to fold back like scrunched fabric, moments overlapping. Ottilie could see a shape at the cliff's edge – the rock where Leo had first told her about wingerslinks, the great winged felines that occupied the lower grounds.

The drop wasn't visible, the cliff stairs drowned in sunlit silver, but she could see them all the same. She remembered leaping down the stairs and sprinting for the wingerslink sanctuary after Whistler had snatched Bill.

Gracie had been out there that day. Ottilie could see her draw those familiar knives. She could still hear her quiet command: 'Take her brother.' She saw the wylers leap and the blood trickle down Gully's fingers. In her mind the drips hit the dirt like a drum beat.

She sensed movement and turned to see Skip marching across the clover field, wearing her hunting uniform like a second skin. It had only been one month since Skip was presented with it. Just a month, and already Ottilie could barely summon the image of the sculkie she had met in the springs.

When Ottilie first arrived with the fledgling recruits, the only girls in the Narroway were custodians – servants. Sculkies, like Skip, worked inside, waiting on the huntsmen. When the dredretch threat became too great to leave the girls unable to protect themselves, Ottilie and Ramona Ritgrivvian, the only female wrangler, had begun training them in secret. That secret had finally come out when the sculkie squad joined the huntsmen in the battle at Richter.

Despite the battle, the victory, the lull and the looming war, time insisted on passing as it always had. The new fledglings, freshly picked and trialled, had arrived from Fort Arko. By the time the directorate changed the rules about allowing girls to join the Hunt, it had been too late to involve them in the trials. Instead, those who had fought at Richter automatically joined the fledgling ranks with special honours. There was no denying they had earned their place – and now numbers were more important than anything.

Ottilie remembered the day Skip had finally become a huntsman. Conductor Edderfed had stood at the centre of the Moon Court, the wind howling overhead and the group of girls gathered at the front.

She and Leo had been late. Flyers usually worked alone but, ever since Richter, Ottilie and Leo had begun hunting together whenever they could. They both preferred to be there to watch the other's back.

On that day, they had been held up by a troublesome vorrigle – a vicious winged dredretch, like an over-grown, hairy vulture with poisonous spines along its featherless wings. Vorrigles were tough to take down. They had finally shot it at the same time. Both claimed victory, but they would never know who it truly belonged to. Hunting had once been a deadly game – a fierce competition to be named champion – but no-one was keeping score anymore.

Late, they slipped into the Moon Court. Leo made to head for the elites, not caring about disturbing the ceremony and no doubt eager to draw attention as he paraded to the front. But Ottilie held him back, forcing him to stand with Maeve.

Maeve and Alba were two of the few members of their old sculkie squad who had not opted to join the Hunt. Both were taking part in the new mandatory training for every resident of the Narroway, but, as Alba had said from the beginning, she didn't want to be a huntsman. Instead, she kept her old job helping her mother, Montie, in the kitchen.

Maeve confided that she would have liked to join, but she wanted to focus on getting her magic under control. Of course, she didn't tell anyone else her reasons. Maeve had been accused of witchcraft once, and nearly exiled to the Laklands as a result. In truth, Ottilie was glad Maeve was staying a sculkie – there was far less chance of injury, and they needed Maeve at her full strength now more than ever. Having a witch on their side gave Ottilie hope – especially for Scoot. A witch had turned him to stone. Surely another witch could cure him. They just had to figure out how.

Conductor Edderfed cleared his throat. It was strange to see him standing there. Captain Lyre always addressed them at ceremonies, but he had been gone for weeks. He'd travelled east to All Kings' Hill to ask the king to send reinforcements to the Narroway.

The conductor looked grim. There was a deep crease between his brows, as if the coming words were sore for him to speak.

'Some of you will know the legend …' His voice was as full and deep as ever, but there was a stiffness to his delivery that Ottilie had not heard before.

'It is a myth, nine hundred years old, of a great monster that terrorised the west. Haunting the wetlands, it earned the name fendevil.'

Ottilie knew this story. Alba had told her about the legend of the first dredretch and the princess responsible for its demise. How interesting that Conductor Edderfed felt the need to wash it with the word *myth*. Alba had always said that the bones of the story, at least, were true.

Someone nudged Ottilie's elbow and whispered, 'This was Captain Lyre's idea.'

She jumped and turned. Ramona Ritgrivvian had arrived. There were flecks of blood on her cheek, and a smear of mud trailed across her eyepatch.

'I can't believe I nearly missed this!' Ramona muttered. 'We just lost two horses.' Her fiery hair was escaping from its braid and her uncovered eye was hooded and grave. 'A clan of pikkaminers – they say they came out of nowhere.'

Ottilie pictured the grey, spindly creatures with their needle fangs and bladed feet. They would have gone straight for the horses' legs, sliced through tendons to get them to the ground and then swarmed ...

She twitched, dislodging the images.

Ramona had said, *out of nowhere*. Ottilie only hoped that didn't mean what she thought it meant – more dredretches freshly called to the surface. An increase in numbers was the last thing they needed. But it was not just the thought of more monsters that made her nerves jitter and jump, it was the suggestion that Whistler was active – making moves against them.

The bone singers, once stationed as scorekeepers and mystical protectors of the forts, were really Whistler's salvaged disciples. She lent them her power and they performed rituals over the bones, initiating resurrections under the pretence of preventing the very thing they were enacting. But as far as Ottilie knew, Whistler alone could summon dredretches from below.

Was Whistler out there again, wandering the Narroway? Sneaking up on huntsmen? Ottilie had seen her lurking so many times in the past. The hooded figure …

They believed she was once a pure fiorn, like Maeve. A witch with the ability to turn into a bird. But, twisted by rage and hatred, Whistler had begun summoning dredretches and controlling them. As a result, her winged form had turned monstrous, akin to the creatures that had become her army – a force she intended to use against the king of the Usklers, her nephew, Varrio Sol.

Ottilie imagined Whistler watching from the shadows as the pikkaminers toppled the horses. She paled. 'The riders?'

'They survived,' said Ramona. 'But it's a terrible thing, to lose your mount.'

Ottilie felt a rush of phantom panic. She couldn't even imagine losing her wingerslink, Nox.

At the fore of the courtyard, Conductor Edderfed was still speaking in that strange, stilted manner. 'The legends tell of a creature like a wingless firedrake. A scaled thing, five times the size of a horse, fangs the length of spears and breath of blue flame that could destroy all in its path.

'But the monster needed none of these weapons, for anyone who came within striking distance dropped dead. They did not know it, but it was a dredretch – the first on record in the Uskler Islands.

'Armies could not defeat it. Our people were dying … the story goes that the king's youngest daughter, Seika Sol, lured the beast over a cliff, where it washed down a river and out into the sea. She became Seika Devil-Slayer.' He paused, clearing his throat. 'With her image you will be marked, and by her name you will be honoured.'

There was none of Captain Lyre's flair. No weight or wonder in the tale. Just fact, delivered as if he did not consider it factual.

Ottilie couldn't help but notice most of the wranglers were looking particularly stony. Wrangler Voilies had fixed a sickly smirk on his shiny face. Beside him, the scruffy, one-eyed Wrangler Furdles leaned over and muttered something in his ear. Voilies' smirk seemed to suck inwards, as if he had just had a sip of hagberry juice. Wrangler Kinney, the gold-toothed wingerslink master, sat closest to Conductor Edderfed but looked pointedly away, out over the girls' heads, his thumb tapping irritably on the whip tucked into his belt.

'Edderfed was against all this "fuss",' said Ramona, leaning close. 'But Captain Lyre argued that the girls would feel so set apart, and so behind in training – he wanted them to have something special to hold onto.'

'Why would Conductor Edderfed care about giving them a special name?' whispered Ottilie. It was utterly baffling that, after everything, they were still having arguments about the girls' place in the Narroway.

'The legend of Seika Devil-Slayer is a funny one,' said Ramona. 'In the past, it got mixed up with some dark rumours and the royals eventually buried the story. But a princess defeating a monster, that's a tough one to keep down. Whispers managed to bleed through generations.'

'What dark rumours?' said Ottilie.

'Something to do with witches. Witchcraft always rears its ugly head whenever a girl does something unexpected or extraordinary.'

Fear was such a strange reaction. Ottilie didn't think she would ever understand that sort of thinking. She looked to the front. This was the end of the sculkie squad. They had become the Order of Seika – soon to be known as the Devil-Slayers. Behind Conductor Edderfed, Wrangler Morse lifted a curtain, revealing a bronze shield mounted on the wall with an engraving of a duck on its centre.

Why were there ducks everywhere? There was a painting in Captain Lyre's chambers and a carving on the well in the canyon caves. Back in the Usklers a duck marked the hatch that led to the Wikric Tunnels. Now there was this shield, and another was stitched onto the uniforms of Fiory's newest recruits.

Ottilie noticed Conductor Edderfed didn't even look at the duck – but Ramona was smiling. This must have been Captain Lyre's doing, too.

'That's Seika Sol's mark,' said Ramona. 'After she defeated the fendevil they made it the royal insignia – it was for centuries, but Viago the Vanquisher changed it to a battleaxe as soon as he became king.'

'Whistler's father?' said Ottilie. Viago the Vanquisher was the king responsible for the dredretch infestation in the Laklands. A century ago, when the Lakland army helped save the Usklers from the clutches of the Roving Empire, it was promised that all old feuds would be forgotten. A vow was made that the Usklers would never invade the Laklands again.

The damnable act of the Usklerians breaking that vow, and the resulting monstrosities of war, poisoned the land – sinking down into the soil, calling dredretches to the surface and sealing the fate of the Laklands, that desolate kingdom to the west.

Its people had paid the ultimate price for the evil enacted upon them. The Laklanders who survived escaped into the Usklers. Some settled peaceably. Others sought vengeance. To this day, Laklanders were branded *enemies* by Usklerians – because, Ottilie suspected, the Usklerians feared the Laklanders could not forgive them. How could the Usklerians trust anyone they had wronged so deeply in the past?

'You're missing it,' Leo hissed.

Ottilie thought she caught a wet gleam in the corner of his eye. With a grin, she snapped her head to the front just in time to see Conductor Edderfed present Skip with her uniform at long last. After seven years in service to the Narroway Hunt, Skip was finally a huntsman.

Now here she was on this misty summer morning, wearing that uniform, a look of deep concern darkening her face. 'I just talked to Alba,' she said. 'She told me about the burns on Ned's arm.' She narrowed her eyes. 'We're going to have to watch him.'

Ottilie tensed. She'd told Alba at breakfast that she was worried about Ned, and she found it slightly irritating that Alba had already passed it on to Skip. It didn't need to be a secret, but Skip's attitude made her defensive. 'What are you getting at?'

Skip glanced around and lowered her voice. '*Well* …
it's Gracie Moravec all over again, isn't it?'

A fierce protectiveness swelled. 'No, it is not!' She
remembered Gracie's wyler bite. The way it glowed
like hot coals. She imagined her own skin bulging
and blistering, breaking apart. She clenched her fist.
'They're just burns. They're not from a dredretch – it's
not a bloodbeast thing.'

Bloodbeasts were a fresh horror in the Narroway,
and had become Ottilie's own personal nightmare.
Whistler rewarded her favourite followers by binding
them to a dredretch. By Ottilie's count, there were at
least three out there. Gracie had been bound to a wyler
– its bite was just the beginning. The wyler's burnt-
orange fur had turned white, and the beast had begun
to grow. The last time Ottilie had seen it, it was the size
of a pony. It was now Gracie's bloodbeast, and Gracie
could not only take control of its mind and see through
its eyes, she could do the same with every wyler. Under
her command, the wylers had become a deadly pack,
responsible for the death of Scoot's guardian, Bayo
Amadory, and the serious injury of many others.

'We don't know what they did to Ned in those caves,'
said Skip. 'If he's not healing properly … and Alba said
you were worried about how he looked this morning.
Remember how sick Gracie got?'

'Stop it, Skip!'

She arched a brow. 'Why did you see him so early anyway?'

'He was just saying happy birthday.' Ottilie wasn't sure why, but it felt like a lie.

Skip's face softened. 'It's your birthday!' She cracked a crooked smile and caught Ottilie in a hug. 'Go mess some monsters to celebrate.'

Ottilie snorted. 'You sound like Leo.'

'It's a pity they're not doing points since the bone singers all turned out to be evil. Beating him would have been fun.'

'You're in different tiers – you wouldn't have been against each other,' said Ottilie. 'And fledglings spend half the time training anyway. You don't get nearly as much hunting time.'

'Listen to you schooling me about the Hunt.' Skip grinned. 'Just like old times, only backwards.' She laughed. 'I better go – got to check on Preddy in the infirmary.'

'In the what – why?' Ottilie spluttered. This was what it was like now; a brief moment of laughter, of feeling like things were normal again, and then reality would smother the sun. 'What happened?' Had Preddy been hurt on their hunt?

With the exception of the fourth tiers, who got a year off from acting as guardians, the elites were already paired up with the new fledglings. So the directorate had decided to pair the Devil-Slayers with second-tier huntsmen in the order most suited to them.

After an assessment of her skills, Skip, who had been having secret horse-riding lessons with Ramona since her first year at Fiory, was placed with the mounts, and assigned Preddy as her guardian. Although pleased to be working with Preddy, Skip insisted it was a sneaky insult to allow the fourth-tier elites their year off, and pair the girls with the far less experienced second tiers instead. Ottilie was inclined to agree.

Gully had been partnered with Fawn Mogue, one of the first members of the sculkie squad. It turned out she was impressively gifted with a cutlass. Ottilie, for whatever reason, hadn't been given a fledge. She suspected it was because they thought her less capable of teaching. She didn't care too much – she was still getting used to flying Nox on her own. Preddy had been riding horses since he could walk. He was far more qualified to be a mentor. Still, even he couldn't avoid injury ...

'Preddy's fine – a scratch,' said Skip. 'He just needed it cleaned.'

Ottilie let out a breath. 'I'm late.'

Leo hated being late, and she didn't want him to go out there alone.

4

The Philowood Tree

The two wingerslinks swept low across a basin of krippygrass, cutting through a swarm of stingers. There was a throaty grunt from behind and Leo flipped to sit backwards in Maestro's saddle, shooting an arrow into the gaping mouth of a sword-tusked olligog.

The lumbering terror staggered and rolled with a muddy splatter. The bluish scales on its stomach seemed to reflect the midday sky before sinking beneath the grass.

For Ottilie, hunting was about more than monsters now. She was always distracted; one eye on the dredretches and the other seeking signs, any clue that might lead her to Bill. But there was nothing. Every day – nothing.

Their hunt took them north, towards the Withering Wood. Ottilie would never forget the first time she had visited that festering patch of forest. Of everything she had seen, nothing disturbed her more than the withering sickness. And it was spreading. As they flew over woodlands that had only weeks ago been breathing and bright, Ottilie's chest tightened. Blackness licked the tree trunks, curling like claws around branches, suffocating the trees until their leaves drooped and dripped like stalactites.

'Something's moving down there,' said Leo.

Ottilie felt a strange humming in her pocket. It was the necklace, with its little shard of dredretch bone, that Bonnie had given her weeks and weeks ago.

Ottilie had visited the bone singer in the burrows, begging for answers – for a way to cure Scoot. Bonnie hadn't been able to help, but she had given Ottilie the necklace – the one that Whistler gave each of her bone singers, sharing a little of her magic and protecting them from attack.

Ottilie had carried it with her ever since. She wasn't sure why – perhaps to remind her Whistler was out there. But it had never done this before. This strange vibration. It was unnerving.

Nox tensed. Ottilie reached for her bow and nudged her to circle lower, but the wingerslink lurched backwards, refusing to descend.

Below them, Leo growled, 'Get her under control, Ott! She shouldn't still be pulling this stuff!'

Ottilie nudged her more firmly, but Nox just circled higher. 'She doesn't want to go!' She couldn't blame the beast. The rotting stench was unbearable. They could hardly breathe down there.

Leo threw up his hands. Then, after signalling for her to wait, he took Maestro down. Ottilie didn't like it. He shouldn't be going alone. Nox liked it even less. She snarled, beating her wings and rocking from side to side.

'What's wrong?' Nox was throwing Ottilie about so much, she couldn't focus through the trees. There came a flash from below and Ottilie's heart faltered.

'Down,' she growled, thinking only of Whistler, of that impossible black light that broke when she changed into her winged form.

She had known it was coming. Everyone knew Whistler would not stay hidden for long.

Nox understood her. Leo was down there and they had to go to him. She swept in spirals, giving Ottilie a chance to see what was happening below. The air temperature rose with their descent. The stench snaking into her lungs felt like a violation. She coughed and pulled herself together.

Leo and Maestro had landed in a deadened clearing near the darkest patch of the Withering Wood. They were fine, and there was no threat in sight. Leo, still mounted, had nocked an arrow and was staring intently at the vast, still vertical, corpse of a tree.

It resembled the husk of a spider. What was left of its branches drooped to the ground in jagged arms, creating a cage around a hollow trunk.

Something was happening in the heart of that ancient shell. There was a crack, like bones breaking, and another flash of lit black. The air roared and whistled like wind through slits in stone.

Nox landed beside Maestro and Ottilie felt a familiar wave of nausea as a sheet of hot air smacked her in the face. They were trained to ward off the dredretch sickness, a sickness that was fatal to anyone exposed for too long. But Ottilie had always struggled – even with the help of the warding ring she had been given as a fledgling. Like everyone else's, it was engraved with a line from the lightning song, an old rhyme Gully used to chant. *Sleeper comes for none.* The sleeper was the collector of the dead. The words were a promise of protection, but they had changed after the battle at Richter. Another line took their place: *pay for what you've done.* Only Ottilie's ring hadn't changed because, for whatever reason, Whistler was not finished with her yet.

Ottilie squinted through the dense air – Leo could ward without a ring, but she wondered how he could breathe here without feeling even a hint of the sickness.

There was a crack and a crunch, like a boot on burnt bark. Then it came, as if birthed from the rotting tree. It was shaped like a bear, with sickly yellow fur and two sharp bones, like shoulder blades hooked into horns. A mord.

Ottilie was entranced, her eyes wide with horror. She looked at Leo – he had paled, his mouth gaping. This couldn't be a beast resurrected by the bone singers. Some had fled to join Whistler before the rest were imprisoned, but even if they had crept out here to perform the ritual, why would the bones have been in the heart of a rotting tree? It was too strange. No. This was a fresh dredretch. It had been summoned. Called. And she knew who did the calling ...

Ottilie tore her eyes away, searching for any sign of the witch that haunted her nightmares.

Skin prickled. She turned her head.

Bright eyes in the branches.

Behind her, the mord bellowed and Ottilie heard the ancient trunk cracking apart as the beast rent itself free.

'Shoot it, Leo. Before it's out.'

There was a whoosh and sticky *thud* as his arrow met its mark. She couldn't turn back to look, but as she aimed through the trees, Ottilie heard the splitting and sizzling of the mord coming to pieces, barely free of its birthplace.

'Whistler,' she said, and beside her Maestro swung around.

There was a terrible shriek. They loosed their arrows. A winged creature swooped through the shadows, its storm-painted feathers stirring up the hot air. It was all angles, like a wolf dunked in water, or a bird scrunched and then twisted back into shape. Its beak was hooked, its scaly talons peeling, leaking shadow. Its feathers seemed stiff and sharp enough to slice skin. With a crack and flash, Whistler stood in its place, a dangerous smile on her birdlike face, and in an instant their arrows turned to ash at her feet.

Her silver eyes fixed on Ottilie, she said, 'A pleasure, as always,' before jerking into a lopsided bow.

Leo drew his cutlass. Ottilie considered doing the same, but if arrows were no good against Whistler, a blade wouldn't be much better. Her heart was pounding and her fingers shook on her bow.

'Did you like my gift?' said Whistler.

'What *gift*?' said Leo.

Ottilie couldn't think. She couldn't see past her rage. Whistler had turned Scoot to stone. Angry tears welled.

'It wasn't for *you*.' Whistler waved her purple sleeves at him.

Leo shifted in the saddle. Ottilie could feel his confusion.

'My girl likes to know things, to understand things, don't you, dear?' said Whistler with a somewhat awkward wink.

My girl ...

Ottilie imagined bitemarks breaking skin and felt a burning sensation along her arm. She pictured Gracie's smile and a glinting blade. She refused to meet Whistler's gaze.

Whistler shambled forwards and flapped her arms in the direction of the hollow tree. 'My gift ... this is very special – letting you in on a secret.' She lifted a sleeve-shrouded finger to her lips, then pressed her hand to a branch. 'This is the heart of the Withering Wood. The first dredretch I ever summoned came through this opening.' Her voice was almost wistful, but it was a cover. Ottilie caught the danger lurking just beneath – like a crocodile's eyes breaking the surface of calm waters.

'Opening?' said Ottilie.

'Think of it as a gate at the top of a deep stairway,' said Whistler.

A stairway from the underworld? The hellish place far below where only the worst creatures belonged?

'Why would you show her that?' said Leo.

But Ottilie was too caught in her thoughts to wait for the answer. 'That's why the withering sickness spreads from here,' she said, scanning the tree. She remembered hearing something about a philowood tree at the centre of the Withering Wood. This must have been it. 'You poisoned this land when you opened that gate! And every time you summon a new dredretch, the sickness spreads.'

'It was already poisoned,' Whistler snapped. 'Otherwise there could never have been a stairway, let alone a gate.'

Already poisoned? Ottilie knew bad things could imprint the land like they could a person.

'Poisoned by what?' said Leo.

Whistler's face had turned thunderous, and Leo leaned back in the saddle. Ottilie had sensed this before. When Maeve felt something deeply, Ottilie could feel her mood like a change in the weather. Whatever Whistler's memory of this place was, it was something so horrible that even an experienced witch like her could not contain her emotions.

Whistler was glaring at Leo, and Ottilie grew, if possible, even more afraid. A vision of grey stone crusting over his gingery hair flashed in her mind. She had to distract Whistler.

'But what about the other patches we've found,' said Ottilie. They had been popping up here and there – little stretches of the sickness, far from the Withering Wood. 'What are those? More gates?'

Whistler's eyes lit up. 'I used to have to raise the dredretches here. Every single one. But as the years passed, the Narroway weakened ... so many lies, so much violence. It takes its toll. Now I can summon one wherever I like. One day this land will be as fertile for dredretches as the Laklands. And then no-one will have to summon them. They'll sniff out the way on their own. It's been a long game.' Her lips curled. 'But worth it.'

Ottilie leaned forwards. She wanted to understand it all. Whistler had said *fertile*, but Ottilie was sure she meant *damaged, wrecked, infected*. She needed to know why Whistler was doing it. Why the philowood tree? Why punish the king? What had he done? What had happened in this place?

Without really knowing why, Ottilie shifted to dismount.

'Ott,' Leo muttered.

So many questions. She couldn't help herself. The one she wanted answered most of all burst from her lips. 'Where's Bill?' she demanded. 'What are you doing with him?'

'Never you mind what I'm doing with him,' said Whistler, stomping in an impatient circle.

Ottilie freed her feet from the stirrups. She wanted to get near Whistler, to make her talk.

'*Ott*!'

It was infuriating. The Hunt was searching for Whistler, and here she was, but there was nothing they could do! They couldn't overpower her and drag her back to Fiory. They couldn't do anything but listen to what she decided she wanted them to know. No, not *them*. Ottilie.

Whistler laughed. 'Enjoy my gifts. While you can. There's a dry storm brewing.' With a swish of violet sleeves and a flash of black, she spiralled into the air.

Ottilie wanted to chase after her, to claw at her feathers and yank her back. Whistler had just wanted to taunt them – to show she could flit in and out of their notice, unharmed. She hadn't told them anything useful. They had no way to stop her. All they could do was brace for impact.

Ottilie could feel Leo's glare. She turned. There was fear in his face.

'It's all right. I don't think she'll come back.'

He narrowed his eyes, and she realised that wasn't what he was afraid of.

'She likes you too much.'

She looked away. 'What do you mean?'

'Just what I said.'

But he didn't know the half of it. He didn't know what Bonnie had said about the words on the ring – that Whistler had not given up on her yet.

And, *my girl* ... What did she mean by it?

'What was she talking about – *gifts*?' said Leo. 'I thought she said the mord was the gift. Do you think that means there are more around?' He scanned the trees.

Ottilie considered it. 'I think she meant *clues*. The mord was a clue, see, so she must have dropped more of them, just then, when she was talking to us. She likes giving out clues. I think she finds it fun. She's done it before.'

Ottilie remembered the book about the royals that Whistler had given her, Alba and Skip months ago. A hint that the Sol family was at the heart of all this. Later, after Whistler had revealed herself and fled Fiory, the directorate burned her entire collection – every book and scroll – all except those that Alba, Skip and Ottilie managed to swipe from the pile in Director Yaist's chambers, just in time.

'I think she wants me to figure something out,' said Ottilie with a confused squirming inside. Whistler collected people, and Ottilie refused to be one of them. But if Whistler was providing answers, Ottilie wanted to hear them.

She racked her brains, trying to remember every word Whistler had just said. It was no good. Her nerves had made a muddle of her memory.

– 5 –

Dreamwalking

It was as if they were frozen in the middle of a deep breath. Whistler's presence had only ever heralded disaster. If she had decided to show herself, it must mean tragedy was imminent. There had been no word from Captain Lyre. Was the king sending his men? When were the reinforcements coming? Every day, the number of dredretches seemed to grow closer to what it had been before the battle. And, with at least three bloodbeasts out there, organised, intelligent attacks made up for any losses.

Every morning Ottilie wondered if this was the day that everything was going to change. No-one could guess what Whistler's next move would be. She had failed to take Richter; would she try again? It was in the prime position for her to build her army with the Lakland dredretches. Wondering about it was keeping Ottilie from sleep.

One such night, there came a soft tapping on the shutters. Curiosity defeating fear, Ottilie unlatched the window and let the cool breeze waft inside. The moon spilled into the room, carrying a dark shape in the stream of light.

A black owl landed softly on Ottilie's bed. She smiled. 'You're out late.'

After a series of prickly snaps and an action like a magical sneeze, the feathers quivered, then seemed to suck inward and explode out in the shape of Maeve Moth. Ottilie had seen it before, but it was a marvel every time.

'Quick!' said Maeve, leaping up. 'It's Ned.' Her distress chilled the air.

'What happened? Is he all right?' Terror gripped her. This was what she had been waiting for – something terrible, something wrong.

Maeve didn't even pause for Ottilie to put on shoes. She leapt across the room and threw the door open, beckoning for Ottilie to follow.

Heart hammering, Ottilie grabbed a vial of water from her shelf and scrambled for her glow sticks.

Greenish light sputtered to life as she and Maeve rushed along the dark corridor.

'I didn't know who else to tell, after everything that happened with Gracie ...'

'What has this got to do with Gracie?'

The green lights bobbed and bounced along the narrow walls, pricking Ottilie's nerves. She remembered Skip's words: *it's Gracie Moravec all over again ...*

'Something's wrong with him,' said Maeve, her voice thin. 'I saw him out by Floodwood. He's not himself. He's in some sort of trance!'

They sprinted out into the grounds, too breathless to shape words. Ottilie took the lead, heading for Floodwood, hopping and skipping as her bare feet crunched on sticks and prickles. Leaping over a patch of whiskerweed, she caught sight of something moving ahead.

It took her a moment to identify the lanky shape. Then she realised it must be a shepherd – one of the dusky wild dogs that guarded the grounds – but it was smaller than the others, perhaps younger, only half grown. And just ahead, weaving through the trees, was Ned.

He was in his nightclothes, and barefoot, like her. But unlike her, he took no care where he stepped. His path was strange. It wasn't leading him anywhere, but it didn't seem aimless.

The shepherd was stalking Ned, snarling. The dog knew something wasn't right.

Ottilie hurried up to him. 'Ned?'

He didn't seem to hear.

She reached out as if approaching a panicked horse, but found she was afraid to touch him. Circling to face him, Ottilie held the glow sticks aloft. Gracie's eyes burned red when she was in a trance – commanding the wylers or seeing through her bloodbeast's eyes. Ottilie saw it all too often in her dreams. But Ned's eyes weren't glowing, and Ottilie puffed a breath of relief. Something *was* wrong with him, though. He didn't see her, but he was seeing *something*.

She forced her jaw to unlock. 'Do you think you can get inside his head?' Maeve had shared Bill's thoughts and memories with Ottilie before.

'I didn't think of that!' said Maeve. 'Yes! Here.' She grabbed Ottilie's hand and carefully reached for Ned.

The sounds came first. Angry voices. The crackle of flame. Then, like water settling, the canyon caves smoothed into view.

Ottilie gasped, her eyes darting, immediately looking for Bill. But she knew he wasn't there. Maeve had said the caves were abandoned, and … It took Ottilie a moment or two to remember she was not really there. This was Ned's dream, and these were not the canyon caves as she knew them.

Grand staircases zigzagged up the walls. Ornate arches were carved into the entrances to tunnels, and the well, a crumbled ruin when Ottilie had seen it, was smooth and sturdy. Her eyes swept the stone, searching for Seika Devil-Slayer's mark – and there it was, clearer than she remembered it, a simple duck carved into the side of the well.

Just beside it lay a long iron box. A coffin. Open.

Twelve figures stood in a circle around a pit of fire. Their clothes were strange, ancient. Both men and women wore their hair braided into intricate swirls, like crowns. Only one let hers hang loose.

When was this? Ottilie was sure they had fallen into the deep and distant past. She searched the figures, seeking any clue as to who they might be. The firelight licked at their faces, revealing expressions ranging from revulsion to rage to deepest sorrow.

She followed their focus and jerked backwards. She had taken it for shadow and smoke, but there was a person chained up, standing in the pit of fire. No. Not a person – a creature. Its whole body was covered in grey scales. She didn't know if it could see, because dark sockets gaped in place of its eyes. It stood unmoving, unbothered by the flame.

One of the twelve was speaking. '... you are found guilty by your coven of a crime so unspeakable that we will not utter it here in this sacred place.'

Coven? Ottilie knew that word. These people were witches.

The scaled creature's mouth curved into a horrifying smile, revealing rotting gums and fangs whittled down like the thinnest arrowhead at the tip.

'You have stripped yourself of humanity. You are no witch. You are no human. You are hereby made nameless. There has never been another of your kind, and there will be no other. You have lived as this sleepless beast for one day – and it will be your final day.'

'You cannot kill me,' the creature hissed in a voice like a whip shredding flesh.

Ottilie shivered. So, it was a sleepless witch: a witch that would never grow old, that could never die.

Her heart hammered. That meant it was out there somewhere now – still alive. It had to be. No matter how long ago this was, how many centuries had passed ...

The crime they spoke of ... she knew the rumours. To become sleepless, a witch had to consume their own newborn baby. It was horrifying. Unthinkable. Those very rumours had sparked the witch purge that wiped out countless innocent women during the Roving Empire's occupation of the Usklers. Whether this creature had been a man or a woman Ottilie could not tell. It occurred to her for the first time that the ritual could probably have been performed by either parent.

Why had she never considered that before? Why had no-one? They had only buried women.

A man spoke from the circle. 'It is true, your spirit is tied to this plane evermore. We cannot undo this. Your soul will live on, locked inside your immortal bones, but this will be your prison – buried, eternally alone.'

The first speaker spoke again. 'You will not walk, or talk, or see. You will not act. You will only feel.'

'You cannot touch me,' said the creature.

The witch with loose hair stepped forward. She was tall, but undoubtedly the youngest of the circle, and somehow familiar. Ottilie wasn't sure why. Did she remind her of Whistler? No, that wasn't it …

'You underestimate us,' she said.

The circle of witches clasped hands and the cavern seemed to yawn awake. Hot air lifted, swayed, then swirled, and the flames around the creature spiralled into a whirlwind. It laughed, rattling the iron chains until they snapped like dried vines.

Facing Ottilie, it stepped out of the wildfire.

Panicked, she stumbled backwards, losing her grip on Maeve's hand and dropping her glow sticks. The vial shattered and the green light winked out. Ottilie's heart was pounding. She was drowning in darkness.

A twig cracked, the shepherd growled, and someone grabbed her from behind.

6

A Sinister Secret

'Maeve!'

'Ottilie?' said Maeve, from a few feet away.

Hands gripped her. It wasn't Maeve. 'Ned?' she whispered.

Ned didn't answer, but his hold loosened a little.

'Maeve, can you make some sort of light?'

'I can try.'

For a moment nothing happened. Then it was as if the air had lifted off like a blanket. She felt breathless until the world settled and countless tiny embers popped into existence, casting a glow mightier than reason.

Despite everything, a smile tugged at her lips. It was as if the stars had drifted down to say hello. The young shepherd rocked back on his hind legs, sniffing at the air.

'Careful,' said Maeve. 'They'll burn you. I can't control where they go.' She glanced nervously around the surrounding woodland – but Floodwood was so damp there was no risk of starting a fire.

Resisting the draw of the embers, Ottilie turned her attention to Ned. The light seemed to have calmed him. He released his grip and stepped back, looking down at his shaking hands.

'Ned?' she said again, still not entirely sure he had come back to himself.

His dark eyes met hers. 'What happened?'

'We were going to ask you that,' said Maeve, and Ottilie was bothered by the coldness of her tone. She was undoubtedly thinking of Gracie again. Even though Ottilie didn't want to admit it, she was thinking of Gracie too. With each blink, red eyes flashed in the black.

'I think you were sleepwalking,' said Ottilie, and explained how they had found him. 'We saw ... Maeve showed me ... I think we saw what you were dreaming.'

His eyes widened. 'You saw *it*?'

She knew immediately what he meant. 'Is that what you've been dreaming about, Ned? That thing in the fire?'

He nodded. 'It wasn't always like that. It was a person first, a witch and then … then …' His voice shook, and he couldn't continue.

Ottilie didn't need him to. That creature was what had become of a witch that enacted the sleepless ritual. Alba had read that no witch had ever truly attempted it. It was all false accusations and lies. But the coven in Ned's dream had said it was the first and last of its kind. It was so long ago, perhaps people had forgotten it ever existed. But what had happened in the end? It seemed like the coven were trying to imprison it – perhaps in the iron coffin, waiting by the well. The well that was now a ruin …

Ned coughed, and Ottilie's eyes snapped to his arm. All thoughts of the sleepless witch flew from her mind. Something dark was oozing through Ned's sleeve. She grasped his forearm. Ned winced and pushed back his sleeve to reveal the star-shaped burns, his fist clenched in pain.

Just like Gracie's wyler bite, Ned's burns were glowing like hot coals. Ottilie hovered her hand above them and felt heat, as if they were three tiny campfires along his arm. She watched, transfixed, as their light began to dim.

'It's just when I dream,' said Ned, shame weighting his words.

Ottilie looked at Maeve. 'Don't tell anyone.'

Maeve's face darkened and she opened her mouth to retort.

'I kept *your* secret! You owe me.'

Maeve shut her mouth, her face stony.

It was Whistler doing this to him. It had to be. She had marked him for a reason and now she was showing him something – pieces of the forgotten past. But why?

A shepherd bayed in the distance. The young dog responded, then hesitated, giving Ned one last sniff before bounding into the night.

Ottilie's eyes swept the darkened woodland, and memories of yickers scuttled into her thoughts. She remembered scrambling through the trees with Scoot in their fledgling year, running for their lives, the winged spiders swarming.

Sorrow sunk in. She blinked and saw him at Whistler's feet – stone creeping. 'We should get inside,' she said.

They had just settled in Ottilie's bedchamber when someone tried the latch. She had bolted it from the inside.

'Ottilie,' hissed Gully. 'Let me in!'

She pulled him inside and bolted the door again. It was surely after midnight, but the huntsmen moved in and out at all hours, especially now that the boundary walls were so excessively manned.

'I couldn't sleep,' said Gully. 'I thought you'd be awake so I came to see you, but you weren't here – where have you been?'

Ottilie wasn't sure how to explain. She twisted her clammy hands together and glanced at Ned, who had flopped into the chair by the window. Gully followed her gaze, his eyes sweeping Ned's dishevelled nightclothes and muddy bare feet.

'What happened?'

'Sleepwalking.' Ned mustered a half-smile. 'They found me in Floodwood.'

'He's been having nightmares about a sleepless witch,' said Maeve.

'Maeve! I told you not to tell anyone!' snapped Ottilie. She hurried to the window and closed the shutters, trying to lock the secret inside her room.

'I didn't think you meant *Gully*. Anyway, I didn't say anything about his arm.'

'What about his arm?' said Gully, looking accusingly at Ottilie. 'Tell me what's happening.'

Ottilie half sighed, half growled. She had been intending to tell Gully, but Maeve's readiness to spill the story made her anxious.

'His wound's not healing, and it burns when he dreams about the witch.' She tried to make it sound like it was a perfectly normal ailment. 'We need to find a way to stop it happening. Maybe Alba could research –' she stumbled. Did Alba need to know more than she already knew? Ottilie didn't want anyone else knowing. She wasn't sure how people would react. Skip was already saying they needed to watch him. What if the directorate found out? They wouldn't risk letting him stay at Fiory. The mere hint of a link to Whistler and any one of them would be cast out, or worse. She couldn't handle it, not with Scoot still frozen in stone and Bill captive … nothing could happen to Ned.

She took a breath and turned to Maeve. 'What happened to the witch book after they confiscated it?'

Months ago, on the night they first met Whistler, Skip had snatched the book from Whistler's tower and given it to Alba, who studied it in secret until Maeve caught wind and stole it for herself. The directorate had taken the book after Maeve was accused of witchcraft. Gracie, then Maeve's closest friend, had saved her by declaring herself a witch, even though it was not true. It was her last human act, and the only kind thing Ottilie had ever witnessed from Gracie.

'I have it,' said Maeve with a twinkle in her eye.

'What?' said Gully. 'How?'

'Well.' Maeve looked pleased with herself. 'I think they burned it. But it showed up under my pillow one night, all sooty and stinking of smoke.'

Ottilie frowned. This sounded like Whistler's doing. Had she rescued it from the fire and delivered it to Maeve? Was this another one of her games?

'Do you think someone put it there?' said Ned, as if reading her thoughts.

Maeve shook her head. She didn't seem worried. 'No. I think the magic in the book brought it back to me.'

'But how can you know that?' said Ottilie.

'Because that book was calling to me for months before I stole it from the root cellar,' said Maeve. 'The day I stopped that jivvie scalping Leo on the wall' – she nodded at Ottilie, who had witnessed the whole thing – 'I was flying around the Bone Tower, following the call. I didn't know what it was, or why, but I was drawn there.

'When Alba had it on her, I kept following her around. Then I heard you talking in the library and I finally knew what had been calling me. And when she hid it in the root cellar I knew where to find it. When they burned it, it must have found a way to come to me on its own and put itself back together ... something like that.'

Gully's eyes were wide. He had always been fascinated by the idea of witches and magic.

'Why was it calling you?' said Ottilie.

'Just because you're a witch?' said Ned.

'I think it wanted to get away from Whistler,' said Maeve. 'It chose me over her. It's really special, that book ... it knows just what I need to read. It opens to the right page and symbols change into letters I can understand. Sometimes I feel like it's talking in my head, rather than me reading it at all. I'm not a good reader, usually.' She paused, as if unsure she should continue. 'Gracie taught me how, but I've never really practised.'

Ottilie remembered how much difficulty Alba had had reading the book – Alba, who was the most voracious reader she had ever met. It sounded like the book really had chosen Maeve. Good. It was what they needed.

'Maeve, will you see if there's anything in there about blocking dreams, a potion or ...' She didn't know the right words. 'Something ... something that will make it stop.'

'And the sleepless witch,' said Ned, sitting up straighter. 'Anything about why I'm –'

'That's not as important,' Ottilie cut across him. 'If you stop dreaming it won't matter anymore. You said your arm only burns when you dream. So, we stop the dreams and maybe it will heal. It'll all go away.'

A streak of annoyance crossed Ned's face. Ottilie didn't care. She couldn't bear it, couldn't risk finding out more. Ned's burn looked exactly like Gracie's bite when it glowed. Whatever the purpose, Ottilie knew it would be terrible. They didn't need to find out. They just needed to make it go away. At least this was something they could work towards – something they might be able to beat back.

Ned looked like he was about to argue, but Gully got in first. 'Do you hear that?' He slid off the bed.

Ottilie strained her ears. She could hear it too: hoofbeats. 'It's probably just mounts coming in from a night patrol.'

'That's a wagon,' said Ned.

Ottilie opened the shutters. He was right. A wagon passed through the well-lit main gates, flanked by six mounts. As soon as the gates closed behind them, the wagon burst open and a tall figure pitched out and hurried up the path.

Ottilie thought for a moment that the person had three legs, but then she realised the third was in fact a cane. Captain Lyre had returned from All Kings' Hill at last.

❧ 7 ❧

The Colour of Nothing

The elites found out first: the king was coming.

It should have been a comfort, but the arrival of an army guaranteed a battle. There was no ignoring it. Richter was just the beginning. They were at war.

Ottilie had seen almost nothing of the world beyond the Swamp Hollows, her tiny corner of the Usklers' western island. But she remembered the maps in *Our Walkable World*. For years it was the only book she had access to, so she nearly knew it by heart. She could picture tiny stick-figure soldiers marching across a kingdom of faded ink.

The Usklers was made up of three islands that were divided by two narrow channels: Crown Canal and

Pero's Passage. Usually, dredretches could not cross saltwater. Not even in flight. Salt was poisonous to them – paralysing, if not fatal. It was why the huntsmen carried weapons of salt-forged steel. A special brand from the northern salt springs that would not rust a blade.

According to Leo, the king's army had crossed Crown Canal and trekked the width of the western region to the edge of the Narroway. The border was land. There was no stretch of seawater to save them. If Whistler intended to attack the Usklers, they might well lose the entire western island. Everyone from the Swamp Hollows would be gone: her mother, Freddie; her neighbours, Old Moss and Mr Parch – they and everyone Ottilie had ever known, and so many more. All the towns and villages she had never visited, all the wilderness she had never had a chance to explore, it would all become dredretch territory – a withered realm.

The king's soldiers were camped in Longwood, along the Narroway border. Once each station – Richter, Arko and Fiory – emptied the warding rings from their vaults, the soldiers would be able to enter the Narroway and begin training at Fort Arko.

Ottilie found it concerning that they just happened to have enough rings to go around. Whistler had made those rings – why had she stocked the Hunt with so many? But there was nothing to be done about it.

The king's men couldn't join the fight without rings. The dredretch sickness would knock them down in an instant, and there wasn't enough time to teach them how to ward. Ottilie still hadn't mastered it after more than a year of training.

The king himself, Leo revealed, would be coming to Fiory.

'But why?' she asked, leaning forward to rest her arms on Scoot's infirmary bed. Her fingers brushed a cutting of lullaby vine that Alba and Montie had scattered around his stone body. The feathery, pale blue flowers were known to bring good dreams.

Someone – Ottilie suspected Gully – had placed three fat sunnytree flowers in a jar by the bed. Apart from offering a metallic muddy smell, those flowers did little other than brighten up the room.

No-one else liked to go behind the partitions – they found Scoot too unnerving – so it was private enough to risk reading the stolen books. Ottilie liked to be there, as if just being near him might help her find a cure.

She had just given up on her book when Leo arrived. He and the rest of the elites had been called to a secret meeting with the directorate and she had been waiting to hear the news.

'They didn't explain why he's coming here,' said Leo, in answer to her question. Lowering his voice, he added, 'But Ned thinks it's because he doesn't want to be where the action is. Whistler could easily attack them before they're trained at Arko, and Richter is already weakened and too close to the Lakland border.'

'But we're right in the middle here,' said Ottilie. 'There's nowhere to run.'

Leo shrugged and twisted in his seat, looking through the gap in the partitions to make sure no-one was listening to them.

'You can't tell anyone. It's supposed to be only the elites who know. I don't even think his men know he's coming here. They said he's not bringing them. We're going to stand in as guards.'

Ottilie screwed up her nose. 'Why bother coming at all if he's just going to hide? Why is he even still the king? Everyone knows about all his lies now.'

The Narroway Hunt was born of trickery and deceit. To save his own neck, the king had spread the lie of the rule of innocence, claiming only children could fell dredretches. But at Richter, Whistler had revealed all.

'Everyone in the *Narroway* knows the truth – not the Usklers,' said Leo. 'Who knows what he's told everyone else. They probably don't even know the Narroway Hunt exists, let alone the dredretches. Well, I guess his army must … but anyway, you can't just dethrone a king with a snap of your fingers. It takes time, and the right people to make moves. The heir would have to step up.'

'Who is the heir?' She realised she didn't know. The king didn't have any children, just two daughters who had died young. She winced as she remembered his second daughter had died under Ramona's care.

'Varrio's cousin Odilo – Lord of Rupimoon Rock.' Leo's face darkened.

'You know him?'

'I saw him once, when I was really young – but I still remember it. He was riding up to the palace and something frightened his horse. His guards got the horse under control but he jumped off and had them hold her while he beat her right there in the street.

'I remember hearing all sorts of rumours about what went on up on the north island. When I misbehaved, my father would threaten to send me over Pero's Passage as a punishment. So even if we did get rid of this king, it's not as if there's a better one waiting.'

Ottilie scowled. 'At least he doesn't come with a vengeful witch attached.'

'As far as we know,' said Leo, mustering a grin.

'Who comes next then? There must be at least one good family member!' Was it impossible to be born into power and not be corrupt?

Leo thought for a minute. 'I don't think Odilo had any sons. Before I came here, his only daughter went missing, but daughters can't rule anyway – so second in line would be his brother, Wolter Sol. I don't know much about him.'

She frowned. Once, it would have surprised her that daughters couldn't ascend the throne, but now, she might have guessed that was the case. When had she ever heard of an Usklerian queen? But the bigger question was, why were so many Sol daughters having accidents and going missing?

Wearily, she rested the top of her head against Scoot's stone arm. So, the king was coming to Fiory. What did it matter? What use was he? His presence was putting them in more danger. If anything, he would just fix Whistler's attention on their station. Ottilie herself drew too much attention already. She sat back, twisting her ring. Why hadn't Whistler given up on her? What indication had she given the witch that she was still bendable?

My girl ... She wasn't Whistler's girl. Not in any way. She was the daughter of Freddie Colter and – well, she didn't know who her father was. But he couldn't be connected to Whistler. Could he? Ottilie recoiled and tucked her hand into her pocket, putting the ring out of sight. She resolved to work harder at warding, determined to remove it.

Almost all her friends did without them. Gully had stopped wearing his since the wyler had bitten off his thumb. Preddy had taken his off just before spring's end. Ned and Leo hadn't worn them in years. Even Maeve had realised she didn't need hers, probably because she was part bird. The dredretch sickness was specific to humans. Maeve still wore it, though, fearful that a sculkie seen without her ring would rouse suspicion of witchcraft again.

Scoot had still worn his … Ottilie grimaced, staring down at the ring on his stone thumb. Something caught her attention. The very tips of his fingers had brightened to white. White was not a living colour. It was absence, nothing. She didn't know what it meant, but it couldn't be good.

She tore her eyes away. It felt like water filled her up, weighting her limbs. It was all too much. Whistler reappearing, Ned's dreams, the king coming, and now this.

Her breath was short, her head spinning. The ground was opening up. She was going to drop into the deep, dark places below where the dredretches roamed, waiting to be called, to follow the song to the surface and destroy everything living, everything good, everyone she loved.

Something gripped her, pulling her out of her chair. Leo set her on her feet, but she wilted like a soggy weed. He locked his arms around her and squeezed her tight.

8

Lullaby

It was night by the time Ottilie left the infirmary. Leo had gone up to dinner, but she couldn't face noise and people and food. There were new questions. She had to ask Alba and Maeve about the white stone, and no doubt face an answer that plunged her into panic once more. She had just wanted to sit still a little longer. Alone with Scoot, with nothing moving, frozen in time with him.

When she did eventually leave, Ottilie took a detour. Weaving through the dark lavender fields, she came to the healers' herb garden. It smelled of wild roses and lemon thyme, like soft smiles and the beginning of things.

Holding her pocket vial aloft, she searched for the familiar feathery flowers and found a pale-blue vine snaking up the stone fence. Then, cuttings in hand, she made for Ned's bedchamber.

Ottilie paced back and forth outside the door. It was such a simple thing. Nothing to be nervous about – just some flowers to bring good dreams. Finally, shakily, she knocked.

No-one answered, but the doorway was leaking light, so she knew he was inside. Steeling herself, she said, 'Ned? It's Ottilie.'

There were footsteps, and some other sound – a clattering, like scattered shells – and then the door slid open.

Ned didn't smile at her. She felt her face tense as she realised this might be the first time he had not greeted her with a smile. But there was no time to dwell on it, because a long, dark nose emerged and started snuffling up and down her legs. Ottilie nearly jumped. The shepherd withdrew and growled in a way that seemed more an expression of displeasure than a threat. She knew that growl. The dog could smell Nox's scent on her.

'There's a shepherd up here ...' she said, voicing her thoughts aloud. Ottilie recognised him from the night she had found Ned in Floodwood. He was a young, lanky thing, like an overgrown pup. His black fur had a blueish tinge and strange patches of white that she hadn't seen on many of the shepherds.

'He won't stop following me,' said Ned, warmth creasing his eyes. 'He just showed up at my door the other day. The shepherds don't normally try to get inside – I guess no-one thought to stop him. He sleeps here now.'

The shepherd was still growling.

'Penguin. Enough.'

Ottilie nearly laughed. 'Penguin?'

Ned flashed a quick smile, and a knot loosened somewhere inside her.

'The colours,' he explained. 'Reminds me of the fairy penguins back home. He answers to *Pen* too.' He looked down at the shepherd fondly. 'Fast learner.'

'Will they let you keep him up here?'

He shrugged. 'See what happens.'

Silence fell and, not for the first time, Ottilie wondered at the freedom these boys had. She would never have risked keeping a shepherd in her room. Who knew what sort of trouble she would be in if she was found out?

Ned's gaze caught the lullaby cuttings in her hand, and Ottilie suddenly felt very foolish.

'It's for your sleep,' she said quickly, stumbling over the words. 'To help stop – well, I don't know if it actually – to bring ... I mean, it's supposed to bring good dreams. I thought it might help.' The heat rose to her face and she longed to turn and run in the opposite direction. A memory surfaced: Skip saying something about boys only getting flowers if they were dying or if someone wanted to marry them. Ottilie cringed inwardly and wished she could sink into the floor.

Ned's eyes flicked back up to hers, and her thoughts stopped flailing long enough to notice how gravely tired he looked. She had to stop being so sensitive. This wasn't about her.

His reactions delayed, Ned's face lifted a little. 'Thank you.'

She held out the cuttings, but he didn't take them.

'It might not do anything,' she prattled on. 'But it's something ... until Maeve works out a proper cure.'

Ned took a step back, shaking his head. He hadn't invited her in, but she didn't want to have this conversation where they could be overheard, so she stepped into the room and shut the door behind her anyway.

'Why are you shaking your head?'

Ned sat down on the end of his bed. 'I don't want to stop the dreams.'

'What?' She was suddenly fearful. 'But your arm, and the sleepwal–'

'I know. But the dreams are trying to show me something important. I can feel it, and I want to know what it is.'

'It's too dangerous.' She glanced at his arm. 'You have to stop it.'

'It's not really up to you.'

'I know that.'

'Do you?'

Her face heated again. It was true, she had taken charge the other night, but Ned had been shaken and in pain … someone had to. She realised he hadn't actually agreed when she'd asked Maeve to look into stopping his dreams.

'But Whistler is the one who did that to you. If the dreams are trying to show you something, it's coming from her.'

Ned looked up at her, his brow creasing. 'Ottilie, I know everything you know.'

Her eyes narrowed. Was it really him resisting this? Or was it Whistler's influence?

He read the look on her face. 'This is why it's so hard to say. You don't trust me, because of this.' He gestured to his arm. 'I'm not bound. It's not like Gracie … or anything else. I'm in my right mind. Well, mostly. It's just lack of sleep.'

Ottilie wanted to rush forward and peer into his eyes, search for any hint that his decisions weren't his own. It wasn't just for his sake. If he was some sort of spy, or if his dreams were some weapon Whistler could use to harm them all, if it was a key part of whatever terrible scheme she was cooking up, then it wasn't just his business, it was hers, too – all of theirs. Her hand clenched around the lullaby cuttings and the stems wilted in her grip. Had Skip been right? Did they need to watch Ned?

He was tracking her expressions and she felt guilty. She didn't know what to say. He, too, seemed lost for words. There was something missing from his face. There was no twinkle, no glimmer of laughter. He was really worried that she didn't trust him. The terrible thing was that now, after this, she wasn't sure she did.

Ottilie tried to smile, or nod, or offer some gesture of goodbye, because she seemed to have forgotten how to say anything other than 'don't be stupid' or 'you have to stop the dreams'. Ned turned away and looked out the window and Ottilie took the opportunity to depart.

◄ 9 ►

Varrio Sol

'Who are they?' Six huntsmen Ottilie didn't recognise had just entered the Moon Court.

'No idea,' said Gully. 'Maybe they came with the king – they're wearing green and grey. That's the Arko colours.'

Ottilie was sitting alone with Gully. She couldn't face anyone else right now: not Skip with her distrust of Ned, or Leo with his concern for her, and especially not Ned himself, who, Ottilie couldn't help but notice, was avoiding her too. She had never realised how much Ned looked at her before, but she was keenly aware of the absence of his glances.

Maeve Moth slipped into the seat behind her and leaned forward. 'I found something.'

Ottilie's stomach twisted. 'About the white stone?' She had asked both Alba and Maeve to look into why Scoot's fingertips had changed colour, and had been secretly hoping that neither would come up with any answer.

Maeve blinked in affirmation. 'I was going to wait to tell you, until ...' She gestured to the front of the courtyard, where the directorate was assembling. 'But it's pretty urgent.'

Ottilie swallowed the painful lump in her throat and nodded for Maeve to continue.

Maeve's eyes flickered. 'It's the final stage of the transformation. Heartstone is pure white and permanent. Once he turns completely white we won't ever be able to change him back.'

'What?' said Gully. '*No.*'

Ottilie twisted right around in her seat, her heart pounding. 'How fast does it happen? When will we ... how long do we have to fix him?'

Maeve shook her head. 'I don't know,' she said blankly. Maeve's voice often flattened when she was upset. Ottilie now realised it was because she was trying to control her emotions. Considering that her feelings tended to light fires, stir wind or chill the air, it made sense that she had to clamp down. 'Some turn white straight away – others take months. The book says some people's bodies fight against it. It's just the tip of one hand so far. That's something …'

'Can people last years?' said Gully.

Maeve shook her head. 'The longest on record is eleven months.'

Ottilie needed to see Scoot *now*, to measure it, check how far gone he was. She jumped to her feet, but Gully grabbed her sleeve and pulled her back down. 'Look.'

Beyond the dais, a door opened and Captain Lyre appeared. Ottilie had rarely seen him so subdued. Today, he wore the face she had only seen across a funeral pyre.

'May I present Varrio Sol, King of the Usklers and Lord of the Laklands,' he said, lacking his usual showmanship.

Ottilie narrowed her eyes. Viago the Vanquisher had laid waste to the Laklands a hundred years ago, yet his descendants still boasted the title.

There were gasps and whispers. Everyone rose to their feet. Captain Lyre gestured to the door and silence fell as the king entered the Moon Court.

Ottilie peeked up over the bowed heads. Varrio Sol was a hollow-looking man. He had broad shoulders that rounded into a slight hunch. This was exaggerated by the chestnut fur cloak he wore, despite the mild weather. It looked unsettlingly like wingerslink fur. Ottilie guessed he was just bones beneath it, and that his bulk was made up of his many-layered black-and-gold clothes.

There was something else that she couldn't put her finger on. Beneath his circlet crown and grizzled hair, his face was angular, almost wolfish. There was something familiar about his eyes. Perhaps he reminded her of Whistler? She was his aunt, after all.

The king slumped onto the grand throne usually reserved for Conductor Edderfed. There were no trumpets, no fanfare, only stiff silence. The bone singers had always played the music – and those who had not flocked to Whistler were imprisoned in the burrows.

Once he settled on the throne, his bulky shoulders curving forwards, the crowd straightened their backs. The king flicked his fingers at them. They sat, and Captain Lyre moved forward to speak.

Captain Lyre's energy usually brightened the room – it could make things seem less serious, sometimes even fun. Ottilie imagined being greeted on their first day in the Narroway by this sombre version. How much scarier, how grim and violent life as a huntsman would have seemed.

Now he was explaining everything Leo had already told her, and Ottilie stopped listening. There was a strange energy in the room. It wasn't just Captain Lyre's sullenness. It was coming from the huntsmen themselves.

Here was the king – the man responsible for everything. And they all knew it. Whistler had told them. She had tricked him; knowing his violent, warmongering ways, she had told him that if he sent his armies out to fight, he would die. And he had been too cowardly to question it, to even test it.

When the dredretches appeared in the Narroway, Varrio Sol had been so frightened by Whistler's words – her false hex – that he had created the Narroway Hunt to deal with the threat. He had kidnapped children into service: traded them to keep his crown.

Now he had come to help them clean up his mess, but what use was he? His soldiers had never even seen a dredretch, and he was hiding here at the fort he considered the safest.

Captain Lyre's disdain was mirrored all around, so when the huntsmen were dismissed, Ottilie was surprised by how many of them remained to meet the king. A great line formed before the man on the throne, and one by one they moved forward and bowed as Captain Lyre introduced them.

'*Leo*!' said Ottilie, as she spotted him heading for the line. 'What are you doing?'

'I want to meet him,' said Leo with a grin.

Gully snorted, but Ottilie just gaped.

Leo shrugged. 'He's the king.'

'So?'

Leo didn't seem to have a better explanation. She turned away from him just as one of the Arko huntsmen approached. He was the youngest of the lot, with brown hair, a nasty scar across his jaw, and shockingly green eyes.

'Are you Gulliver Colter?'

Gully didn't answer him.

Ottilie frowned. She'd never noticed him struggle with speaking to strangers before. 'Yes, he is,' she answered for him.

The boy's eyes lit up. 'I'm Murphy Graves,' he said, with a slightly lopsided grin. 'I've been wanting to meet you!'

Ottilie recognised the name. Murphy Graves had spent a good part of their fledge year at the top of the rankings – coming in second, behind Gully, in the end.

Gully managed a somewhat nervous smile and said, 'Oh, hello.'

'And you're Ottilie?' Murphy said, ignoring Gully's odd behaviour. 'You two are famous!'

She laughed. 'Are we?'

There was a whistle from across the room. The other Arko huntsmen were heading out, and one of them was waving Murphy over.

'Better go. Congrats on making champion, Gulliver.' As he walked away he called back, 'I was looking forward to taking you on this season – too bad they've stopped scoring!'

Gully stared after him. 'It's Gully,' he mumbled, too quietly for Murphy to hear.

Ottilie elbowed him in the ribs. 'What was that?'

'He had really green eyes.'

'I saw,' said Ottilie, with a bemused smile. She couldn't remember Gully paying any attention to appearances before.

'I have to go hunt now,' said Gully, and he hurried over to Ned without another word. Ottilie smiled and turned away. Something caught her eye. Alba was waving her over.

She and Maeve were in a corner. Maeve turned and Ottilie was relieved to see she had brightened. 'Alba's found something that could help Scoot and Ned.'

Ottilie felt a jolt of panic – what had Maeve told Alba? Not about the dreams, surely? She had promised!

'His burns,' added Maeve quickly.

She relaxed. Alba already knew Ned's burns weren't healing. Ottilie had told her that herself.

Alba grabbed Ottilie's arm, clearly bursting to share the news. 'There's a legend about a spring in these parts – a *healing* spring that can cure any ailment!'

'A healing spring?' Ottilie raised her eyebrows. 'But is it real?'

'There's enough sources to suggest that it might be,' said Alba. 'The legend says that the water springs from the site of an ancient heroic deed. Places … the land … it remembers things. Water soaks up memory, and in that particular spot, the memory is so powerful that it makes the water magic. The water acts as a conduit –'

'A what?' said Ottilie.

'A way we can access the magic,' said Alba. 'Absorb it …'

'But you have to get it from exactly the right place,' added Maeve. 'Because as the water moves away from that spot, the magic is …'

'Diluted,' Alba finished for her.

'Weakened,' said Maeve.

Ottilie's heart raced. 'How are we going to find it? How will we know where the right place is? Do I just start dipping cuts into water everywhere to see if they heal?' She wasn't joking. She would do it, if that's what it took.

Alba shook her head with a sad smile. 'It's going to be basically impossible to find without more information. It could be anywhere. It could even be in the Arko or Richter zones. We're going to keep researching. I'll let you know as soon as I have more clues.'

Ottilie wanted to stay hopeful. She wanted so badly for this to be the solution. 'So, so … once we find it,

Scoot and Ned just have to drink it, and then …' she faltered. Scoot was a statue – he couldn't drink.

'He wouldn't have to drink it,' said Alba. 'Just come into contact with it. But it has to be before he turns fully white.' She squeezed Ottilie's arm. 'Pure heartstone is … there won't be anything we can do after that.'

'But,' said Maeve.

Ottilie braced.

'Because magic is involved with their …' Maeve searched for a word. '*Problems*, it's a bit harder to fix. But still possible. The water has to be poured by the caster of the spells –'

Ottilie's hope winked out. 'But that puts us back where we started! Whistler's not going to help us. We might as well just ask her to undo the magic – it's the same thing.'

'The caster of the spells, *or* someone of their bloodline,' said Maeve, her eyes sparking again.

Ottilie spun and stared at the wolfish figure on the throne. Would he help them? Surely he would. It was just pouring a little water on a statue – and on Ned, one of the Hunt's prized elites – why would he say no?

The only thing they had to worry about now was keeping him out of Whistler's clutches. Until Alba could gather more information about this healing spring, they had to keep Varrio Sol safe.

Ramona's Right Eye

The next day, Ottilie planned to meet Leo at the base of the Dawn Cliffs. His hunt would be half done, but at least they could work together for part of their shifts. She was on her way to the lower grounds when angry voices drew her ear.

Ottilie traced the sounds to the pentagonal courtyard, where the rankings were still frozen. Drawing closer, she recognised Captain Lyre's voice. The other voice was new and, with a thrilling jolt, she realised it was probably the king. She slipped around the corner and ducked behind a raptor statue to listen.

'Announce it!' snapped the king. He wasn't looking at Captain Lyre, but was instead staring up at the ranking walls.

Ottilie followed his gaze and, with a painful scrunching feeling, took in her name at the top of the second tiers. Scoot was just below, in second place, and Gully was third. She had seen it before, but didn't like to look at it – to see Scoot's name up there. Especially because Ottilie knew why she, Scoot and Gully were ranked the highest. The scores were frozen just after Gracie's attack – the day that Whistler revealed herself and Bill was taken, then Ned too, shortly after. The wylers they felled that day had shot them to the top of the rankings.

Seeing it marked on the wall stirred up some of Ottilie's most horrific memories and deepest fears. It was a reminder, too, that Whistler still had Bill, and there was nothing she could do about it. The thought made her feel like someone was trying to tug out her guts with a fish hook.

'This is no time for celebration,' Captain Lyre said through gritted teeth.

Ottilie was surprised to hear him speak so bluntly to the king.

'You of all people know the value of lifting spirits,' said the king. 'I thought you loved parties. Or have you changed? Do I not know you anymore? It has been several years since I saw you last.' He gestured towards the rankings. 'You've been so busy here, with your *games*.'

'Watching over them,' snapped Captain Lyre. 'Trying to give them some semblance of a life after you condemned them to this!'

'You didn't put a stop to it, though, did you?' mocked the king. 'You didn't rise up. You were always a coward.'

'We've been over this, Varrio,' said Captain Lyre, swinging his cane in frustration. 'I didn't know any of this nonsense about a hex … not until Whistler rendered our western fort a ruin so she could give a speech about how much she loathes you!' He thumped the cane on the paving. 'Yes, I discovered the rule of innocence was false years ago, but I trust you remember how you silenced me?'

The king grunted. 'Of course. You should be thankful I did not go back on my word, after this debacle with the clawed witch. How you could not recogn–'

'Whist– *Fennix* was set up here as the head bone singer long before I ever came to the Narroway, as you well know! If you had ever dared to travel further west than Wikric you could have recognised her yourself.' Captain Lyre smoothed his pointed beard, his brow so low it cast shadows over his eyes. 'How could I have known? As I understand it, Fennix Sol went by another name when she was your mystic – and I never even met her when she lived in All Kings' Hill. How could I possibly have guessed? For all I knew she'd look like an old woman now. She's nearly a century old!'

'She's a witch,' spat the king. 'Of course she has not aged.'

'Whistler is no sleepless witch.'

He was right. If Ned's dreams were accurate, then there had only ever been one sleepless witch – and that distorted thing, whatever had become of it, would not be able to pass as a human. Whistler must have slowed her ageing by other means.

'Speaking of witches,' said the king. His gaze snapped to where Ottilie crouched, and her heart leapt into her throat. Had he seen her? His eyes slid over the stone wings to her left. Ottilie nearly jumped out of her skin when Ramona walked past. She had been so absorbed in the conversation, she hadn't heard her approach.

Captain Lyre's back straightened. Ottilie thought his fingers twitched on his cane.

Ramona inclined her head – it was not a bow.

'Ramona, how delightful,' said the king. 'We were just speaking of you.'

Ottilie was confused. When had Ramona been mentioned? Or was he just saying that to unsettle her somehow?

A grin split his face. 'Tell me, one of you. Why is a *girl's* name marked on this wall?'

Ottilie flinched as the king unsheathed his massive sword and leant the tip against her name.

Neither answered.

'I did notice, in our little assembly yesterday, a handful of girls sitting with the huntsmen. At first I wondered if you'd gone soft and allowed the custodians to sit down during Hunt gatherings, but now I fear you have actually allowed women to join my Narroway Hunt.'

'They earned their positions,' said Captain Lyre carefully.

'They have more right to it than any boy you kidnapped and forced to join. They volunteered,' said Ramona, her face a mask of grim calm.

The king's expression grew thunderous. 'It is an abomination!'

Ramona snorted.

Ottilie swallowed her cry of horror as the king lunged and grabbed Ramona by the throat.

So quick she might have missed it, Captain Lyre unsheathed his secret blade. Metal glinted in the sun and then slid back. The cane was just a cane again. Captain Lyre gripped the bird head handle, stepped forwards and said, 'Please, Varrio!'

'Please, *my king*,' he snarled, the tip of his nose brushing Ramona's cheek.

'Please, my king,' said Captain Lyre immediately.

'Not you,' said the king. '*Her.*'

Ramona looked like she was about to spit in his face.

Still holding her by the throat, the king lifted a hand and ran a thumb over her eyepatch. 'Do you want to know why we do not allow women to hold such positions?' He ripped the eyepatch away, revealing the knotted, sewn-over socket where her right eye should be. 'Because they are *incompetent*,' he hissed, tossing the crocodile skin eyepatch to the ground. 'You will discharge these girls from the Narroway Hunt.'

'This is no time to make your army smaller,' said Captain Lyre, his eyes fixed on Ramona.

The king finally released her. Whatever his decision about the girls, he didn't say. Instead, he took a step, crushing the eyepatch beneath his heel. Turning his back on Captain Lyre and Ramona, he said, 'Announce my banquet, *Captain*, and see to it that Ramona puts the patch back on. If she doesn't, run her through with that blade in your cane – not wearing it is an offence punishable by death.'

Without another word, the king stalked out of the courtyard.

Ramona forced a deep breath and bent to pick up the eyepatch, but Captain Lyre got there first. He brushed it off carefully on his blue coat and passed it to her. Ramona placed it back over her missing eye. A strand of her fiery hair was caught in the strap. Captain Lyre stepped close and freed it, his eyes fixed on hers.

◆ 11 ◆

Trapped

Ottilie was so late for her shift she barely had time to absorb what she had heard. Not much had made sense to her, but this wasn't the time to riddle it out. A distant mind was a death wish beyond the boundary walls.

Nox flew southeast, following the flow of the Sol River. Ottilie glanced at her left glove. There was a fresh scab beneath it. She wondered about dipping it into the river, just to check, but didn't think she could face the disappointment. The healing spring could be anywhere and river water was in constant flow – happening upon the right spot would be almost impossible.

Raging from recent rain, the waterfall ahead was so loud she could hear little else. But something caught her eye, just below: two mounts bolting through the scattered peaking-pines. Ottilie recognised the horses immediately. The towering velvet brown was Warship, although Preddy preferred to call him John, and just ahead was Skip riding her spindly black-and-white, Echo.

Leo would be waiting, but Ottilie couldn't resist hovering so that she could help if she had to. Following overhead, she watched Echo leap over a fallen branch and weave through the trees. Ottilie knew Ramona had taught Skip how to ride, but had never imagined she could be this good.

Their pursuer was just a fat shadow on their tail. Preddy and Skip shot out of the woodland into a stretch of misery moss, named for its bluish tinge. They curled in opposite directions, hooking back and closing in on what Ottilie had thought was one dredretch, but was in fact *three* horrahogs. These porcine terrors had midnight fur that dripped with violet oil. They emitted a smell that reminded Ottilie of the time she and Gully had hidden a rotting lungfish inside their neighbour Gurt's already stinky old boot.

The horrahogs split apart in the confusion, but Preddy and Skip circled, keeping them surrounded. Preddy shot one through the head with an arrow. Skip fired and missed. Even from high above, Ottilie could read her frustration.

Skip leapt from the saddle, spear in hand. The horrahogs charged, coming at her from both sides. Skip twirled, spinning her spear as a horrahog hurtled past, and lunged low to pierce its middle.

She released the spear, rolling out of the other beast's path. Pulling a cutlass from across her back, she narrowly avoided the horrahog's razor-sharp tusks and dragged the blade down its side.

With both dredretches reduced to their festering bones, Skip looked up at the sky. Cupping her hands to her mouth, she hollered, 'Enjoying the show?'

It was astonishing how talented Skip was. Ottilie had barely been able to tackle a jivvie in her early fledgling days. Of course, Skip had trained with the sculkie squad and fought at Richter. These days she put more hours into training than anyone Ottilie knew – even Leo – but it was still impressive. Ottilie would never admit it, but she was jealous of how seamlessly Skip had slid into this role.

Preddy waved and Ottilie considered landing, but Nox tensed. Ottilie strained her ears. She couldn't hear anything beyond the now-distant roar of the waterfall. Nox tilted and swerved in a sharp circle, shooting back over the trees towards the Dawn Cliffs.

Something was wrong. Was it Leo?

Nox dipped below the edge of the towering cliffs. Cool vapour wafted from the falls and flecks of water sprayed her face as they swooped lower. Finally, she heard it – Maestro's distressed cry.

Her muscles curled and bunched. She hated that sound. Why was she so late? Why had she spied on the king and lingered to watch Skip hunt?

Don't be Whistler. Don't be Gracie. Don't be anything!

Swinging left, Nox swooped over the top of a wiry thicket. Jagged shadows carved up the sunlight and blooming vines cast an eerie violet glow. Ottilie could see them – Maestro and Leo had been backed in deep by a pack of lycoats. The trees were too thick and Maestro couldn't take off.

Nox landed in the clearest glade. Ottilie jumped down, bow in hand. Twigs and thorns tearing at her clothes, she waded through the scrub.

With sickly yellow fur and wrappings of shell-like armour, lycoats looked like blunt-nosed dogs dragged from the grave. Ahead, Maestro knocked one aside with his massive paw. Leo shot another, managing to pierce a sliver of flesh. Viper quick, he released more arrows, and by the time Ottilie was near enough to get a clean shot, he had knocked the last one down.

He looked over, a triumphant grin on his face, and said, 'You're late.'

A disgruntled Maestro beat his wings, tossing his head skyward.

Ottilie gestured to the tangle of branches. 'Did they chase you in?'

'No.' Leo laughed. 'We followed them. Maestro made a fuss.' He gave the wingerslink a rough pat. Maestro rumbled and tried to shake him off. 'Doesn't like small spaces.'

Ottilie patted his pale fur. 'Me neither,' she whispered.

Maestro curled his head down and pressed his face against her side.

'All right, enough of that,' said Leo.

Maestro tensed. Ottilie was about to say, 'Don't be jealous,' but was interrupted by the beating of wings and a bloodcurdling squawk.

'Squail,' muttered Leo. 'Where is it?'

The call of a squail could render a person unconscious in a matter of minutes. Nothing could stop it – only felling the beast. Ottilie's skin prickled all over as another call joined the first, then another and another.

Leo swore as innumerable red-and-black birds, like half-roasted owls, swooped into the thicket, alighting on every tree limb in sight.

He and Ottilie began firing and the squails fell, but there were more and more of them and Ottilie was growing dizzy. Something drew her eyes up: the biggest one, paler than the others, amber and grey, with fuller feathers. Some bone singer's bloodbeast was high in the trees.

It was their only way out. If she shot that one, the usually solitary squails might scatter. Ottilie didn't think about the bone singer bound to its life. This was about survival. She aimed high. Her vision reeled and snapped back. She released the arrow with a shaking hand and it flew low, to the left. The bloodbeast fixed its shadowed sockets in her direction. Could it even see her through those things? Could the bone singer?

Her blood drained to her toes. She fell to her knees, a sharp rock digging into her shin. Her arrow supply was nearly used up.

Leo swayed on Maestro's back, his eyes sliding shut.

'Leo!' It was like trying to shout in a dream.

Tossing her bow aside and wrapping her scarf over her ears, Ottilie crawled over to Maestro, who was standing frozen so that Leo wouldn't fall. He was only half-conscious, gripping the saddle.

Ottilie drunkenly guided Maestro to tip sideways so that Leo slid off. She caught him as best she could, but his slack muscles were heavy as sacks of grain. Free of Leo, Maestro lunged and attacked any squail within reach, his beautiful wings catching on the thicket, violet vines tangling in his claws. He thumped and snapped and swiped, but the squails retreated into the knot of branches.

They couldn't fight, couldn't escape. Distantly, Ottilie could hear Nox roaring, crashing through the scrub. She would not be able to save them. There was only one thing that might. Shielding Leo with her body, Ottilie did the only thing she could think of. She knew the risk. It was a direct link to Whistler, but it was the only way. Ottilie drew the bone necklace from her pocket and slipped it over her head.

— 12 —

Captive

The world dissolved, but somehow Ottilie remembered to breathe. Something nudged her shoulder. A huff of hot breath – Nox had reached them. The thicket reassembled. Ottilie didn't know if the squails were still squawking. Her head was crowded with an unworldly song.

She clutched Leo's arm, pulling him closer. The bone necklace was supposed to make dredretches stop attacking. That was what Gracie had told her at Richter. She only hoped Leo's proximity to her would keep him safe as well.

She blinked. The song hushed, sinking lower, mingling with her pulse. The squails stilled. Their squawking ceased, but they didn't fly away. She looked higher – it seemed even the bloodbeast would not attack them now.

She felt Leo stir. They were both out of arrows. His eyes twitched open. He was white as salt. 'What's happening?'

Before Ottilie could explain, a voice spoke inside her head. 'Tea?'

'What?' said Ottilie out loud.

'Ott?' Leo leaned away from her.

She grabbed him and muttered, 'Stay close.'

'What? Why?'

'I would like you to join me for tea,' said the voice, and this time Ottilie recognised the speaker.

'Why would I do that?' It was absurd.

'Who are you talking to?' said Leo, pulling away again.

Ottilie wrenched him back, her eyes darting up to the trees. The squails had stopped screeching, but they could still attack him with their deadly talons.

'Because,' said Whistler. 'If you grace me with your presence ... I will give you the goedl.'

Ottilie nearly jumped to her feet. 'Bill? *Why?*'

'The canyon caves. Tomorrow, at midnight. You know the spot. Come alone, and leave the old cat outside.'

'Is he all right?'

The voice disappeared.

'Whistler!'

'Ott!' His eyes narrowed, Leo grabbed the necklace. Ottilie tried to pry his fingers open, but he held fast and began lifting it over her head.

'No, Leo, *stop*! They'll start again if you take it off me!'

He paused, but didn't release his grip. 'Why can Whistler talk in your head?' he demanded.

'Because of this,' she said, her fingernails digging into his hand. 'Just this! But I have to keep it on so we can get away.'

His nostrils flared. 'No, I don't like it!'

'Then let's get away from here and I can take it off!' Ottilie moved towards Nox. 'Stay close,' she said, scanning the branches for any sign that the squails might attack.

In silence, they squeezed into Nox's single saddle. The wingerslinks didn't know what to make of dredretches that weren't attacking. Tail flicking and ears flat to her skull, Nox slunk through the trees and Maestro walked tentatively behind. The squails watched them go but didn't follow. Breaking the tree line, Ottilie didn't dare take off the necklace. Behind them, the flock of squails spiralled out of the thicket and swept northward until they were just specks of dirt marring the perfect sky.

Leo was furious with Ottilie. She had never told him about the bone necklace; she didn't really know why she still had it. She had planned to show it to Maeve, thinking it might be a useful weapon against dredretches. But she had never actually handed it over.

Did it really matter? Ottilie had no doubt that if she hadn't used it yesterday afternoon, she and Leo would not have survived. That was the truth, and now Whistler was offering her a chance to get Bill back. Knowing that her friends would make a huge fuss, Ottilie had begged Leo not to tell anyone about it. He had lasted a day so far. But with everyone so busy, that didn't mean much. Now it was raining, so all shifts beyond the boundary walls were cancelled. Most of her friends had the night off – and, as per the king's orders, Captain Lyre had arranged a banquet in his honour. With nothing to do but talk and eat, Ottilie didn't know what Leo might say.

Wet weather keeping them from the uncovered Moon Court, the huntsmen gathered instead in Fiory's grandest hall. Ottilie had not been inside it since her first day at the fort. She still remembered Captain Lyre standing in front of the arched windows holding a birdcage aloft.

Tonight was uncommonly warm and windless. They had opened the windows, filling the room with the sound of falling rain. Ottilie was horrified to see that the bone singers had been dragged up from their cells and caged in the corner of the room. They sat, looking as dishevelled as ever, playing their instruments as the huntsmen feasted.

Gully was tense beside Ottilie, regarding the cages with narrowed eyes. 'How can they expect us to have a party *now*' – he nodded towards the bone singers – 'like *this*?'

'It's all because of the king,' said Ottilie. She noticed Captain Lyre's face was lined and grim, but Conductor Edderfed was happily devouring a turkey leg as if there were no prisoners in the room. Wrangler Voilies and Director Yaist were growing steadily drunker and offering the king simpering smiles. Wrangler Furdles kept throwing his chicken bones through the bars, sniggering when he hit a bone singer, until Wrangler Morse moved to stand sentinel beside the cage.

'Aren't they afraid of them?' Ottilie asked Skip, who was sitting nearby. 'Don't they think they're witches or evil mystics or something?'

'Iron manacles,' said Skip.

Iron was supposed to block magic. It was why witches were buried in iron coffins.

Sure enough, Ottilie spotted Bonnie strumming a harp, her wrist bound with an iron chain attached to the cage. The soft music was interrupted here and there with the rattle and clank of their fetters. This was something the king found very amusing. He prowled past, leering in and smiling cruelly.

Two Arko huntsmen had been assigned as the king's personal guards: Murphy Graves and Banjo Adler. Ottilie could tell they weren't happy about it. The rumour was that Murphy and Banjo had accompanied the king to Fiory and impressed him when they dealt with a giffersnak that dropped onto the roof of the carriage. He had rewarded them by *honouring* them with the role.

The pair were standing by the drinks table talking to Bacon Skitter, and Ottilie noticed Gully's eyes kept flicking to Murphy Graves.

'You look at him a lot,' she whispered, trying not to smile.

Gully's eyes snapped to the ceiling. 'No more than you look at Ned,' he muttered, glancing sideways at her.

'Can I talk to you?' said Ned.

Ottilie jumped, turning to find him behind her, his brow furrowed. Out of the corner of her eye she caught Leo squeezing into a seat beside Preddy and immediately engaging him in conversation.

With a sigh, Ottilie followed Ned across the room. He stopped just out of earshot of a group of the new fledglings, who kept shooting uneasy glances at the cages. Ottilie couldn't imagine how those fledges were feeling about this new life that had been forced upon them. It was a wonder there hadn't been an escape attempt.

'What were you thinking?' said Ned, fixing his eyes on hers.

'I have to go. She said she'd free Bill.'

'Not about that. Of course you can't do that – it's obviously a trap and you know it. I'm talking about the necklace!'

'What?' She hadn't been expecting this. She didn't have her arguments lined up.

'Leo said she can talk in your head when you wear it! Why would you keep that?'

'Well, I don't wear it! Only yesterday, and it saved me and Leo. I'm glad I kept it.'

Ned's lips thinned. 'You've got some nerve telling me I have to stop the dreams because Whistler's making me have them, when you've been walking around with that thing in your pocket!'

'I …' He was right. Wait. No, he wasn't. 'I can control when I use it. It's completely different to the dreams.'

'Why would you even want to use it?'

'Because it stops the dredretches attacking. It's *handy*! I'm not getting rid of it. Especially not before I –'

'You can't go tonight!'

'That's not up to you,' she said, cringing as she realised they were the same words he had used when they'd argued about stopping his dreams.

Ottilie was painfully aware of how close he was standing. She had to look up to see his face properly. He was glaring at her, but she realised it wasn't anger in his eyes. It was fear. Ned reached forwards, his fingers twitching as if he intended to take her hand – but he didn't. Instead, he stepped back and walked away from her, right over to Gully.

What followed was the worst fight Ottilie had ever had in hushed tones. It was just Gully at first, then Skip and Preddy joined in, all three refusing to let her go to meet Whistler. Ned and Leo stayed back and she glared at them, furious that they had spread the word.

The adults in the room were growing louder and louder. Laughter boomed and cracked. Stories were told with shrieks and shouts. Men yelled over one another. Everything felt wrong. The bone singers' music seemed to lag, as if time had slowed, and beneath it all Ottilie and her friends fought on.

Eventually she hissed, 'Fine! I won't go.'

'You swear?' said Gully.

Ottilie looked into his eyes and lied.

✦ 13 ✦

A Midnight Meeting

Ottilie had just pulled on her boots when a black owl soared through her open window. Maeve transformed in mid-air and stepped lightly onto the floor. She had come so far from the frightened girl who once accidentally set a tapestry alight above Wrangler Voilies' head.

Ottilie slid her cutlass into the sheath across her back. 'You can't stop me.'

'I'm not here to stop you. I came to make sure you're still going.'

Ottilie had not expected that. She peered through the shadows, meeting Maeve's hopeful gaze. 'Course I am.

She said she'd let Bill go.' Nothing could stop her. They were no closer to finding the healing spring, Ned was still dreaming and Scoot was still stone, but she could rescue Bill.

'I'm coming with you,' said Maeve.

It was tempting, but Ottilie was scared that if she didn't follow Whistler's instructions, she might not hand Bill over. 'You can't come.'

Maeve took several steps forward, her expression pleading. 'I'll go as the owl, and I won't come into the caves. I'll stay outside.'

It worried her, but Ottilie was such a bundle of nerves she couldn't turn down the offer of company. If everything ran smoothly, Whistler would never know Maeve was there.

Nox dropped Ottilie on a ledge at the passage opening, then the wingerslink and Maeve flew to the top of the cliff to wait.

The last time Ottilie had entered these caves, it had been a trap. When they had come to rescue Ned, she and Leo had been ambushed by a bone singer and a horde of dredretches. Ottilie had lost part of her ear in there, and if it wasn't for Maeve, she might have lost much more.

She had thought the difficult part would be leaving Fiory, but it wasn't. It was here on this ledge, at the entrance shaped like a lightning bolt. Her insides squirmed and her feet refused to move.

She took a deep breath and thought of Bill. He had helped her even though he was afraid. He had led her through the tunnels all the way to Wikric and then, a year later, he had stowed away, entering monster-infested territory just to find her.

Ottilie shook out her shoulders, held her glow sticks aloft, and walked into the caves.

What was ahead? There had to be some sort of trickery involved. Did Whistler still have her lined up for a binding? Was there a particularly foul dredretch waiting for her by that crumbling well, ready to become her bloodbeast?

With a shaking hand, Ottilie drew her cutlass. She had to take this opportunity. She might never get another chance. The bone necklace hummed in her pocket, and with a jolt Ottilie realised why – it hummed when Whistler was near.

Clenching her fingers tighter on her cutlass, Ottilie rounded the final curve to find Whistler seated at a great chunk of rock laid with a blue tablecloth. Resting on the uneven surface was a jar of embers, like a fistful of fireflies. The amber glow illuminated a single teapot, painted orange, and two purple cups.

'Ah,' said Whistler, shambling from her perch on a rock. 'Welcome!'

Ottilie froze, her eyes combing the cavern. There was no sign of Bill – no sign of anyone, or *anything*. There were no dredretches nearby. Whistler must have kept them at a distance to put her at ease.

Waving her sleeve at the rock opposite her own, Whistler chirped, 'Sit, sit, sit.'

'Where's Bill?' said Ottilie, still frozen in the mouth of the cavern.

'He'll be along.'

Begrudgingly, Ottilie moved forward and balanced on the very edge of the rock, ready to leap up at any second.

An amused smile tugged at Whistler's lips as she poured the tea. Ottilie only wished her hand would stop shaking as she reached out and pushed the cup away. Some of the honey-coloured liquid slopped onto the tablecloth. Both Ottilie and Whistler stared down at the swelling puddle.

'You don't have to drink it if you don't want to,' said Whistler. '*Rude*,' she muttered, as if Ottilie couldn't hear.

'What do you want? When do I get to see Bill?' Ottilie blurted, her heart still hammering.

Whistler smiled. 'You're a rumbler, my girl. That's what I like about you.'

'A rumbler?' Her eyes darted all around, wary of attack.

'A bringer of change, a mistress of floods, a drawer of tides. You remind me of me.' Whistler lunged forward as if to take her hand.

Ottilie lurched backwards, the white tips of Scoot's fingers fixed in her mind. 'You don't bring change – you bring misery!'

Whistler merely smiled and raised her hands like a scale. Tipping them up and down, she said, 'Misery to some. Joy to others. You can't please everyone.'

Ottilie scowled. Whistler seemed to think this was a big joke.

'I offer choices. Choose right and you've nothing to fear.'

'I've already told you I'm not going to switch sides.' Ottilie didn't know where she found the rush of courage. 'Why are you wasting your time? Don't you have more important things to do? What are you waiting for?'

What was the point of all this? Why did Whistler even want to talk to her? *You remind me of me* ... That was troubling. But what did Ottilie have to do with anything?

'Astute,' said Whistler. She lifted her teacup delicately to her lips and took a loud, messy slurp. 'I am waiting. Stuck for a bit.' She took another gulp, her birdlike eyes fixed on Ottilie over the rim of the cup.

'But I am offering you safety and salvation, girl. Do you consider that a waste of time?'

'What do you mean, *stuck*?'

Whistler didn't answer. Instead, she slammed down her cup and said, perfectly calmly, 'I think, when you know more, you will come around to my way of thinking. Our hearts are aligned. You just don't know it yet. I want to tell you a little about who I am.'

'I want to see –'

'And when I'm done you can see your friend.'

Ottilie bit back her retort.

'Some of it you already know, so forgive me if I tread over old ground.'

Despite herself, Ottilie leaned forward. Whistler caught the movement and her eyes glittered.

'Years ago,' she began, 'my father, fresh from destroying the Laklands, gained the title *Viago the Vanquisher*.' Whistler said the name as if it were an insult. 'I have told you before,' she continued, 'that after he broke the promise and destroyed the Laklands, the dredretches emerged and a rumour took root. People began to whisper that my family was being punished – they called it the Vanquisher's bane. They said that my mother was barren, like the Laklands, and the Sol line would end. But, ten years after the war, she finally fell pregnant. My parents rejoiced, believing this proved the bane was not real.'

Whistler's lip curled. 'But then the baby was born. *Me*. A daughter with a misshapen hand – and the rumours twisted into a new shape. They said my mother could birth only monsters, like the land that my father had destroyed. And when I started showing signs of magic ... you can only imagine how that fuelled the fire. The clawed witch, they called me.

'With the birth of my younger brother, the rumours – the legend – found its final form. My brother, Feo, was healthy, *normal* – no twisted limbs, no magic. So, they decided, my parents included, that *I* was the bane, *I* was their punishment, their curse, and from then on all Sol daughters have carried my burden.'

Disgust darkened Whistler's face. 'My family believes females are bad luck – that they carry on the bane, and are destined to be the ruination of the Sol family and the lands they rule.'

Ottilie narrowed her eyes. 'But ...' She looked Whistler up and down. 'They were right. You are a' – she thought of the giant winged creature – '*monster*,' she whispered, 'and you're destroying everything ...'

Ottilie expected her to lash out. Strangely, Whistler smiled a self-satisfied smile. 'Have I taught you nothing? Hexes, curses ...' She shook her head.

Ottilie frowned. True, she was yet to hear about any form of curse that had not turned out to be a complete lie ...

'There's always a choice,' said Whistler abruptly. 'No matter how trapped you find yourself, there is always free will. I was no curse, just a young innocent girl, but my life was shaped by people's belief in that curse's existence.

'At seven, I was imprisoned in my father's dungeons, allowed out only to use my magic to help punish his prisoners, or force them to speak. My mother abandoned me, forgot me. I never saw her until years later, long after I escaped at age twelve.'

'Where did you go?' Ottilie felt a twinge of guilt – was she just satisfying her own curiosity? This wasn't why she'd come. How was this helping Bill?

'Many places,' said Whistler. 'I studied magic, honed my craft, visited far-off lands where witches still practised freely, unthreatened.

'I returned to the Usklers long after my father died. My brother, Feo, was a good king, but I was wary of his son, Varrio, who I found to be a freakish double of my father.

'When my brother passed and Varrio became king, I watched from afar. I saw him become a cruel, war-hungry ruler. He invaded the independent islands to the south-west, conquering land for the sake of it, massacring entire communities, crippling ancient civilisations and leaving the dregs to rot.

'I heard rumours he was planning on expanding the Usklers by launching an assault on the Triptiquery Principalities – the Usklers' closest neighbour and strongest ally, and our salvation in the Lakland War.

'Just like my parents, Varrio and his queen had difficulty producing an heir, and rumours of the bane were revived. When the queen bore his first child, I heard it was a girl – the first Sol daughter since myself.'

Varrio's first child … Ottilie had never known much about her. She had died long before Ottilie was born.

'I feared for her and immediately installed myself at the palace.' Whistler's voice had changed. It softened and swelled at the same time. Ottilie sat up a little straighter.

'Varrio had never met me before. As far as he was aware, the clawed witch, Fennix Sol, was long dead. I used a false name and had myself instated as the Royal Mystic to watch over the princess.'

Just as Ottilie had sensed in the Withering Wood, Whistler's emotions billowed out. Ottilie could almost see them, like smoke swelling. She knew the princess had not lived long. Was this what Gracie had meant by vengeance? Was Whistler's vendetta against the king something to do with the young princess?

'Enough history!' snapped Whistler, and Ottilie saw the shadow of the winged beast in her eyes. 'Does it sound to you, Ottilie, like I was a curse?' she growled. 'Like this innocent girl after me was cursed?'

'Of course not.' Ottilie's fingers twitched towards her knife. She felt strangled and shivery all over, as if Whistler's emotions were pressing in on her. 'But now …'

'Now, yes, *now*,' snarled Whistler. 'That's the point. I made a choice to give them all what they feared most, to become the terror that they believed I, and every Sol daughter after me, would become.

'I aligned myself with the same breed of monster that my father's callous ambition brought forth. And now, I *will* see the end of the Sol line, and bring about the ruination of all they rule.'

Ottilie felt as if spiders were crawling up and down her spine. 'What happened to the princess?' she dared to ask.

Whistler leapt out of her seat. Ottilie rolled sideways, ducking behind the stone table, waiting for an attack that didn't come.

'I'm giving you a gift,' said Whistler icily.

Ottilie peeked above the blue tablecloth to see Whistler strolling away from her.

'I don't want any more gifts,' she said, staying low to the ground.

Whistler turned, her eyes bright. 'You want this one, possum.' She rested a hand on the crumbling well.

Ottilie stared at it, her mind humming. She had never considered it before. From Ned's dream, it seemed that a coven of witches had once inhabited these caves, and here in the middle of it all was a well. She'd seen it before, of course, but she hadn't thought ...

Despite everything, hope sparked. Ottilie jumped up, her eyes fixed on the ruin. It could just be ordinary water, but Whistler's smile suggested that the well contained exactly what Ottilie had been hoping for – the healing spring.

— 14 —

The Well

'I'm giving you a choice,' said Whistler, 'and I think you will be pleased.'

Ottilie tensed, her hope burning hot.

'As I see, you've guessed. This well was built over the legendary healing spring.' Whistler paused, and Ottilie felt a strange urge to laugh. She could have run over and hugged the ruin.

'Here is my offer,' said Whistler. 'Either you or Bill may lower a pail and leave with its contents.' Her smile twitched wider. 'The other remains with me.'

Ottilie's heart sank.

Only one of them would be free to leave. If she left with the water, she might be able to cure Scoot and

Ned, but Bill would still be a captive. If she remained … There was no choice, really.

'Where's Bill?' It was a struggle to keep her voice steady.

Whistler swung her sleeve towards the entrance to a dark tunnel. To Ottilie's horror, Gracie Moravec appeared, holding a rope that bound Bill's wrists.

Gracie had changed since their conversation at Richter. Her eyes had once flashed red when she sent commands to the wylers, but now they seemed permanently lit with that fiery glow. There had always been something strange about the way Gracie moved, but there was a new wildness to her movements, a stiffness to her legs and an odd tilt to the turn of her head.

Ottilie met her gaze and saw no trace of the girl she remembered. It may as well have been the white wyler staring back at her. With a jolt, she realised it probably was.

She needed to get Bill away from her, now. Ottilie hurried towards them, but was halted by Whistler's raised arm and cry of, 'Ba, ba, ba!'

Bill's shoulders curved, and his eyes flicked here and there. When his gaze met Ottilie's, he looked more nervous still. He blinked at the well and then back at her. What was he trying to say? That she must leave with the water? Ottilie gritted her teeth and shook her head.

What had happened to Gracie was a fate worse than anything Ottilie could imagine, and she feared Whistler would do that to her, too. But Bill would not change her mind.

He opened his hands over and over, like he was miming a book. He began to mouth something, but Gracie turned and bared her little white teeth. Ottilie wasn't close enough to be sure, but it looked as if they had narrowed, tapering to pointed tips. Bill closed his mouth tight.

'What is your decision?' said Whistler.

Ottilie was still watching Bill. His eyes darted to the well.

'We don't have all night.' Whistler flicked her sleeve and Gracie twirled her knife, pointing it in Bill's direction.

Ottilie hesitated.

Gracie smiled and lunged for Bill.

His yelp of fear was like a spear through her heart. 'BILL GOES!'

Gracie paused mid-lunge and Ottilie ground her teeth, her heart beating wildly. She had never hated Gracie more. How could she have chosen this? She was a beast. A minion. Just another one of Whistler's monsters.

'Very well,' said Whistler.

In an instant, the ropes that bound Bill uncoiled, slithered across the floor and knotted around Ottilie's wrists. She gasped as they pulled tight, burning her skin. Whistler ducked to pick up the loose end.

Bill stumbled forwards. 'No, Ottilie!'

'Enough, Bi–' Whistler's cry was cut off as an arrow flew across the cave, catching on her sleeve and yanking her arm backwards, causing her to twist and fall.

The rope tugged and Ottilie pitched onto her knees. At the same time, her head whipped to the side and she saw Gully leaping from a ledge.

Why was he here? How did he know?

Whistler was gathering herself. She turned to Gully, rage warping her features. Ottilie's whole body shuddered, but the screech of an owl distracted Whistler. She waved her hand and Maeve transformed back to a girl in mid-air. Maeve rolled and crashed to the ground, skidding across the cavern floor.

Whistler had dropped the rope. Ottilie struggled away from her, but couldn't get her hands free. She was useless.

Where was Gracie? Ottilie turned and saw she had stopped still, her eyes glowing brighter. Ottilie's bowels turned to water as she realised Gracie was calling the wylers to her. She blinked and saw Scoot and Bayo. Glittering frost. Pools of red. Droplets on wildflowers.

She saw tangled webwood trees. A wyler lunging at Gully. The beat of blood.

Bill raised a tentative hand and covered Gracie's eyes, looking inquisitively to see if it was helping. It was not.

Whistler faced Maeve, readying her strike. Gully shot another arrow. Whistler twisted and turned it to ash. But it was enough of a distraction. With a strained groan, Maeve raised and lowered her hand.

There was a great shuddering and cracking. The ancient ledge above Whistler collapsed and she disappeared beneath a mountain of crumbled rock.

Everyone scurried away from the rolling stones. Dust billowed and Ottilie coughed, gasping for air.

With a yowl of rage, Gracie snapped out of her trance and began clawing at the rocks, trying to free Whistler.

'Run!' cried Maeve.

Gracie's eyes snapped to her old friend. She bared her teeth, more beast than girl, but didn't attack.

Ottilie tried to move, but the end of her rope was caught under fallen rock. Gully hurried over and cut her hands free. 'Come on!' he said, pulling her arm. But she shook him off and scrambled over the loose stones – not to the passage, but to the well.

'The wylers are coming!' cried Maeve.

Ottilie reached the well, snatched at its rusted chain and lowered the bucket. Down, down, down. How low was the water level? It seemed endless …

Finally there was a jolt and a distant echoing thud.

A lump formed in her throat.

The well was dry. That was what Bill had been trying to say. Whistler had said he could lower the bucket and leave with the contents. Air. Nothing.

Tears brimmed and a great heaving sob wreaked havoc on its way out.

A familiar scent: puddles and rain-soaked bark. Bill's clammy hand pressed over hers and, for the briefest of moments, Ottilie let relief lift her up; he was alive. 'Run, Ottilie,' said Bill.

'RUN!' cried Gully from across the cave.

There was a great rumbling, and Ottilie whirled to see a humungous dark shape pushing from underneath the stones. A wing bent up and for the first time Ottilie saw the dark, hooked spikes hidden among the feathers. Whistler had shifted and was rising from the rubble.

Gracie palmed her knives and started running towards Ottilie and Bill. Maeve twisted into an owl and dived, her talons outstretched. Gracie shrieked and raised her arms to shield her face.

'Come on!' cried Gully, and he, Ottilie and Bill bolted out through the passage.

Behind her, Ottilie could hear stones shifting as Whistler struggled to rise, and the shrill shrieks of Gracie's wylers.

They stumbled out into the night, skidding to a halt where Nox was waiting with Maestro. Ottilie looked around, half expecting to see Leo, but there was no sign of him. Gully crawled into Maestro's saddle, and Ottilie pulled Bill up onto Nox.

'Strap yourself in, Bill!'

As he fumbled for the leg straps, she twisted in her seat, staring back through the lightning-shaped opening. Where was Maeve?

Gully was doing the same, dread fixed on his face. His eyes met hers, and she found hopelessness there. But they wouldn't surrender to it. Maeve would come out. They would not move until she did.

'How did you know, Gully?' she asked.

His lips thinned. 'You don't think I know when you're lying?'

But they were too anxious to say more. The seconds ticked by. Any moment the wylers would come and they would have to take flight. Whistler herself could be after them.

Ottilie heard claws scraping behind them. She looked at Gully and he shook his head. Maestro shifted his feet, eager to get away. Nox emitted a low growl.

A wyler shrieked, and a flash of orange arced over their heads. But it wasn't leaping – it was falling, tossed from the talons of a shining black owl that shot out above as the wyler plummeted into the canyon, disappearing into its night-drowned depths.

15

Horror and Heartstone

They landed in the lower grounds. High above, silhouettes of wall watchers blotted the torchlight. What did they think of Nox and Maestro going out in the middle of the night? They weren't scheduled to, and the wrangler in the tower would certainly have taken note.

Ottilie didn't care. The Hunt could punish her if they wanted. Rescuing Bill was more important. She felt tingly with joy at the thought. But her happiness staggered under the weight of disappointment. The well was dried up. Their one chance to save Scoot was gone.

She slid down Nox's side and landed heavily on the grass. Blinking back tears, Ottilie helped Bill unbuckle his legs. Beside her, Maestro shook Gully off. Gully glared up from the ground – not at Maestro, but at Ottilie.

'Leo's going to kill you for taking Maestro out.' She meant it to be lighthearted – a sort of joke. But it came out half-whispered, in a voice that hardly sounded like her own.

Gully had learned the fundamentals of flying last year, but he was only a beginner. Maestro, although a difficult wingerslink, was loyal to Ottilie, and Gully knew it. She could only assume Maestro had granted Gully that single flight because he'd sensed her brother's desperation.

Gully was still glaring at her. Ottilie knew she should thank him for rescuing her, but defiance and shame were mixing her up. She looked away from him to Maeve, who was panting on the grass.

Ottilie hurried over. 'Are you hurt?'

Maeve gestured to the scrapes up her left side. Her dress had torn over her shoulder and Ottilie could see a nasty graze. Her chin and cheek were also cut up from when she had fallen from mid-air.

'That was amazing, Maeve. You beat her!'

Whistler had not come after them. Ottilie assumed she was too injured to fly, although if she was anything like a dredretch, she would heal in no time.

'It was only because she was surprised.' Maeve nodded at Gully. 'His arrows – that was the only reason ...'

She crawled up from the ground and drifted over to Bill. 'Hi Bill,' she whispered.

At least Maeve understood that it had all been worth it. Ottilie glanced back at Gully and found she was scared to approach him. They had squabbled plenty of times before, but he had never been this angry with her.

'Thank you,' she said quietly. 'If you hadn't come –'

'I know.' He turned his back.

Ottilie wanted to say, *I'm sorry. I'm sorry for lying, for scaring you, for nearly getting myself captured.* But she didn't. She couldn't say it because, like he said, Gully could tell when she was lying.

None of her friends were speaking to her. Even Preddy only offered stiff politeness, which Ottilie found just as distressing as Skip and Leo's raging, or Alba and Ned's dark disappointment.

She understood why they were angry. She had lied to them and put herself in great danger. If anyone else had done it, Ottilie would have been furious with them. But she couldn't help seeing it as a triumph. They had rescued Bill and escaped Whistler! Although, the thought of Whistler turned everything a funny colour. *You remind me of me* – she couldn't get those words out of her head.

Why was Whistler so determined to lure her there? Bill was a goedl. An ancient species with unparalleled camouflage abilities and a collective consciousness. Young for one of his kind, Bill still struggled with the ceaseless storm of memory that sometimes spun his thoughts off kilter. He had access to a wealth of knowledge collected over eons. The answers to so many questions were at his fingertips, if only he could focus enough to grasp them. Not only that, Bill had a kinship with birds, and they often shared with him things they had spied. Why had Whistler wanted to trade all that away? Bill, with his marvellous mind, for Ottilie – it didn't make sense.

Avoiding her friends, Ottilie spent a lot of time in the wingerslink sanctuary with Maeve and Bill. On a blustery afternoon, they gathered in Nox's pen. Nox leapt into the field with a sullen snarl and Ottilie watched her sweeping in circles, enjoying the wind. Ottilie was transfixed, jealous of her wings.

Maeve was sitting on the floor in the corner, her knees bent up in front of her. Bill was beside her, mimicking her position. The graze on her face had flared to an angry red. She had told the custodian chieftess that she tripped on the rocky path by the apiary.

'But why, Bill?' Maeve was saying. 'Why was she willing to give you up?'

'I couldn't give her the words she wanted,' said Bill, wrapping his webbed fingers around his throat. 'She said she was giving up on me, so I had to be … *a worm on a hook*.' He blinked his spidery eyelashes in Ottilie's direction.

She scrunched up her face.

Maeve looked her over. 'What does she want you for?'

'She says I remind her of *her*.' Ottilie was ashamed of it, but, strangely, she didn't mind confessing to Maeve. After all, who had more in common with Whistler than Maeve? 'She says she wants to save me.'

Maeve frowned and picked a piece of straw off Bill's shoulder, but didn't comment. With a breath of relief, Ottilie remembered that Whistler had offered Maeve a place at her side too. Maeve had been asked twice: once by Gracie, and the second time by Whistler herself.

Maybe Whistler really did want to rescue them, in her own twisted way. Ottilie couldn't consider Gracie's transformation as anything resembling a *rescue*, but to survive in Whistler's world – the dredretch-infested ruin that she threatened to bring about – perhaps becoming a monster was the only way.

It wasn't worth it. How could anyone believe it was?

Ottilie knew why Whistler had been interested in Maeve. She was a fiorn, like Whistler herself. She had probably sensed it long before Maeve understood. But why did Whistler want Ottilie too?

She and Maeve were both unusual girls – both outsiders. Perhaps that was all there was to it. Bonnie had said Whistler liked to think of herself as a champion of unwanted children, and Ottilie and Maeve were unwanted in many regards. Certainly in the Narroway – the directorate had threatened to banish both of them. And Ottilie's mother was more devoted to bramblywine than she was to her children. As for her father, she had never even met him.

Keen to change the subject, she turned to Bill. 'What did Whistler want from you?'

Bill gulped, his eyes darting around as if he feared Whistler were near. 'She wanted me to remember about a sleepless witch.' He shivered.

Ottilie tensed. She had not been expecting this, although perhaps she should have been. A sleepless witch ... like the one Ned had been dreaming about.

It was as if someone had poured ice water down her back.

Why did Whistler need that information? And what did it have to do with Ned? Ottilie shuddered. The sleepless witch had to be out there somewhere – another terror lurking, another horror waiting for its moment to pounce.

'But you didn't know – you couldn't remember?' said Maeve, bending a thick piece of straw. 'Maybe that's just because no goedl ever saw – or knew – anything about it.'

Bill shook his head, his brow dipping low. 'There are bits in there.' He tapped his skull. 'And I can feel more, but I couldn't ... can't ... find it ... see it ... I was too afraid.' He shuffled his bare feet, burying them in the straw.

'So she just let you stop trying?' said Ottilie. That didn't sound like Whistler.

'She said she would have to go with her backup plan,' said Bill. 'It just meant more waiting.' He gulped. 'She was angry about that.'

'Waiting?' Ottilie frowned. Whistler had mentioned *waiting* to Ottilie too.

She twisted her fingers around her elbow. Whistler could attack whenever she wished, and yet she was waiting. She must have been planning something huge. Something to do with the sleepless witch. The thought made Ottilie's stomach turn.

'Has she ever said what she's going to do after all this waiting?' said Maeve. 'I mean, we all just think she's going to attack the Usklers, but do we know *how*? She failed at taking Richter last year. If she's attacking with dredretches, I don't know how she plans to get them past the Hunt. And let's not forget that the Usklers are islands. She could take the west, but the rest ...'

Ottilie pictured dredretches prowling through the Swamp Hollows, the withering sickness strangling the trees in Longwood Forest. The western island was only a third of the Usklerian Kingdom, but it was the largest landmass.

Maeve was right. The rest of the Usklers would be protected by the channels. Dredretches could not cross the saltwater, although ...

'Bloodbeasts will,' said Ottilie, thinking of the knopoes she and Leo had hunted. She had thought before that they had been positioned in Jungle Bay for a reason. Someone was testing them. She remembered them leaping between the Sea Spears, under the command of an unseen bone singer.

'They'll do anything they're told,' she added. 'And any normal dredretch directly controlled by a bone singer, or Whistler, will too.' She rested her head on her knees. It was exhausting.

'Still, only winged kinds will make it,' said Maeve. 'The others can't just swim. The saltwater would end them.'

'*Heartstone*,' Bill murmured. He clapped a hand to his mouth and whispered through the gaps in his fingers. 'She's got lots ... like Scoot ... she's been making it for years. She's going to build big white bridges. It's the only thing dredretches will cross.'

Ottilie snapped upright. 'What?'

'Of course it is,' said Maeve, spitting her words. 'Because it's evil. It's people turned to stone.'

16

A Promise and a Lie

Ottilie returned to her bedchamber to find a note under the door. She had barely read the first line when a shape shifted on her bed. She jerked backwards, but it was just Gully, staring grimly across the room.

'Where have you been?' he demanded.

'Lower grounds.'

He held up a letter of his own. 'Captain Lyre wants to see us – right now.'

Ottilie wriggled her fingers, casting off her fear. It was just Captain Lyre, not the whole directorate, and Gully had been summoned too.

'Why?' she asked, suspecting she already knew the answer.

'Because we went out in the middle of the night when we weren't rostered on,' said Gully, shuffling to the edge of her bed.

Ottilie had no explanation to offer Captain Lyre. No-one knew about Bill, and she couldn't very well tell him she had left to have a midnight tea party with a witch. Before they'd rescued Bill, being in trouble with the Hunt had seemed like nothing compared to meeting Whistler. But now that it was over, punishment was a much more frightening prospect.

'They saw the wingerslinks,' said Gully. 'No-one ever rides Nox but you, and they asked Leo about Maestro and he said it was me.'

'He what?!'

'Ottilie, it *was* me.'

'He didn't need to tell them that!' She scrunched the letter in her fist.

'What else was he going to tell them?'

'Anything!' Her nerves fuelled her anger. 'Nothing! He could have told them he didn't know – how *did* he even know?'

'Because I told him,' said Gully, with a maddening shrug.

She didn't understand why he wasn't angry with Leo.

'Get over it, Ottilie. He knew you'd be in less trouble if I was called in too.'

Ottilie's mouth fell open and rage simmered deep down. He was right. She had thought it herself, just moments ago, but that had been merely a feeling; now she understood where it came from. They were less likely to punish her because Gully had broken the same rule. They would be lenient with him, and therefore more lenient with her. She felt like kicking a wall.

'Don't ever do it again,' said Gully quietly.

Ottilie didn't respond. She didn't know what to say. She would do it again if she had to. She would have done it over and over.

'Don't go without me,' he added.

'What?'

His gaze was steady. He suddenly seemed so much older. 'Take me with you,' he said. 'Don't leave me behind.'

She met his eyes. 'I won't. I mean, I will – I'll take you next time. Every time.'

The anger in the room dimmed on both sides. Ottilie dropped the letter, Gully hopped off the bed, and together they headed for Captain Lyre's chambers.

➤————————————→

Ottilie knocked on the door and Captain Lyre pulled it open. His expression was unreadable, which put her on edge. When he stepped aside, she realised there was someone else in the room. The king was seated at Captain Lyre's desk.

He looked her up and down and then met her gaze with an unbreakable stare. It was the sort of look that Ottilie knew was supposed to intimidate her – and it was working. Her shoulders raised up and her neck tensed, as if someone were standing too close.

It occurred to her that they were probably supposed to bow. Captain Lyre was saying something, introducing them, but Ottilie hardly heard him. He must have offered them a seat because Gully immediately sat in front of the desk and tugged on her sleeve.

Captain Lyre perched on a seat beside the desk, looking wary. She got the sense that the king was here uninvited. Captain Lyre opened his mouth to speak, but the king got in first.

'So, you're the girl?' He leaned back in his chair.

Ottilie didn't know what to say to that. Thankfully, Captain Lyre cut in. 'Ottilie was our first female recruit,' he said. 'And one of our highest scoring huntsmen in the fledg–'

'Hunts-*men*,' said the king, with a spiteful smile.

'We didn't feel the need to change the name,' said Captain Lyre carefully, pinching the tip of his pointed beard.

'I should think not.' The king bared his teeth. 'The Narroway huntsmen have held that name for thirty years. Changing it on account of one little girl seems an extreme action to me.'

Ottilie clenched her jaw. Was this ever going to stop being an issue? She had never been too bothered by the fact that she was called a *huntsman*, preferring that to an alternative name that singled her out. Now, for the first time, she wished they were all simply the Narroway hunters.

But right now, with Whistler preparing to build heartstone bridges and obliterate the Usklers, what did anything else matter? How could the king be focusing on anything other than stopping Whistler?

Ottilie stared at his face. There was something about it. His eyes, perhaps? Not the expression, but the shape. The way they were set beneath his brow. He had a harsh face, but his eyebrows had a habit of dipping down. It was familiar to her, and his sole softening feature, which was easily cancelled out by his callous gaze. She thought again of Whistler's interest in her – she couldn't possibly be linked to this horrible family, could she?

Captain Lyre seemed eager to get back to the point. 'Ottilie, Gulliver – we've received a report that you exited the grounds in the middle of the night without permission. I'm afraid I will need an explanation.'

'It was my fault,' said Ottilie, before Gully had the chance to lie for her. 'I went out, and Gully only followed to bring me back.'

'And why did you go?' said Captain Lyre.

Ottilie thought fast. She hadn't come up with an excuse. She had intended to just refuse to tell them, but now that seemed very foolish. She had to say something, anything …

'Dreams,' she blurted out.

Gully stared at her, his eyes wide.

'Sleepwalking – sleepflying,' she stammered.

'*Sleepflying*?' said Captain Lyre, clearly trying to squash his smile.

'I'm a funny sleeper, always have been,' she said. 'Gully knows.' She nudged him with her elbow. 'He keeps an ear out in case I wander off – don't you, Gully.'

'Y-yes,' said Gully.

'Indeed?' said Captain Lyre, the twinkle returning to his eyes.

Ottilie glanced at the king. He was still staring at her, a cold, amused expression on his face. '*Sleepflying* for half the night?' he said.

'Gully's a terrible flyer,' said Ottilie.

Gully nodded, frowning in agreement. 'It took me a long time to find her – I am *not* good at it.'

'Probation,' snapped Captain Lyre. Ottilie thought he might be trying to cover a snort. Schooling his features, he added, 'In the past we would have banned you from hunting, limiting you to guard duty and wall watch. But … considering the *times* and the fact that the scoring system is no longer in place, I do not see the point in wasting two of our *strongest* second tiers.'

His speech seemed to be for the king's benefit. She remembered Captain Lyre telling him this was not the time to make his army smaller.

'But we will be watching you, and if you break the rules again, you risk dismissal. Do I make myself clear?' said Captain Lyre.

'Yes,' they said together.

The king caught Ottilie's eye. Cruel amusement played on his lips. Ottilie couldn't pick any physical resemblance to Whistler, but there was something in that expression that reminded her of the witch. She tore her eyes away and glanced at Captain Lyre. He gave her a look that seemed to say, *tread carefully*. Ottilie blinked in acknowledgment and he simply said, 'You may go.'

17

Spilt Milk

Ottilie slipped through the partitions to find Montie laying fresh lullaby cuttings on Scoot's pillow.

'You're up bright and early, Ottilie.'

It *was* early. The world was still silver and gold. Ottilie's sleep had been patchy. How could she rest knowing that every night brought Ned more dangerous dreams, every dawn took Scoot further away, and every hour could bring Whistler's next strike upon them?

Montie adjusted the golden flowers on the windowsill – Gully's doing, again.

Ottilie glanced at Scoot's fingertips. The pure white reached his wrist, as if he were wearing a single snowy glove.

Montie lay her hand over his, covering the change. 'We'll find a way to help him,' she said firmly.

Ottilie nodded, a lump forming in her throat. She looked up into Montie's face, then quickly down again. Every time she saw Montie's scars she thought of Gracie. She hadn't told either Alba or Montie that Gracie had been there the night their house was burned, and that Gracie's own parents had set the fire. She couldn't decide if it was important – if it was worth stirring up the memories.

'I'll send some breakfast down with Alba,' said Montie, kissing the top of Ottilie's head and leaving the room.

Ottilie sat alone for quite a while, her eyes fixed on Scoot's hand, until something beyond the partitions disturbed her. The door swung open. The patchies were greeting someone, and Ottilie thought she heard the clatter of claws on the tiled floor.

'How did this occur?' said a patchie.

'Caught it on a brambleberry bush,' said Ned's voice.

It was like breath on embers – little lights flared somewhere deep down.

The clawed thing made a sighing sound and slumped to the ground.

'It looks fresh. This was last night?'

'Night patrol,' said Ned, too quickly.

Ottilie frowned. She knew Ned hadn't had a night patrol. He was lying. He must have been sleepwalking again and injured himself.

She heard the patchie go into the back room and begin filling something with water. Ottilie slipped around the corner and Ned nearly jumped out of his seat.

The little lights flared brighter.

'Night patrol?' she said.

Penguin raised a sleepy head and sniffed vaguely in her direction. The lanky shepherd was lying in an exhausted heap beside Ned's feet, no doubt worn out from dogging Ned on his night-time wanderings.

Ned's eyes flicked up to meet hers and Ottilie quickly added, 'Don't get mad at me.' She raised her hands in surrender. 'I'm not saying anything.' She was in no position to lecture him about his sleepwalking – not when she had gone to meet Whistler in the middle of the night.

To her surprise, he laughed. She sighed with relief and knelt to look at his hand, which was covered in scratches. Brambleberry thorns were nasty. Like cat's claws, they hooked in and cut deep.

'It just needs cleaning,' he said, lowering his good hand to pat Penguin.

Ottilie sat with him while the patchie fixed up his hand. She felt both glad and guilty that the injury gave her an excuse to stay close. After the bandage was fixed in place, Ned followed her through the partitions to visit Scoot. She settled in her usual chair, but Ned froze at the end of the bed, his eyes fixed on the golden flowers in the jar.

He paled, and she wondered if he was still breathing.

'What is it?' She stood up. 'What's wrong?'

He shook his head. The expression was familiar – it was like Bill's *memory* face. 'They locked it in the coffin.' He turned to her. 'The ... that ... witch.'

Ottilie frowned. She had wondered what happened that night in the canyon caves after they fell out of Ned's dream – she remembered seeing the creature stepping out of the flames, the coven seemingly powerless to stop it. The fact that it had been imprisoned offered her less comfort than she would have guessed. It still lived, probably buried somewhere, just waiting to be released.

'Is that what you dreamed last night?'

Ned's eyes flicked back to the sunnytree flowers. 'Maybe – I can't remember. I don't know where I know it from ...'

Ottilie was so focussed on Ned that she jumped when Alba poked her head through the partitions.

'Morning,' she said, meeting Ottilie's eyes with a flat stare.

Gully had forgiven Ottilie, but her friends were still acting strangely around her. Skip and Leo had been much better after they'd raged at her, but Preddy and Alba were still simmering. They were hurt because Ottilie hadn't included them in her plans. But how could she have, when she had been forbidden to go?

'Mum told me to bring you some breakf— oh, sorry, Ned,' said Alba. 'I didn't know you were here too. I've only got —'

'That's fine, no problem. I'm off anyway,' said Ned, his eyes flicking only briefly to her face and then back to the flowers again.

'Do you have a hunt?' said Ottilie. But he had already headed for the door.

Alba stared after him, then looked back at Ottilie, and something changed in her expression. 'Here.' She held out the tray.

Ottilie thanked her and took a bite of the warm brambleberry pie. Alba couldn't be too mad at her, not if she had brought Ottilie's favourite breakfast. Montie had even included saffi milk to calm her nerves.

Alba settled on the end of Scoot's bed, then suddenly lunged forward, leaning over his stone legs.

'What —' But Ottilie saw it before she finished the question. Tray clattering to the floor, she leapt up and gripped Scoot's arm. The white was moving. She could see it, creeping up like frost. 'No, Scoot!' she said, following it with her hands as if she could tear it back. It flooded his entire arm, spilling onto his neck.

'It's slowing,' Alba whispered.

She was right. The progress slowed, then seemed to pause.

Ottilie's heart thundered. They had to find a way to stop it. All of it. Everything. If the healing spring was not an option ... 'Have you found anything, Alba? Anything that could help?'

Alba placed a hand on her ribs and breathed deeply. 'I've been going over the books we stole. It's where I first read about the healing spring. I was hoping something would explain why it dried up, or why it existed in the first place. They say it was the site of a selfless heroic deed – a man tackled a crocodile to save a stranger.'

'But something like that has to have happened somewhere else!' said Ottilie. She was still clutching Scoot's arm, her fingernails bending against the stone. 'There must be more healing springs!'

'There might be,' said Alba, as if she didn't really think so. 'But you have to collect the water at the right spot, and unless there's a legend telling you where to go ...' She shook her head. 'I wondered if the water might have been able to save Gracie and the bone singers – the bound ones, I mean. Maybe they weren't bad to begin with.'

Ottilie opened her mouth, but Alba added, 'We could try to cure them of the binding, at least, and then see ...'

Ottilie swallowed. Alba had a right to know. 'There's something I should tell you. I found out … Gracie told me she was there when those Laklanders set fire to your house. I think it was her parents that did it.'

Alba froze, and Ottilie worried that she had done the wrong thing. It was in the past, so many years ago … Was it bad to put faces on those people? Was the knowledge a poisonous thing? It certainly was in Whistler's case. Whatever the king had done, whatever had befallen his eldest daughter, it had led to this – to the havoc Whistler had wrought, with the worst still to come. But that was Whistler, not Alba.

Ottilie sunk inward and sought a great wrong. She had never been the victim of something so violent and catastrophic, but she had felt something akin to losing a home.

The keeper from the Swamp Hollows appeared in her mind. Bill had told her he made the pickings list for the Brakkerswamp. He was responsible for Gully's abduction. He, who had always been friendly with Freddie, had put her son's name on that list.

Was it better that Ottilie knew it was him?

Yes. It gave her a better understanding of her past. For some reason, it made her feel more in control – she had a firmer grip on her own story. Although the picture was not perfectly clear. Why had he done it? She would probably never know.

Alba made a little coughing sound and twitched her nose. 'Well, Gracie would only have been five or six, same as me. It's not her crime –'

'I just mean she's from bad –'

'It doesn't matter where someone's from – Gracie is not her parents.'

'It sort of seems like she is actually –'

'You know you sound like Leo, right?'

'Look, I guess I just mean Gracie's done bad things on her own. Sounds like even before the binding …' It was impossible, completely impossible to imagine doing anything to help Gracie.

'I'm not defending her,' said Alba. 'I just think that if we can sever the connection to the bloodbeasts they can all be judged fairly.'

Ottilie didn't disagree with Alba. Maybe the bone singers were not the same as Gracie – maybe they hadn't had a choice. Even if they had, perhaps they could be given the opportunity to atone. But after seeing Gracie in the canyon caves, she wasn't sure there was anything left of the girl she once was, and she could only imagine the others were the same. There was no point in discussing it further, though. The healing spring was gone.

For a moment they stood in hopeless silence. The sun shifted beyond the window and a ray of golden light spilled across the bed. Ottilie had the strangest desire to close the shutters. Sunlight was too lovely a thing. It didn't belong here.

'I've been reading through Whistler's books,' said Alba, finally. 'I've found some bits about Seika Devil-Slayer, but mostly the ink's really faded or there are pages missing, so it's hard.

'I want to know how she defeated the fendevil, all on her own without a ring or salt weapons or anything. I just think there might be something there ... not necessarily to help Scoot,' she added, her eyes drooping. 'But if Whistler attacks with the dredretches again, well, the more we know, the better. If Seika had some trick – even if it was magic, the way she lured it over the cliff – it might be something Maeve could learn.'

Ottilie nodded, still staring at the sunlight.

'But so far, I haven't found anything that makes any sense. One thing keeps coming up – it seems to be connected to Seika ... this old rhyme, *The Sleepless Stars*.'

Ottilie didn't know it. 'Is it important? How does it go?'

'*Three circles past* ... something like, *from sleepless stars it cannot hide* ... I can't remember it all off the top of my head. It does mention a *dreamer* though, which made me think of Ned.'

Ottilie scrunched her eyelids, trying to think it all through. Ned's dreams might be linked to a rhyme that was linked to Seika Devil-Slayer – an ancient, long-dead princess who felled the first dredretch. Whistler had inflicted the wounds that were linked to his dreaming, and her secret plans had something to do with the sleepless witch that his dreams centred around. The healing spring that might have saved Scoot was located in the cave where that same sleepless witch had been imprisoned. And sometime in the past, the king who was hiding in their fort had done Whistler a great wrong, impelling her to set all of this in motion. It was one huge puzzle and Ottilie didn't know how to put it together.

— 18 —

Breathing Bones

With a deafening crack, the sky seemed to split open and rain flooded the path. Ottilie was drenched in an instant. She'd lost track of how many times she'd circled the grounds. Her patrol wasn't until the evening, and for once her afternoon off seemed like a punishment rather than a gift. She had tried researching, looking for anything that could help Scoot, but she'd been too anxious to focus. Finally, she had given up and gone out for a run.

Thick sheets of rain slapped her face as she approached the haunted stables where the sculkies had once trained. They weren't really haunted, of course, just abandoned because they were too close to the boundary walls. When she finally reached cover she was greeted by Hero, the leopard shepherd, who slunk over and sniffed in her direction.

'Sorry – no fish.' She held out her empty hands, her skin glossy with rain.

Hero bared her teeth and turned her back.

Ottilie was just stretching her overworked legs when she heard a scuffling from somewhere in the decaying stalls. Her pulse quickened. Hardly anyone ever came up here – not even the sculkie squad since they had become the Devil-Slayers.

Resting a hand on the knife at her hip, she followed the sounds all the way to the open trapdoor. Greenish light was shining out of it. Someone had glowsticks below.

Ottilie heard a soft nicker and her head snapped up. Two horses were locked in the only stall with a working gate. They were restless, stamping their feet and flicking their tails, but she had been so focused on the light she hadn't even noticed them. It was Echo and Warship, which meant ...

'Preddy?' Ottilie called down into the tunnel. 'Skip? What are you doing?'

There were a few moments of silence and then Skip's head popped out of the opening.

'Ottilie? What are you doing here?'

Ottilie was relieved that she seemed friendly enough. She gestured to her sopping clothes. 'I was running and then it started pouring.'

'Oh, same,' said Skip distractedly, looking back down into the tunnel.

Ottilie laughed. 'What?'

Skip tore her eyes back up. 'I mean, sort of. Me and Preddy train here sometimes when the main yards are busy.'

'How is that the same?'

Skip looked back down into the tunnel. 'Can you read it?' she hollered.

'What are you talking about?' said Ottilie.

'You're not making any sense,' said Preddy's voice. He must have been climbing up, because his words were louder by the end.

Ottilie had absolutely no idea what was going on.

Preddy spoke from somewhere beneath Skip. 'When the rain started, we didn't know how long we would be stuck, so Isla was going through the tunnels to get us some food and she saw something.'

'Lucky we found some of our old glow sticks in the barn, otherwise I wouldn't have spotted it!' said Skip, with a proud, toothy grin. She beckoned, then swung down the ladder.

Ottilie followed her down and along the tunnel.

'I saw it here,' said Skip, 'but I can't read, so –'

'You *can* read,' Preddy interrupted.

Skip swatted her hand in his direction. 'Not well. Anyway, I got Preddy to come and see. That's when you showed up after your swim.' She laughed.

'It's right here.' Preddy held the glow sticks high. 'We must have passed it a hundred times but we never looked up!'

Ottilie's mouth fell open. Painted on the ceiling of the tunnel was ... She strained her eyes. Strange markings.

She blinked.

No, not strange – familiar letters. A song or a poem. A section of the ceiling had crumbled off, and what might have been the first verse had been reduced to its final two words: *lead you.* Beneath it, another verse seemed to be fully formed.

'Well?' said Skip impatiently. 'What does it say?'

Preddy cleared his throat and held the glow sticks higher. '*Light of the sun, peak of the sky. Wander no longer, there breathing bones lie.*'

Breathing bones? Ottilie shivered. She didn't know what it meant, but she didn't like the sound of it.

'Midday,' said Skip. 'Light of the sun, peak of the sky – midday.'

'But what about the last bit?' said Ottilie. She looked at Skip, who shrugged, and then at Preddy, who was gazing at Skip with a strange look on his face.

'Preddy?' said Ottilie. 'What are *breathing bones*?'

'What?' said Preddy, with a slight jump.

It was impossible to tell in the greenish light, but Ottilie could have sworn she could see heat rising on his face.

'Breathing bones is a fancy term for … well, sort of … the living dead. Or someone buried who still lives – that's probably more accurate,' he said.

'You mean a sleepless witch?' said Ottilie. Her breath shuddered a little upon release and she was suddenly very aware of the small space and the darkness.

'So it's a rhyme about finding a sleepless witch at midday?' said Skip. She spoke so casually. Ottilie hadn't filled her friends in on Whistler's interest in the sleepless witch. It was too tangled up with Ned's situation. Skip didn't have any reason to think this was anything other than an interesting piece of history.

'Seems to be,' said Preddy. 'I wonder what that used to say?' He pointed up to the crumbled section.

Ottilie didn't really want to know. 'Why would anyone want to find the sleepless witch?' Well, she knew one person who did … had Whistler seen this?

'Maybe just so you know where it is – so you don't accidentally dig it up,' said Skip with a laugh. Ottilie hoped she was right.

Preddy frowned up at the words. 'It's witch script.'

'What is *witch script*?' said Skip. Ottilie didn't know either.

'When I first looked,' said Preddy, 'it was in ancient Usklerian – then it shifted to the modern alphabet.'

'You can read ancient Usklerian?' said Skip.

He shook his head. 'But I know what it looks like – my old tutor showed me samples of it.'

'So you know that it's witch script because the letters changed?' said Ottilie.

'It translated for us?' said Skip.

Preddy nodded. 'That's what witch script does – I learned about it. When it's very old, the magic slows and you can catch the change – which means this must have been here for centuries.'

Why had this tunnel existed so long ago? The Narroway Hunt had only been in operation for thirty years. How old was Fort Fiory? Ottilie didn't have any answers, but it didn't seem like something they needed to worry about.

Still, worry she did. All afternoon and into the evening, she had a strange sense of unease. She felt like she was missing something, as if there was a riddle that she couldn't quite figure out, only she didn't even know what the riddle was.

When it was finally time for her patrol shift, Ottilie couldn't have been more relieved. She had never thought she'd look forward to encountering dredretches, but at this point a skirmish with a flock of jivvies or a wrestling match with a learie was all she wanted to deal with.

19

The Dreamer

'What's that?' Leo pointed below.

They were technically supposed to be patrolling different zones. But, dreading being on her own again, Ottilie had ignored orders and followed him along his patrol route. Leo, to her great surprise, had not said a thing about it.

Nox swept lower. The glow sticks bound to her saddle cast a greenish light across the ground. Ottilie strained her eyes. There was a shape bounding through the webwoods.

'It's a *dog*,' said Ottilie. She could hear its bark, but it couldn't be a shepherd – not this far from Fiory. Not unless ... Her breath caught. 'I think it's Penguin!'

'Can't be,' Leo called down to her. 'Ned doesn't have a shift tonight.'

Swinging back to investigate, they came to a decaying ditch that was poisoned by the withering sickness. Sure enough, a patchy, half-grown shepherd was bounding backwards and forwards, kicking up noxious muck with every panicked leap.

Leo swore and jumped to the ground. Penguin bolted towards him, his barks turning to whines. Ottilie slid down and approached on unsteady legs. She scanned the area, but there was no sign of Ned within the light of their glow sticks.

'Where is he? What happened?' said Leo, patting Pen to try to soothe him.

'He's been sleepwalking.' It just tumbled out.

'I know! You're the only one who keeps secrets from me.'

She felt his words like a slap in the face. She had only been trying to protect Ned. Little did she know he had confided in Leo himself. It didn't matter. She was panicked. If Ned was in the same absent state he'd been in when she'd found him in Floodwood, he would be helpless before a dredretch.

For over an hour they searched for him, switching between looking on foot with Penguin and flying. Ottilie was on the ground again and Leo had disappeared into the dark when a black shadow swooped in front. She whipped an arrow from her back. At her side, Penguin lowered his head and snarled, hackles raised. The wings withdrew and Maeve stepped onto the leafy carpet. Penguin settled in an instant.

She was panting. Between breaths, she managed to gasp, 'The birds told Bill. They saw ... *Whistler*. She took Ned!'

'What?' said Ottilie. Her vision swung. She reached to Penguin for comfort. Cool air beat across her face as Maestro thumped to the ground nearby.

'Whistler's got Ned, Leo!' said Ottilie.

'What! Why?' He jumped down and hurried over to them.

'He was sleepwalking,' said Maeve. 'Beyond the wall. She just snatched him and flew off!'

'But how did he even get out here?' said Ottilie breathlessly. 'You can't just sleepwalk past wall watchers.'

'They were distracted, shooting down jivvies,' said Maeve. 'The gate opened by itself. Or that's what it looked like, but I'm guessing Whistler did it.'

'What does she want him for?' said Leo, his voice thin with panic.

The possibilities swarmed. Ottilie gasped. 'The backup plan!' she said. 'Bill said Whistler gave up on him. He couldn't give her any information about the sleepless witch. She said she would have to go with her backup plan. It must be Ned, and the dreams – it's all about this sleepless witch that Ned's been dreaming about!'

'We have to go after him,' said Leo. 'We have to find him.'

Ottilie dug her fingernails into her palms. Yes, they had to go after him. But where had he gone? 'We have to talk to Bill.'

Bill covered his eyes, rocking back and forth on a stool by the hearth. 'I can't. I'm sorry. I can't remember anything.' He rocked back so far that he nearly fell off the stool. Maeve pushed him upright.

'Nothing?' Ottilie's voice shook. What were they going to do? What would happen to Ned?

Bill just shook his head, his mouth drooping.

Ottilie chewed her lip as she paced in front of him. She and Leo had gone straight to Montie's kitchen to gather food while Maeve found Bill. They didn't know where Whistler was taking Ned, but it seemed foolish to leave without any provisions.

'What are you doing in here?' said Alba, appearing in the doorway with a tray of dirty dishes – probably the remnants of a director's late-night meal.

'Taking food,' said Leo.

Ottilie and Maeve quickly filled her in.

Alba exhaled and placed the tray on the table. 'You're really lucky Mum went to bed early.'

Ottilie barely heard her. She had already turned back to Bill, who was muttering under his breath.

'Are you saying numbers?' said Maeve, leaning forward as if trying to read his lips.

'A number?' Bill stood and looked up at the drying thyme strung from the ceiling. He flipped his fingers, as if counting. 'Two days. *Three* … three threes!'

'Three threes are nine,' said Alba, as if she couldn't help herself.

'Why are we doing maths?' said Maeve.

'What does this have to do with anything!' Leo thumped the table, making them jump. Only Maeve was steady. She fixed him with a glare.

'Years,' said Bill. His bendy feet made sticking noises as he paced the floor. 'In two days, it's nine hundred years since they sealed the iron coffin underground.' He placed his hands over his eyes. 'I remember,' he whispered.

'So?' said Leo. Ottilie could tell he had tried to say it gently.

'Are you sure?' said Maeve.

Bill sat again and tapped his temple.

'Whistler's been waiting,' said Ottilie. 'Waiting for something …'

Alba clapped a hand to her mouth, then reached into her pocket. '*Three circles, circles, circles past ...*'

'What?' said Maeve.

'I've been reading about Seika Devil-Slayer,' said Alba, smoothing out a crumpled piece of parchment, 'and I keep coming across this. *The Sleepless Stars* – an old rhyme. I've been carrying it around, trying to figure out its significance.'

Ottilie's eyes snapped to the parchment – this was the rhyme that mentioned the *dreamer*. Alba had told her about it before.

'A *rhyme*?' said Leo, as if he thought this a complete waste of time.

'*All in a row, the glowing guide. From sleepless stars it cannot hide*,' Alba chanted.

Ottilie frowned. 'I don't underst–'

'*Three circles, circles, circles past, the dreamer seeks it out at last.*'

Bill started rocking again. Maeve patted his shoulder. 'Three circles?' she said.

'I think it means *centuries*,' said Alba. 'I've been trying to work that out for so long – the wording made me think it might be referring to *time* in some way, but I never thought of centuries! But it's three *circles, circles, circles*, like Bill said. Three by three – nine! And the *dreamer*, the *glowing guide*, it has to be Ned!'

Leo thrust out his arm. 'Ned's marks are like three stars,' he said.

'And they glow when he dreams,' Ottilie added. There was no time for secrets now. She twisted her ring around her thumb, thinking hard. There were little clues everywhere. These words, these old rhymes ... Even on their rings. Lines from the lightning song. Maybe the lightning song had something to do with all this, too – it was about a sleepless witch, after all.

Burns like three stars ... Ottilie gasped. 'Hiss, flick and sputter, *three will mark it hot*!'

Alba's eyes stretched to the size of dustplums. 'And *crunch, thud, dig deep down* ... It's about where it's buried! It can't all be a coincidence. It's been nine hundred years since a sleepless witch was buried, and Whistler marked Ned as the guide. The burns must be guiding him to the iron coffin!'

Ottilie's mind was spinning. 'So that's it – it has to be ... it all fits!' she said. 'Whistler wants to dig up the sleepless witch, but Bill couldn't tell her where it was buried, so she had to wait for the nine hundredth anniversary – and for a *dreamer* to guide her. This must be what she's been waiting for!'

'A witch that can't be killed,' said Maeve, going pale.

'She must want it to join her army,' said Ottilie, horrified. 'A sleepless witch would definitely help her get past the Narroway Hunt. And … what … in two days?' She looked at Bill, who covered his eyes with his hands and nodded.

The final piece clicked into place. 'At midday,' said Ottilie. 'If that's what she's planning, then in two days, at midday, that's when she'll dig it up.'

Everyone was staring at her.

'Skip found something marked on the tunnel near the haunted stables,' she explained. 'It was written in witch script – something about finding the sleepless witch at midday … *there breathing bones lie.*'

Alba was frowning, tapping her leg.

'The rhymes, they're all about the same thing,' said Ottilie.

'Like prophecies?' said Alba.

Maeve shook her head. 'It sounds more like a spell to me. You probably have to do a certain ritual to get what you want. Magic is like that. Especially long-lasting spells. I've read about things like this. Maybe you can't dig up the coffin unless you mark the dreamer, who will then lead you there at a certain time, on a certain day. Nine hundred years sounds like a sort of weak point before the turn of the age – before it's sealed forever.'

'The rhymes could be like old records of the ritual,' said Alba. 'Maybe people trying to remember, passing it down through generations. Songs get under people's skin. They live much longer than any written records.'

She frowned. 'But why the nine hundredth anniversary? Marking the dreamer ... all the conditions? Why make it so difficult?'

'You wouldn't want to make it easy,' said Ottilie. 'It's a sleepless witch.'

She bit hard into her lip. Why hadn't she put this together earlier? She knew Whistler was interested in the sleepless witch, and anyone could have guessed why! She had been so scattered, her focus flitting from one thing to the next, with Scoot, the king, rescuing Bill, not to mention her hunting duties ... she hadn't been thinking clearly.

'From what I've learned, you don't get much of a choice about spells,' said Maeve. Her eyes darted to the door, as if she feared she would be overheard and exiled to the Laklands again. 'Especially the really powerful ones. If a witch wanted to magically seal the coffin, but weave in some sort of loophole in case someone needed to get to it ... for whatever reason, nine hundred years might have been the only option – a weak point, like I said.'

'But this still doesn't help!' said Leo. 'If Bill doesn't know where the iron coffin is buried, how are we going to find Ned?'

Ottilie frowned, thinking hard. Something was bothering her, some memory or knowledge just out of reach. She went over the lightning song in her mind, trying to remember the correct order, the original lines as Alba had clarified them months ago:

Flash, smack and crackle, lightning knows the spot.
Hiss, flick and sputter, three will mark it hot.
Wail, whine, dinnertime, sleeper comes for none.
Crunch, thud, dig deep down, pay for what you've done.

'*Lightning knows the spot*,' she muttered. 'When lightning strikes the ground, it means there's a witch buried below.' She remembered Scoot saying that in their fledgling year, the day the yickers attacked them in Floodwood.

'So?' said Leo. 'Lightning strikes all sorts of places. It could be anywhere.'

She was on the very edge. She had the answer. It was like a dusty old book – she just needed to brush it off and hold it to the light. Ottilie thought of the last time she had seen Ned, staring at the golden flowers by Scoot's bed. She remembered the treasure she and Gully had buried beneath their favourite tree, and the bolt of lightning that had sent her fleeing into Longwood so many years ago.

Her mouth fell open.

'I know where they're going,' she said. 'I know where it's buried!'

20

Farewell, Fiory

They waited for dawn. Ottilie had promised Gully she would not leave him behind, so, strapped with every weapon they could carry, they headed for the wingerslink sanctuary together.

'Hello,' said Skip as they rounded a corner. 'What are you two doing up?' She and Preddy were dressed to hunt, and seemed to be heading for the stables.

Ottilie's eyes flicked to the other huntsmen striding in different directions across the grounds. 'We can't stay out here – come with us, quick!'

Preddy hesitated, glancing at the stables.

Gully gave him a meaningful look. 'You can be late, Preddy.'

They explained about Ned and the sunnytree on the way.

'I'm coming too,' announced Skip as they entered the sanctuary.

Leo was standing in front of Maestro's pen. His arms were firmly crossed, eyes shaded by a frown. 'What are they doing here?' he barked.

Alba was there too. She'd ordered them out of the kitchen last night and promised to bring some food in the morning. Shooting Nox a distrustful glance, she tucked the last of the supplies into a saddlebag.

Penguin was pacing back and forth, occasionally snarling or barking at the wingerslinks, who were rumbling in their pens. Shepherds and wingerslinks were not fond of each other, but Penguin had not left Leo's side.

'I'm coming,' Skip repeated, looking Leo in the eye.

He shook his head. 'You're a fledge. Besides, there's no room.' He waved at Maestro and Nox, who were saddled and ready to travel.

'We can double up,' said Skip, leaping boldly over the gate to Maestro's pen. Maestro swung around and snarled. Skip jumped backwards, and it was a mark of how distressed Leo was that he didn't laugh. Watching Maestro frighten people usually brightened him up.

'We need room for Ned when we get him back,' he said stiffly.

'Maestro's as big as a house,' said Skip, eyeing him warily. 'He can take three. You don't know what's going to happen out there.'

'She's coming,' said Ottilie. Skip was wily and tough. They might well need her.

Leo threw up his hands. 'Fine!' He wrenched the gate open. 'We don't have time for this – just hurry up!'

The wingerslinks leapt into the field. Ottilie and Leo were the first down after them.

'Whistler won't hurt Ned.' Ottilie forced herself to sound confident – even though it didn't entirely match her feelings. 'Not before he shows her where to go.'

Leo ground his teeth and stared at his boots. 'You don't know that.'

'I do. I'm sure of it. He can't just tell her where to go. He's only had dreams of a place. He wouldn't know where the sunnytree is. He'll have to feel his way there. Maeve says the burns are going to guide him.' Ottilie didn't understand magic, but Maeve had been studying the old witch book and she seemed sure that this was how it would work.

Leo grunted and walked away from her. 'Pen, stick with Alba, all right?' he said, patting him on the head. The shepherd slid close and leaned against Leo's legs.

Alba crouched down, offering a consoling pat.

Leo and Skip mounted Maestro, and Gully and Ottilie climbed into Nox's saddle. She didn't want to say goodbye. She wanted to believe they would be back soon. Back with Ned. Safe and sound.

Ottilie sensed something to her left. Bill had appeared at her ankle with a black owl perched on his head. His mouth was turned down and his eyes were heavy with dread.

'She's coming with you.' His eyes flicked upwards. 'In case you need a witch.'

Ottilie smiled. She could tell it hadn't been his idea. No doubt Bill had spent a long time trying to convince Maeve not to go, just like he had once asked Ottilie not to go to the Narroway.

'We'll be back, Bill.'

'You've said that before.' His long fingers curled around her leg.

She remembered the last time he had done that, just before Whistler took him and kept him for months and months. 'This time I promise.'

21

Back Onto the Map

They flew via the coast. It was the longest but safest route. They couldn't risk being slowed by dredretch attacks. It was a strange feeling, Nox swooping over the waves, tilting and curving to follow the line of the shore.

The strengthening sun washed the world with gold and the cool salty air was comforting, like gentle hands brushing back Ottilie's hair. Maeve flew ahead, slipping in and out of shifting veils of light. A massive shadow moved beneath them, flashing a fin, then a vast tail, and causing rolling ripples far and wide.

They stopped twice to give the wingerslinks a break, resting first on a pebbly beach, then a rocky cliff. They were just settling near the cliff's edge when something caught Ottilie's eye: a leaking darkness, oozing from a narrow gap in the ragged clifftop. It was like black water, but too thick. It divided into tendrils, sticky roots creeping outwards.

Gully gasped. An army of rokkers, like giant blood-red scorpions, was peeling free of the gloop. The gap in the cliff was widening, the ground half melting, half crumbling. The sludge slipped off the rokkers as they scuttled towards Leo's outstretched legs. He leapt up with a yelp of surprise and kicked out.

Her eyes still fixed on the puddle, Ottilie called the wingerslinks away. Rokkers had a paralysing sting and the wingerslinks could offer little help without endangering themselves.

Ottilie curled her fingers around the bone necklace in her pocket as Skip, Gully and Leo stamped and thumped, having far more difficulty than they might with something larger. If she hadn't been so disturbed, Ottilie could have laughed. But she thought she understood what she had seen. She and Leo had witnessed it before – a dredretch rising. But Whistler was nowhere nearby. She knew that for sure, because the bone necklace was not humming.

This was a patch of withering sickness, and the rokkers had risen on their own. Ottilie had thought the Narroway would have to become a blackened wasteland before that was even possible. She'd had no idea it could happen already.

She heard the whizz and stick of an arrow and turned to see Skip lowering her bow. She followed Skip's gaze to a humungous rokker – the size of a large rat – pinned to the ground by her arrow, its toxic stinger half an inch from the back of Leo's leg. Leo whirled and jerked back, his eyes wide with shock. Regaining his composure, he stepped casually sideways to stomp on the last rokker. He watched Skip pluck her arrow out of the gooey pile of broken shell with a look of annoyance and admiration on his face.

'That's twice you've been saved by a fledgling,' said Skip, winking at Ottilie.

'I would have got it if you hadn't,' said Leo.

Skip flashed a grin, spun the arrow, and wiped it on a patch of rubbery weeds. 'What are they doing so near the coast?'

Ottilie led the wingerslinks closer again. No-one else seemed to have put it together, and she was reluctant to share the unsettling news. Finally, she took a breath and said, 'They rose on their own.' She pointed to the putrid puddle.

Leo frowned, his eyes darting inland. 'Surely not. Maybe they were sent.'

'You think Whistler knows we're coming?' said Gully.

'Why would she care enough to stop us?' said Ottilie. Whistler had never seemed to take them very seriously before.

'I think after you flattened her in the cave, she'd be stupid not to try,' said Leo, nodding in Maeve's direction.

Maeve was perched on Nox's saddle. She responded to Leo's comment with a hoot that could have meant anything, really.

'I supposed if tomorrow at midday is her only chance to do this, she can't risk anything messing up her timing,' said Ottilie. How woeful – the thought that Whistler was tracking them, trying to stop them, was the more comforting option. Ottilie wrapped her arms around her middle. 'Trust me. She didn't send them. They rose on their own. Right there. Look.'

Leo and Skip moved over to inspect the patch of sickness.

Gully kept his distance – taking Ottilie's word for it. 'They ... so what ... they can rise anywhere now? Without her calling them out?' he said, his eyes wide.

She frowned. 'Not everywhere, I don't think. Just places where something really bad's happened.'

Evil sings to them ... Alba had once told her that. Just as an act of goodness had created the healing spring, an evil deed could bring dredretches and the withering sickness. The world was weakening here – that's what Whistler had said. It was becoming more fertile for dredretches, easier for them to find their way up.

'Something terrible must have happened in this spot,' said Ottilie, 'for the dredretches to come without being called.'

Leo looked out to the ocean, glanced westward, then walked to the edge of the cliff and peered down. He turned back. 'Slaver caves.'

Maeve took flight. She swept over the edge of the cliff and disappeared somewhere below.

'What slaves?' said Skip.

'Viago the Vanquisher reintroduced slavery to the Usklers,' said Leo.

'That's Whistler's dad, right?' said Gully.

Ottilie nodded.

Skip arched a brow. 'Nice family,' she muttered.

'I learnt about it in my history lessons before I came here,' said Leo. 'After the Lakland War, a lot of Laklanders went into hiding in the Narroway. The slavers used to hunt them and imprison them in coastal caves. Then boats would come through from Wikric Town and collect them to sell at the slave markets there.'

His casual tone turned Ottilie's stomach. He was just reciting a memory of a lesson. Slaves ... She had known the Usklers had used slaves on and off throughout history, but it had always seemed so distant, almost like a story, not something that had happened to real people – ordered and enforced by real people. But standing here, she could feel it. The reality of it. The horror. It almost knocked her down. She felt a new kind of fear – a crippling distrust. How could people get things so wrong?

Ottilie noticed that, despite his tone, Leo too was unsteady. He looked pointedly away from the edge of the cliffs, his body stiff and his thumb twitching.

Slavery was monstrous, and Whistler's father had reintroduced it. She hadn't thought it possible to resent Viago the Vanquisher more. But she vaguely remembered reading that Feo Sol had outlawed slavery. That was Whistler's brother. She remembered Whistler saying her brother was a good king. How disappointing – devastating, even – that Viago came before him and Varrio after.

Maeve swooped up over the edge of the cliff and stepped onto the grass as a girl. She looked wretched. 'Dredretches must have been coming through for a while – the sickness is everywhere,' she said. 'There's a whole hive of caves in there, all the way down to the ground. They're rotted through. But there are still ...'

She struggled to speak. 'S-skeletons and chains bolted to the walls.'

Ottilie felt her blood drain. She turned back to the pool of sickness – where the world had begun to rot. No wonder …

It was too dangerous to make camp in the Narroway, even on the coast. Curving further out to sea, they avoided the area where the border wall between the Narroway and the Usklers met the ocean. Being seen risked unnecessary complications, so they drifted far enough out that they lost sight of land. It was a wonderfully freeing feeling, being surrounded on all sides by nothing but sea. Ottilie looked to the south and thought of Sunken Sweep, Ned's home. She had never been there … never been anywhere, really. She wondered if she ever would.

The approaching dusk hung a violet veil, still pierced by spears of bronze. They turned northward, heading for land. Gully leaned forwards and gently bumped his head on Ottilie's shoulder. She understood him. They had done it – at some point, out at sea, they had crossed the border. They had left the Narroway.

She remembered the escape plan in their fledgling year. How strange that they had finally achieved that goal. But everything had changed. Back then, they had been desperate to return to the Swamp Hollows; now, Ottilie didn't know where home was supposed to be. Flying Nox, Gully with her – she wasn't sure there was a closer thing to home than this.

The sleepy sun flared, dipping lower, and they flew inland. Seeking fresh water, Ottilie spotted a slip of silver and whistled to Leo, pointing.

Nox and Maestro tilted to land, finally touching down by a gentle cascade where the river curled over a rock shelf and into a wide pool. Dusk settled. A great mass of black shapes swooped out of the treetops and everyone tensed. Leo whipped out his bow and Ottilie's hand flew to her own before she realised what it was – bats. Just bats. It had been years since she had seen so many animals out in the wild. She smiled as the bats scattered across the hazy sky, some dipping down to skim the water before swooping back up to join the colony.

Ottilie freed her feet from the stirrups. A heavy black shape plunged ahead of them, landing with a skimming splash. Gully grabbed her elbow. She turned her head and whispered, 'It's a swan.'

She slipped out of the saddle. Her stiff, flight-weary legs stumbled sideways and she let herself fall, the palms of her hands pressing into the Uskler mud.

— 22 —

Deep Breath

Skip was sitting against a log, her arms wrapped around her knees. Leo and Gully were riffling through their bags in search of food and Maeve was struggling to conjure a fire. By the light of the glow sticks, Ottilie saw a strange expression on Skip's face. She wondered if Skip remembered the Usklers at all. She had lived half her life in the Narroway.

'It's so loud here,' said Skip.

Ottilie strained her ears, not sure what she meant. But then the sounds pushed to the front — crickets chirping, mosquitoes buzzing, the owls and other night singers, the possums with their strange call, like rasping breath, the howl of the driftdogs far off near the coast. The world was full and alive again, like it was supposed to be.

Maeve huffed and let her hands drop to the dirt.

'You can make a rock wall collapse on Whistler's head, but you can't make a campfire?' said Leo.

Maeve shot him a look so dark that Ottilie stepped between them.

'Don't anger the witch,' said Skip.

Maeve slumped to the ground. 'I'm so tired! I think that's why it's not working.'

Gully crawled forwards. 'Course you're tired – you flew all the way here by yourself. I can do it if you like.' He dug around for the flint they'd packed and went to work. When sparks flared, Maeve flicked her fingers and a great fire caught. Gully gasped and dropped the flint, and everyone scattered.

'Sorry!' said Maeve.

Gully's mouth was open. 'That was *amazing*!' He shook out his singed hands and grinned. 'You're amazing!'

'Bit of warning next time, Moth,' said Skip with a snort.

Ottilie grabbed Gully's hand to check for damage, and he winced. 'Come on.' She pulled him over to the water's edge to dip his fingers in. Gully was still looking back at the fire with wonder in his eyes.

A loud splash caught Ottilie's attention along the stream. She looked across to see Nox swipe at the water, sending a silver fish flying onto the bank. Maestro slunk in behind and snapped it up. Nox bared her teeth and turned back to the water, waiting for another catch.

'What are we going to say to them?' said Gully quietly.

'The wingersli– oh … you mean …'

The sunnytree was so close to the Swamp Hollows. Once it was done – if they made it through – they would have to go and visit. Ottilie tensed at the thought. She wanted to see them all so badly, and yet she was afraid that Old Moss and Mr Parch would be angry, that they wouldn't understand, that they would try to make her stay. She didn't even know what to expect from Freddie.

One thing she had decided – Ottilie was going to ask about her father. She was going to find out who he was. If she was somehow connected to Whistler, she wanted to know about it. There did seem to be some sort of power in blood – a chain of links reaching back to the first to walk the world. But for Ottilie, it didn't necessarily relate to family. Children with two parents had always been a rarity around the swamps. Family had never been about blood. It had been about the people who were there. The people who loved her and looked out for her. Blood had always seemed different from family, and looking back at her friends around the campfire, that impression pressed deeper.

She turned back to Gully. 'We have to save Ned first,' she said. 'And stop Whistler, if we can. Then we'll ... figure something out.'

<hr />

The birds woke Ottilie just before dawn. She was no stranger to sleeping on the ground, but it had been a long time since she'd had to deal with the stiffness. Leo was leaning against Maestro's side. He was pale, possibly from broken sleep. Ottilie knew that look in his eyes, knew the way his jaw was set and his fingers were clenched. He was nervous. She tried to shoot him a smile, but couldn't quite manage it.

Leo dug into the food bag and tossed Ottilie an apple. Gully yawned and sat up beside her. She passed him the apple and he screwed up his face.

Ottilie pressed it harder into his hand. 'Eat it or you're not coming,' she said.

'Fine,' Gully croaked, tearing a shred of the red skin off with his teeth.

Skip wandered over from the river with an armful of filled waterskins.

Leo was staring at Maeve, and Ottilie followed his gaze. All around her, the fallen leaves were lifting a little off the ground and floating back down with her breath. It was mesmerising. So peaceful. Ottilie watched the leaves lift and fall, breath after breath, and wished she didn't have to wake her.

Maestro appeared at Leo's shoulder. His ears flattened forwards. He reached tentatively with his paw, making a vague swatting motion, then lunged forwards, crushing the leaves with his two front paws. Maeve woke with a yelp. She looked up at them all and narrowed her eyes. 'What?'

'You were making the leaves dance,' said Gully, grinning while he picked at the apple.

'Shouldn't we be going?' she snapped, clearly trying to shift the attention away from anything strange she may have been doing in her sleep.

Silence fell. They had to go. There would be no more stopping. They would fly directly north – over Wikric, along the River Hook – straight for the iron coffin buried beneath the sunnytree.

~ 23 ~

The Corpse

Ottilie had never seen so much of the world, and she had never been in a worse state to appreciate it. They stuck to the wilds as best they could manage, but there was no time to lose, and the straightest route north took them over some areas of civilisation.

She wondered what the townsfolk would think of the two mighty wingerslinks flying high above. She couldn't imagine how she would have reacted if she had seen such a thing. Would she have thought them monsters? It was highly likely. After all, she had never heard of a wingerslink before she met Maestro. They were not native to the Uskler Islands. The Hunt sourced their wingerslinks from the highlands of Southern Triptiquery.

Her breath caught as they flew by a sprawling mass of grey buildings, sliced down the middle by the River Hook – Wikric Town. She looked over to see Skip gazing over Maestro's side at her old home. Scoot's, too, she remembered.

They passed over rolling hills on the outskirts of town, and Ottilie saw lofty manors perched up high, far beyond the crowded city. She wondered if that was where Preddy was from. It seemed likely. Were his cruel parents and five siblings just now waking up inside one of those palatial buildings?

Leaving Wikric behind, Ottilie could see the very tips of Longwood's fingers, thickening and branching out into the vast forest that ran all the way to the northern mouth of the river and to Scarpy Village, where Montie and Alba had lived. And halfway between here and there was the Brakkerswamp – her old home.

The flight was far quicker than Ottilie's first journey between Wikric and the Swamp Hollows. Before she knew how to feel about it, Nox was landing in the field of krippygrass, her hefty paws sinking into the soil. She lifted them one after the other with a rumble of distaste. Maestro landed beside her, sending watery mud flying in every direction. Nox swung her head and snarled.

'Shh,' said Ottilie, nudging the wingerslink with her foot.

Nox snapped at her boot, but Ottilie barely noticed. She was looking ahead. She and Gully had stopped visiting the sunnytree after lightning had struck it. They had never come back for their treasure. She didn't know a lot about trees, but she was quite sure that a lightning-struck tree should be merely a stump, if that, seven years after the impact.

The tree was dead – there was no denying that. It was split down the centre, but the halved trunk had not fallen, or even diminished in breadth. The branches still stretched out just as before, but its bark was black as night, with no golden flowers in sight. It reminded her, horribly, of the Withering Wood.

Ottilie jumped off Nox and hurried towards it. There was no black oil dripping, no rotting dredretch stench. Cautiously, she pressed her hand to the singed bark, but it was not slimy or spongy – just a dried-out corpse. Around its base was a circle of mud, with sparse spears of krippygrass that were shorter and darker than those in the rest of the field.

She considered what was buried beneath her feet. Not their treasure, but something deeper, darker … She took a few steps back, her heart pounding.

She turned to find Gully behind her, scooping back mud with his hands.

'What are you doing?' called Leo in alarm.

'It's nearly midday, we need to get into position,' said Skip.

'Gully, come on,' said Ottilie, pulling him backwards.

'I just want to see if our stuff's still there!'

'We don't have time!'

Gully shook her off. Ottilie was about to give in, let him dig it up, but she felt the bone necklace humming in her pocket. 'She's coming!' She wrenched Gully backwards.

Maeve soared out of the trees, finally making Gully pay attention. She had been scouting, hoping to get an idea of which direction Whistler would come from.

'They're on foot,' said Maeve breathlessly, stepping out of the air. 'Coming from the southwest. They're not far – they'll be here right on midday.'

Ottilie, Leo and Gully spoke together:

'Is he all right –'

'How did he look –'

'Is he hurt –'

'He's not himself,' said Maeve. 'He's like the walking dea–' She paused, noting their horror. 'But unharmed, from what I could see,' she added quickly. 'She must have done something to make him stay asleep – she's tied herself to him with a bit of rope. She's on her own, no bone singers or Gracie or anyone.'

'Good,' said Ottilie, feeling slightly relieved. But her hand shook as she pulled her bow from her back. Whistler on her own still outmatched them. Their only hope was surprising her again.

Quickly, they got into position. Maeve changed back and led the wingerslinks, unable to hide anywhere close, to the distant Brakkerbend Hill. Skip and Leo slid into a ditch, finding extra cover beneath the high grasses. Ottilie and Gully crouched in the mud behind the sunnytree itself.

Ottilie could hear her heart beating as they waited. She could see the little X she had carved on a branch so many years ago, and tried not to think of what was buried beneath it.

Finally, after what seemed like an age, Ned appeared, wandering into the field of krippygrass as if he were in a dream. Behind him was Whistler with her uneven gait.

Ottilie felt Gully twitch beside her. 'Wait,' she whispered.

As Whistler came closer and closer, Ottilie lost sight of her through the cracks in the tree trunk. She would wait for Leo's call. He had a full view – Leo would see when Ned was out of the way.

Wait, wait, wait …

Something didn't feel right.

Too much time had passed. The shard of bone hummed in her pocket and Ottilie realised her mistake too late.

A swish of krippygrass.

A hand snatched.

'Too slow!' Whistler hissed as her fingernails dug into Ottilie's arm, and she pulled her sideways into the mush.

— 24 —

Dig Deep Down

Ottilie couldn't think. Her eyes snapped to Gully; charred roots had burst from the mud, twisting up, pulling him down, leaving only one arm free. She recoiled as rough fingers curled around her limbs, dragging her lower. Her legs sank into the mud. She was sprawled on her stomach, the roots lashing her down. She couldn't breathe.

Whistler was standing above them.

She must have known – sensed that Ottilie was there because of the bone necklace. With a groan, Ottilie remembered it was a direct link. She could feel when Whistler was near, but it went both ways. Everyone had told her to get rid of it and she hadn't listened and now she was sinking, drowning. She had ruined their only chance, doomed them all …

Leo hadn't given the signal. What had happened to him and the others? What had Whistler done? Ottilie looked up at the witch, terror and hatred blazing. Her vision swam. She was panicking, but something caught her attention. Behind Whistler, she could see Ned. The light had returned to his eyes.

Whistler didn't know – she thought he was still sleepwalking. He shook his head at Ottilie, warning her not to give him away. So quick it made her twitch, he snatched at the rope that bound him to Whistler, wrenching the witch off her feet.

Gully tossed his cutlass to Ned, who was already lunging forwards. Catching it in one hand, he plunged the blade. It was a whisker from her heart when the blade turned to dust.

Whistler flicked her sleeve and Ned was blasted backwards into the ground. Ottilie couldn't see him through the grass. Terror engulfed her. She didn't know if he was alive – if any of them were. Only Gully, breathing beside her. He gasped as the roots whipped up to snatch his free hand and Whistler staggered upright, her eyes rolling and flashing like a billowing storm.

Ottilie's legs sank lower. The pressure was more than she could bear. Fear clouded her vision. Something scratched at her fingertips. She managed to turn her head just enough to see Gully straining to reach out, touching his hand to hers.

Maeve was their only hope. But where was she? She was supposed to tie up the wingerslinks and follow Whistler.

'Relentless.' The pointed tips of Whistler's boots appeared in front of Ottilie's nose.

Ottilie didn't look up. She didn't want that hateful witch to be the last thing she saw.

'You're here for your friend, I assume?'

Ottilie pressed her fingertips more firmly into Gully's.

'It's rude not to look at someone when they're speaking to you,' snapped Whistler. She sighed. 'Oh, all right then.' The roots withdrew an inch or two and Ottilie's panic eased. Whistler bent down and clutched Ottilie's chin, her fingernails like claws beneath the sleeve. 'I do hate to hurt you, my hatchling.'

Ottilie wrenched her chin out of Whistler's grip.

'But you do insist on fighting me. A rumbler. But you're aiming your wrath in the wrong direction.' Whistler stood upright and leaned against the blackened tree trunk. She paused, meeting Ottilie's gaze. 'You've met him now, I know. What did you think of my charming nephew?'

'He's yet to turn one of my friends to stone.'

Whistler's face darkened, and with it the sun itself seemed to dim. 'How much clearer do I need to make it?' She growled. 'He is the cause of it all. Everything. Your friend is stone because of Varrio Sol.'

'My friend is stone because of *you*.'

'Varrio Sol *destroys* innocents. He made an army of children so he could keep his crown.'

'To battle monsters that you control!'

'*Enough*!'

Ottilie had crossed the line, and she knew it.

'You had your chance,' said Whistler. 'I tried to save you, but time's up. I have none left to waste. *Three circles, circles, circles past* … such a helpful rhyme. I let Gracie pick the guide to mark. She'd been watching closely – knew you all best.

'I did hope Bill would tell me where to go much sooner, but he couldn't remember, poor beetle. Disturbing memories … But Ned here did very well.' She waved her sleeve backwards to where Ned was hidden beneath the krippygrass.

'It was an interesting choice. I worried he was too sensible, but I was pleasantly surprised. So helpful of him not to make a fuss about the burns and the dreams. And you, dear, so good at keeping secrets. If word got out that he was dreamwalking I'd have had to snatch him much sooner, and I don't much fancy keeping prisoners if I can avoid it. It's not my style.'

Why was Whistler saying all this? It must have been to hurt Ned. That meant he was still conscious, still alive, perhaps just lashed to the ground like her and Gully. Ottilie's thoughts buzzed. She needed to keep Whistler talking – anything to keep her from freeing the sleepless witch. Or at least to distract her until Maeve came. Surely Maeve would come.

Ottilie tried to steady her nerves. 'Why do you hate the king so much? What did he do?'

Whistler ducked to the ground and leaned in close. Ottilie could taste the misery on her breath. It was like flowers ripped from their roots and left in water too long – sharp, dead waste.

'Maia was his daughter's name.' Her eyes flared as if daring Ottilie to speak it. 'She was neglected. Ignored. I raised her like my own until she was six years old. She had a sore throat when he sent me away. A mere cough. I thought it would pass.

'I wanted to stay in Varrio's favour, so I went to the North Island – to Rupimoon Rock, as instructed – to lend my services as Royal Mystic to his cousin. I began to suspect something was amiss when Odilo kept me longer than necessary. But I returned too late. When I arrived back at All Kings' Hill, she was gone.'

Whistler snapped upright and paced back and forth. Tendrils of chilled air curled through the midday warmth. 'Maia had developed a dangerous fever and was sent westward, they said, to a famed healer. But I didn't believe it. There were no healers better than those at the Hill – none better than myself. I left immediately, following them west, catching up to them on the road to the Laklands.'

Her expression shifted. There was something fresh, an urgency, almost like she was pleading for Ottilie to understand how truly terrible the king was.

'That was his plan, you see.' She wrung her hands beneath her sleeves. 'Fearful of the Vanquisher's bane, the curse of the Sol daughters, he wanted to let her die of this natural fever and bury her body far, far away, as far from All Kings' Hill as horses could take her.' Darkness veiled Whistler's eyes, and bitterness sharpened her words. 'No-one thought anything of it. She was going to see this fictitious healer. If she died on the road … well … what could he do?'

Ottilie's gut twisted. The king had sent his own daughter away to die?

'And she did,' said Whistler, blankly. She seemed to pull backwards, curving in on herself. 'I don't know when. By the state of her body I would assume it was two or three days before I caught up. They were halfway through the Narroway by then, nearly at the Laklands. I believe she was going to be taken all the way – dumped in the Laklands to rot with the rest of my family's shame.

'When I found them, my rage was beyond control. I had not hurt anyone since I was a child, not since those days of being imprisoned in my father's dungeons. When I was done with the six men and the nurse who were ferrying her westward, their remains encircled a great philowood tree. I buried her there, beneath its protective branches. But the wrong that was done to her rotted it through.'

'The Withering Wood,' said Ottilie, twisting to watch Whistler pace.

'I could feel it,' said Whistler. 'The potential. In my sorrow and rage I called it forth. A dredretch. An underworld beast to punish him for what he had done, to destroy the Usklers just as my father's treachery had destroyed the Laklands. That was when the withering sickness took root and began to spread. But it was born of him, of his evil, his neglect, and all seven who saw it through.'

'Who you murdered,' wheezed Gully. The roots must have been pressing on his ribs. 'You don't think the murder of seven people helped it along?'

Gully was right. Whistler said everything she did was because of the king, but she also said it was her choice. She owned that choice: to become a curse. She had turned herself into a greater monster than the one she wanted to destroy.

'You answered evil with evil,' said Ottilie. 'You're no better than he is.'

Whistler bared her teeth in a snarl.

'And now what are you doing?' said Ottilie. 'Making an ally of the sleepless witch! Someone responsible for the death of their own child, just like the king – but already punished and locked up where it can't hurt anyone. And you're going to *free* it? That makes no sense!'

To Ottilie's great surprise, Whistler cracked a smile. 'How well you understand me,' she said.

Whistler turned her back. With a great sweeping of her sleeves, the ground began to rumble. Ottilie's hands shook in the mush. She pictured the creature from the canyon caves: that scaled thing crawling free of the soil, baring its fangs, loose at long last.

The mud drew back like a rolling tide. Ottilie wanted to scurry away, to cover her head, to hide. But something bronze glinted in the sun. It was familiar. She had seen its likeness somewhere else ... further south, on the road to Market Town.

Here, beneath the sunnytree, was a bronze hatch. Ottilie strained against the roots. Her knees breached the mud as she leaned closer. She could just see the engraving of a duck carved in the centre of the circle.

Seika Devil-Slayer's mark was here. Why?

Whistler was watching her, a smile playing on her lips. 'Do you want to come and see?' she said. With a flick of her wrist, the hatch flew open. Sunlight spilled into a narrow stairway.

Ottilie didn't know what to say. Did she want to come and see the freeing of the sleepless witch? No, she did not. But if she said yes, Whistler would have to unbind her.

She nodded.

Whistler waved her sleeves and the soil seemed to pushed Ottilie upwards, until she was birthed from the earth. The roots uncoiled and withdrew, leaving only her hands tied behind her back. Ottilie gasped and struggled to her feet, her mud-blackened legs visibly shaking. With a hiss that reminded her of an aggressive goose, she felt a lifting and lightness as every weapon she carried seemed to implode, leaving little trails of ash leaking from her clothes. She glanced at Gully, still bound to the ground, but Whistler said, 'Invitation only.'

'Don't go with her,' Gully pleaded.

But she had to. She was free now, apart from her hands. She might get a chance to stop it – somehow. 'I'll be back.' Her words wobbled. 'I promise!'

'Come on, my walking map,' barked Whistler, turning back to Ned.

Ned struggled to his feet, his hands bound like Ottilie's.

'Keys first,' said Whistler.

Ottilie and Ned looked at each other, neither knowing what she meant.

'That's you,' Whistler whispered, looking pointedly at Ned.

A *key*? Ned was a key? He was going to open something? Maybe the iron coffin. Ned was clearly drawing the same conclusion. He grounded his feet and glared at Whistler, silently refusing to move.

A wide smile spread across the witch's face. 'You both do exactly as I say or I plant him like a seed.' She clicked her fingers and Gully was sucked chest-deep into the ground.

Ottilie yelped and Ned immediately took the first four stairs in one jump.

Whistler gestured for Ottilie to go next, so, throwing one last look back at Gully, Ottilie followed Ned down into the dark.

25

Wander No Longer

Ottilie could feel Whistler's breath on the back of her neck. Descending into darkness, with a witch behind her and no hands to feel the way, was worse than any nightmare she'd ever had.

She felt for the next step with her foot. 'Why is Seika Devil-Slayer's mark on the hatch?' she asked, determined to keep Whistler talking.

'Because her coven put the coffin down here,' said Whistler in a bored voice.

'She had a *coven*?' said Ned, from below.

Whistler snorted.

'Do you mean the witches that imprisoned it?' said Ottilie.

Whistler simply clucked. There was something here she was not willing to divulge, which, Ottilie realised, meant it must be important. She tucked it away. It was something she would have to find out if they made it out alive.

'Why is that duck everywhere else?' Ottilie had wondered about it for so long. 'It's on the hatch that leads to the tunnels under Wikric, and on the well in the canyon caves, and I've seen it around Fiory, too.'

'They haven't told you about the origin of the forts?' said Whistler, with a laugh. 'Of course they haven't.'

'What about the forts?' said Ned.

'The three forts in the Narroway were initially places of worship,' explained Whistler. 'Where followers of the Lore came to pay tribute to the Old Gods – Fiory, Richter and Arko. Did you never wonder where the stations got their names?

'People made pilgrimages from all over the Usklers – most of the tunnels you've encountered were formed for their use when the fendevil was stomping around, and travelling above ground was too dangerous to risk. The tunnels under Wikric were built for similar reasons – in case the beast ever went on a rampage through the city. People were safe from the sickness underground.

'Oh.' Ottilie had never much wondered about the tunnels. Coming from the Swamp Hollows, where the entire community lived in tunnels and caves, she just thought they were the usual thing. But of course, the caves and tunnels by the Brakkerswamp were all natural formations. These other tunnels, it seemed, were not.

'Even before Seika Sol defeated the fendevil, she was revered as a living goddess,' said Whistler. 'The Narroway was, unofficially, her domain. I'd wager that's why you're not taught about any of it. The men in charge wouldn't want you to know about that sort of thing.

'Covens of witches had been living in the canyon caves for years, experimenting with the healing spring. And after the fendevil didn't rise again from the sea, it was in the Narroway where witches forged the first salt weapons. It's also why the coven moved the iron coffin all the way out here. They wanted it out of the *hallowed land*.'

'Why does no-one know about this?' said Ned. Ottilie couldn't even see his outline anymore.

'Because after the witch purge everyone wanted to forget about everything to do with witchcraft, including the legendary princess whose symbol marked the royal house.'

A faint scuffling interrupted her.

'Try not to break your neck, Ned. I need a functioning key,' snapped Whistler.

'Bit of light would be nice,' he muttered.

Ottilie smiled, impressed by his nerve.

'Oh all right, then.' Whistler made a puffing sound and a thousand bright embers burst to life around them, floating just above their heads.

Ottilie exhaled. The stairway seemed to expand and the tightness in her chest slackened with a twitch.

'So, it's true then?' said Ottilie, breathlessly. 'Seika Devil-Slayer was a witch?'

'Why do you think she was considered a goddess?' said Whistler. 'She was a fiorn.'

'But –' Ottilie was so accustomed to the current attitude towards witches, she found it very hard to imagine that Seika gained divine status for the same reason so many others were buried alive centuries later. The fact that she was a fiorn, too … If Maeve were exposed, she would be chained up and carted off to the Laklands.

'Once, fiorns were considered Fiory's chosen children,' said Whistler.

Ottilie was sure she had heard that before.

'It's a rare gift. In Seika's lifetime, she was the only known fiorn in the Usklers. She was worshiped by her people, witches in particular, from a very young age. She could change into a duck. That's why the royal house adopted the image – to honour her gift. The Sol family, at the time, considered it solid proof of their divine right to rule. And people loved to see the mark all around them, because it made them feel protected – it reminded them that they lived in a kingdom loved by the gods.'

There was something peaceful about the image of a duck. It was comforting. Certainly more comforting than a battleaxe.

'That, of course, was well before the Roving Empire invaded, muddied our faith and withdrew, leaving the Usklers unsure of itself and the Lore a mere collection of myths.' Whistler sighed. 'And how gleefully my father changed the symbol when he took the throne. Seika was all but forgotten by then. But we knew. Our family remembered.

'I'm surprised it wasn't changed before his reign. But my father loathed witchcraft, perhaps more than any who came before him. He was born into a world that had already turned against witches. I believe he would have hated them anyway. He always hated any power he couldn't take for himself.'

Ottilie watched an ember float by. She understood the jealousy, but not the rest.

'Witches were peaceful helpers and healers,' said Whistler. 'These tunnels are nine centuries old – it was witch magic that fortified them, preserving them in case they were ever needed again. Yet Viago the Vanquisher imagined those powers used against him. Like Varrio, he was a coward.'

Ottilie was beginning to realise that Whistler saw her father and nephew as one and the same. She wanted to learn more. Talking to Whistler was like getting lost in a fascinating history book – albeit one that might grow teeth and leap for your throat.

Ahead, the sound of Ned's footsteps changed. He had reached the bottom of the stairway.

Ottilie's pulse quickened. The sleepless witch was somewhere near. Her eyes snapped up from her feet. There was nothing, just a stone wall, but something was carved into the rock. The embers moved to hover in front.

Daring and sound,
loved, trusted, and true.
One key to the lock,
and he will lead you.

Light of the sun,
the peak of the sky.
Wander no longer,
here breathing bones lie.

Ottilie recognised it immediately, and noticed with a shiver that the last line now read *here breathing bones lie*. In the tunnels under Fiory, she was sure it had said *there*. But of course it said *here*. Because they had arrived. They were finally at the very place she could not imagine anyone ever wanting to go.

Her eyes skimmed the first lines. *Daring and sound, loved, trusted and true. One key to the lock, and he will lead you.* It was describing the dreamer, the key, the guide – Ned.

'I'd have picked you, Ottilie,' said Whistler.

She could feel eyes on the back of her head. Her neck prickled as if a beetle had crawled out from beneath her hair.

'But it does specify a *he*, and you never know with magic.' Whistler flicked her wrist and Ned gasped. Behind his back, his sleeve caught fire. The roots shrivelled and fell away. His entire forearm was alight. Ottilie took the last steps at a leap. Heat scalded her skin as she reached him, but she had no hands to help.

'Calm down,' said Whistler. 'You're a key – do what keys do.'

Ottilie looked frantically for some sort of lock. There was nothing!

Whistler clicked her tongue and jerked her head at the wall.

Taking the hint, Ned pressed his palm against the stone.

Ottilie was frozen in terrified fascination as, from the star-shaped burns, three streams like molten rock snaked around his arm and slithered into the carved lettering on the wall, making the words *wander no longer* glow red and gold. With a deafening crack, the rock blackened and spilt apart, crumbling to dust that whipped her skin like a sandstorm. She coughed and blinked. 'Ned! Are you all right?'

'He's fine,' muttered Whistler. '*Honestly.*' She shoved past Ottilie and entered what must have been a tomb.

Ned was holding out his arm. For a moment he and Ottilie just stared. His sleeve had burned away and the burns on his forearm were raw as ever, but he was otherwise unmarred.

Whistler's back was turned. Snapping out of his shock, Ned ducked behind Ottilie and tried to tear away the roots that still bound her hands.

'Stop trying to free her!' snapped Whistler, as if they were two misbehaving children. 'Come and see.'

Reluctantly, Ned released the roots, but stayed close by her side so that their shoulders touched as they entered the tomb. It was a rough, rounded space, empty but for the same iron coffin Ottilie had seen in Ned's dream.

She was so nervous that even walking felt strange, as if she had only just learned how and might topple over at any second. Her breath was coming out in funny little hisses. This was it. It was happening. She couldn't think of a single way to stop it.

Whistler ushered them forwards, waved her sleeves, and the lid flew open with bang.

26

Blood

Ottilie braced for calamity. She imagined the grey-scaled creature bursting from the coffin, its pointed teeth bared at her throat.

Nothing happened.

Had she died? Was this what happened after death – did time fix at the final beat, like fish in a lake that froze through?

No. She was still alive. Ned was beside her, breathing. Whistler's sleeves were twitching. But nothing emerged from the coffin. Ottilie looked at Whistler, to see if she was surprised, but Whistler was watching *her*. Catching her eye, she gleefully ushered Ottilie forward.

Ottilie inched closer and peered into the iron coffin. It was empty. Her heart hammered – was the witch already out?

She looked again. There *was* something in there. In the belly of the coffin lay a pale pipe.

A musical instrument, here in the sleepless witch's coffin? Ottilie looked at Ned. He was frowning, and seemed as confused as she was.

In the light of the embers she could see bronze metal embedded in the pipe, twisting around it as fine as a spider's web.

Whistler plucked out the pipe, tucked it into her belt and made for the stairs, as if she had just done something as ordinary as picking a piece of fruit. She said nothing about it, and seemed perfectly pleased with herself.

Was this what she'd wanted all along – this pipe? For what? Where was the sleepless witch? Ottilie had thought she understood what was going on – most of it, at least – but she had known nothing.

She felt as if she had hit her head, as if her memory had been wiped by some spell. She had to keep reminding herself to breathe. She made to follow Whistler, like a dog trailing its master, but the witch stopped in the entrance and whipped around, her eyes stormy.

Ottilie's bound hands reached up her back, aching for the cutlass that was just dust.

'You know everything now,' said Whistler, with no glimmer of mirth. This was serious. She was done playing. 'You have no excuse. This is your *last chance*. Join me and survive, or choose your end, here.'

Ottilie didn't know what to do. What would happen if she said no? Would Whistler attack her and Ned right there in the tomb? Would she go up and hurt Gully?

Vying for time, she asked the question that had been haunting her for months. 'Why does it matter to you so much? Why *me*?'

Whistler met her gaze and said, 'Because you remind me of her. You are what I imagine she would have been, had she lived.'

It was so simple; such an ordinary thing.

That couldn't be all there was to it. Could it? Ottilie's mind ticked and ticked. What was Whistler trying to say? Ottilie reminded her of Maia ... but why? Was this what she had been dreading? Ottilie knew her mother, knew her story, but her father was completely unknown to her. Whoever he was, was he somehow connected to Whistler? To the Sol family?

Whistler was still watching her, a flicker of amusement returning to her eyes. 'Don't get carried away – you have no relation to her by blood.'

Ottilie's head spun. She didn't know if she was relieved or not. To be sure, she was thankful not to be a Sol – as far as she could tell, they were all rotten to the core. But how could she be relieved that Whistler simply liked her for who she was? A blood link was innocent. Beyond her control. But this … what did it say about Ottilie?

'I'll admit I did wonder for a while,' said Whistler. 'You seemed so familiar – there was something in you that touched me. The thought that you might be a lost Sol daughter was a thrilling prospect. Varrio's second daughter died, but he's not the only one to carry the name.'

Perhaps Whistler had thought she could mend a piece of herself if she could save a different Sol. It was probably why she tried to rescue unwanted children. But a Sol daughter … that was about as close as she could come to turning back time and saving Maia.

Whistler was watching her, and something in her expression made Ottilie wonder if she could read her thoughts. She certainly seemed more agitated as she snapped, 'I had some time to kill, waiting for my map to cook.' She flicked her sleeve at Ned. 'So I looked into your family.' A smile formed.

Ottilie felt unstable on her feet.

'But you are a true child of the swamps – you are the daughter of Freda Colter.' Whistler paused, staring Ottilie right in the eyes. 'And Odis Igo, the Swamp Hollows keeper.'

Ottilie's heart seemed to shrink and stick.

The keeper was her father. The keeper, who had always favoured Freddie, but still allowed her to rot in their tiny hollow. The keeper, who had sold Gully to the Narroway Hunt. Hot tears gathered behind her eyes. She could have been sick.

'It means nothing,' said Whistler, her voice softening. 'Your spirit is kin to Maia's – to mine. I felt it when you snuck in to the Narroway to save your brother. You have a great sense of what is right and wrong. You loathe injustice. The Usklers have rotted through. You know which is the right side.'

Ottilie could barely speak. But her thoughts smoothed. The king had sent away the person who mattered most to Whistler, and the keeper had done the same thing to Ottilie. Did Whistler think she wanted revenge?

She remembered Bonnie saying that Whistler had found her curled up with the goats when her father had been in a rage. Whistler chose people who had been deeply wronged and offered them a chance at vengeance, and – she thought of the bloodbeasts – unimaginable power.

'There is a place for you with me.' The embers flickered and flared. 'You can help us right wrongs.'

Ottilie was speechless. She pictured Gracie, bound to a wyler, her pointed teeth bared and her knives spinning.

'You can take your pick,' said Whistler. 'I was going to give you the kappabak. When they found out you were a girl and tried to force you out, they took away all of your power. I thought the most powerful beast was a fair trade. But now I know you better, I'd probably hand you the learies.'

Like it was a gift. The learies. It was a learie that had savaged Scoot – that would have killed him had Whistler not healed him in time. Ottilie could still see that scaled feline with the scorching tail. She imagined pressing her hand to its lion-like face and, for one bizarre moment, she wondered what colour the binding would turn its dark scales ...

Ned spoke up. 'You don't know a thing about her.'

Whistler's eyes flashed. She raised a finger to her lips and said, 'Shhh!'

With a thump, Ned dropped to the ground.

Ottilie jumped to his side, smacking her knees hard into the stone. Tears of pain sprung, but she hardly noticed. What had Whistler done? She blinked and saw Scoot, grey stone creeping ...

Ottilie wanted to shake Ned awake, to search for a pulse, but her hands were still bound.

'Calm down, he's just sleeping,' said Whistler. She almost sounded disappointed.

Ottilie glared up at her, angry tears spilling. 'You hate the king because he harms innocents. You're *mad*,' she snarled. 'You stopped being human when you started messing with dredretches!'

Something flickered in Whistler's eyes, but quickly faded. She answered coldly, 'I have told you, I will save anyone who *wants* to be saved.'

Whistler stepped towards her and it took all of Ottilie's strength not to scuttle backwards across the floor.

'Now here it is,' said Whistler. 'The last chance. You won't get another.'

She made no threats. She simply offered, holding out her hand.

Ottilie's heart was pounding in her ears. Ned was asleep on the ground, maybe forever. Maeve was missing. Something had happened to Leo and Skip. Gully was half swallowed by the ground. Scoot was stone and they had no way to fix him. She didn't know where the sleepless witch was, and the keeper ... the keeper was her father.

She was suffocating in a tangle of anger and fear. She could hardly summon her voice.

'*No.*'

She wasn't sure if she actually spoke the word, but Whistler's face darkened and more than half of the embers snapped into blackness.

'That is your choice,' she said, backing away from the entrance.

Between them, the dust gathered into stones, and the stones tumbled and rolled, piling one on top of the other. The wall was rebuilding itself.

'I will spare you the death that awaits you in war,' said Whistler, her voice less human than Ottilie had ever heard it.

Ottilie tried to nudge Ned awake with her knee, but he slept on. Whistler was going back up the stairs – and Gully was out there! Ottilie wanted to leap up and over the wall. She nearly did it. She moved in her mind, but her body stayed put. She couldn't leave Ned, unconscious, sealed in. She knew Gully would have done the same thing.

The rock wall reached higher. Whistler turned away, and something freezing wrapped around Ottilie's legs. For a second she thought it was just Whistler's emotions chilling the air, but something trickled down her boot – damp, ice cold ... From nowhere, water had begun to pool.

27

Light

Her thoughts were falling debris. Whistler had gone above. Gully was up there. Water covered her boots. Her hands were bound. Ned was going to drown!

With darting eyes, she scanned the space. There was a narrow ledge up on the wall. If she could just get him up there ... but she had no way to try. Ottilie shuffled across the floor. Kneeling, she roughly manoeuvred his head and shoulders up onto her knees. The water smoothed over his legs.

It was like freshly thawed ice. Her only hope was that shock might wake him. Water wrapped around her knees, reaching up to Ned's ears. She gritted her teeth and jerked her legs out from under him.

Ned splashed backwards into the water, his entire head submerged. The water smoothed, his face blurred beneath the surface, and for a horrible moment she thought she had drowned him. But then he lurched upwards, coughing violently. Ottilie was so relieved that, had her arms been free, she would have thrown them around him.

Panting, his chest heaved as he managed to rasp, 'What happened?'

'She locked us in and flooded the place.' Ottilie pointed to the rebuilt wall.

Ned scrambled to his feet, still gasping for air. 'But … where's the water coming from?'

'Nowhere,' she said, hopelessly. 'Everywhere.'

Ned rushed to the wall and pressed his palm against it over and over.

Nothing happened.

He swore and turned back to Ottilie. The water was nearly at his knees. He hurried over and pulled at the roots still binding her wrists. 'Can you swim?'

Ottilie nodded. She and Gully used to swim in the clear creek above the Brakkerswamp. It had been a long time, but she was sure she would remember how. 'Can you?'

'Sunken Sweep,' he said, as if that were answer enough.

What good was it, though? The water would get above their heads and they would have to swim, but it would not be long before it reached the ceiling.

Ned struggled and struggled with the roots binding Ottilie's arms, and finally one strand snapped. The roots unravelled and her hands were free.

'We have to find a way out,' she said, flexing and bending her hands. Her wrists stung where the roots had rubbed away skin.

They waded back and forth, searching for any crack or cleft. Some of Whistler's embers were still alight, but they were slowly drifting down and drowning one by one. Some lights shone beneath the surface like a blurry, upside down sky. It was getting harder and harder to see.

She couldn't stop worrying about what had happened to Gully. She had abandoned him to Whistler. But she couldn't have left Ned unconscious.

The water was up to her shoulders. It was freezing. Her skin sucked inward and her whole body burned. Before long, she could think of nothing but getting out of the icy water. She swam to the ledge and pulled herself up so that just her knees were covered.

Ned followed and Ottilie helped him up. They stood out of the water, arms wrapped tightly around their middles, shivering side by side.

'I'm so sorry,' said Ned. Ottilie could hear the chill in his voice, as if icicles dripped from every word. 'I should have tried to stop the dreams.'

Ottilie shook her head and unstuck her cold-clenched jaw. 'There was no way to stop them. This is my fault,' she whispered. 'I should have got rid of that bone necklace. That's how she knew we were here. Our plan might have worked if I hadn't given us away.'

She hugged herself so tightly she might have cracked a rib, only she was too cold to feel it. She knew they would be warmer if they huddled together. Ottilie rocked on her feet, but found that, even now, she was too nervous to try it.

Ned was shaking his head. 'None of it matters.'

He stared down at the coffin. The solid iron seemed to sway beneath the water, as if it wasn't really there at all, just a memory or a dream. Everything felt that way now – unreal.

'What was that pipe?' said Ned. 'What does she want it for?'

'I don't know.'

This was what Whistler had been waiting for. They would know her plans soon enough.

Even if they managed to escape and reach the Narroway, they might plunge headfirst into a war. It should have been the only thing Ottilie was worrying about. And yet, as she stared at that swaying coffin, her mind kept floating back and forth over the same thought – the keeper was her father … the keeper … she knew who her father was … the keeper … all that time …

It was easier, she supposed, than thinking about what might have happened to Gully and her friends. Easier than worrying about what Whistler was going to do with the pipe, where the sleepless witch really was, or whether or not the white stone had swallowed Scoot whole.

The keeper, who had never even spoken two words to her directly, who put Gully's name on the pickings list …

The water rose higher and higher. It reached Ottilie's waist. Her voice shook as she said, 'I don't know how we're going to get out of here.'

Ned didn't seem to know what to say. Instead, he stepped close and put his arm around her shoulders. Neither could meet the other's eye. Ottilie leaned in to the warmth, but she wasn't sure where her arms should go, or how to stand, or even breathe. But she didn't want to move.

The water rose until her shoulders were just above the surface. There was a higher ledge, much further up. She pulled away from Ned and began running her fingers over the wall, trying to find a way to climb it. There was nothing. They would have to wait until the water lifted them.

Ned found her hand underwater and entwined their fingers. Ottilie remembered the first time he had taken her hand, and how her heart had sunk when he released it. The embers were dying all around them. She could hardly see more than a dark outline of his face.

He must have been thinking the same thing, because his thumb brushed across the tip of her nose, like he was trying to remember how she looked, and for the space of a blink, Ottilie didn't care that she was freezing and terrified and in the dark.

It was the water lifting to cradle the very base of her skull that snapped her back to reality.

Fear pressed down and she shuddered beneath the pressure. Her feet lifted off the ledge. She couldn't stand any longer without her nose below the waterline. Above, the last of the embers were like dying stars winking out at the end of time. Darkness swelled. She would float up and up until she was taken by the sky.

Ned reached out and held her up. He was tall enough that he could still stand, and for a moment he tethered her to the world and she felt grounded again.

Over his shoulder, Ottilie noticed something: a tiny ember disappearing into the rock wall.

'What?' Ned turned to look.

'I think there's a gap up there.' She pointed. 'A light went through.'

'Are you sure it didn't just hit the wall and go out?' Despite his words, his voice was hopeful.

'I need to get higher to see.'

Ottilie climbed onto his shoulders and what she saw made her heart leap. The ember had slipped in behind a rock, illuminating its edges. 'I think there's an opening! We just need to move some rocks.'

She had to leap from Ned's shoulders to reach the ledge above. Dangling from the edge, her muscles pulling so tight they threatened to snap, she managed to clamber onto the jutting rock.

She looked down. There was no way for Ned to get up. She began shifting the rocks herself. It was so dark that she had to do a lot of it by feel. Her fingers were nearly numb. It was like working through six pairs of gloves, yet somehow every scrape still burned and throbbed.

It was slow but, piece by piece, an opening formed.

Below her, the water was rising. Ned was treading water, and finally he was high enough that she could pull him up. She heard his teeth chattering as they shifted the last of the rocks. The ember was still hovering there, just bright enough to illuminate the engraving of a duck on an ancient triangular door.

Ottilie managed a shaky laugh. Whistler didn't know everything! She hadn't known there was a second entrance to the tomb. There was no latch, only an old wheel. Ned and Ottilie pushed as hard as they could until finally, with a great scrape, it began to turn. The door pressed inwards, revealing a tunnel beyond.

They crawled through. The water had already reached the ledge and was beginning to spill into the tunnel. Together they pushed with all their might and shut the door behind them.

'We need to move,' said Ottilie. 'If that tomb keeps filling up I don't know how long the door can hold the water back.'

'We can't go too fast,' said Ned, and Ottilie sensed him feeling his way around the tunnel. 'We'll hit our heads.'

It was pitch black. They had no glow sticks, none of Whistler's embers. Nothing. But they were free.

'Come on,' said Ottilie. 'Let's go.'

⟋ 28 ⟍

Glow

The journey was slow. Ottilie's throat felt like it was lined with bark. She wished she'd thought to gulp down some of the water that had nearly swallowed them up. The door seemed to be holding fast, and she could only assume Whistler's spell had ended – perhaps when the water reached the ceiling of the tomb, or when there were no longer any beating hearts inside.

All she could think about was what had happened when Whistler went back up. Would she have left Gully alive? And the others? What had become of them all? Leo had never signalled. Maeve had never come. There had to be a reason.

Ottilie felt as if someone was scrunching her heart like a damp ball of cloth, because she knew the truth. If Whistler had intended to kill her and Ned, why would she leave the others alive?

She took a great gasp of air and focused on her feet. One foot after the other. Aside from the fact they were climbing upward, she did not know where they were headed. She was just getting the horrible feeling that they had not travelled far at all when a faint light appeared ahead. She froze, wary of company, then edged forwards and saw a trail of pale fungi emitting a silvery glow.

'What is that?' said Ned, reaching towards it in awe.

She searched for the word. '*Lumi.*' The glowing fungi. 'It's really rare, and *so* valuable! There were rumours that there was some in the tunnels around the Swamp Hollows. Gully and I used to hunt for it, but we never found any!'

Ottilie couldn't believe her eyes. There was an absolute abundance. The lumi lined the tunnel walls for what might have been miles, lighting the way around low-hanging rocks, narrow crevices and tight bends, until finally it grew sparse and the trail stopped.

They both scraped some off the walls and held it aloft. It wasn't slimy like she had imagined, but spongy and smooth. Removed from its roots, the glow dimmed a little, but they could still see where to step.

The tunnel narrowed and they had to walk sideways, occasionally ducking down to crawl, until finally they came to a tight gap. Ottilie inched forward, the sharp rock pressing in on both sides, but the space ahead kept her calm. There was a drop beyond. Peering below, she saw a vast cavern, with lanterns and rugs and window shutters on the holes in the cave walls.

Her breath caught. Ottilie knew where she was. This was the keeper's hollow! She swayed on her feet, but couldn't tear her eyes away. She took in every single part of it. Once, this would have seemed like a palace. A bed on legs, not an old chaff-stuffed mattress on the floor. Covered lanterns that were still lit, despite his slumber.

The keeper could not have known what rare treasure clung to the walls of the tunnel not far from one of his mouldering armchairs.

The cavern stank of meat-rot and old smoke. There was a small fireplace in the corner and she wondered where the smoke went. Perhaps through the cracks and into another tunnel, or someone else's hollow.

Ottilie drifted into a strange state of calm. Her head was light, her thoughts distant. She felt spectral, an invisible visitor – like when she'd entered Ned's dream.

Tucking the lumi into her pocket, she began to scale down the wall. When she reached the bottom, she crossed the damp, mud-crusted rugs that lay over every inch of the floor. Stopping at the edge of the bed, she stared at the man she now knew was her father.

The keeper managed the Hollows, and Ottilie remembered him as a figure of great authority: quick-tempered, but prone to sudden bursts of what he himself announced was generosity. Ottilie had once thought it was generosity, too. The extra scraps of food. The occasional blanket from his own supply.

Striding to the fireplace, she could feel Ned watching her as he followed close behind. He didn't speak, no doubt cautious about waking the sleeping man, even though he could not know who it was.

Ottilie took hold of the iron poker. She thought of how thin she and Gully used to be and, without thinking twice, she reached out and prodded the keeper's mountainous stomach.

He swatted at his stained silk nightshirt with a wet grunt, then gasped awake, staring at the two damp intruders.

Ottilie withdrew the poker, her eyes narrowed. Would he recognise her? Did he know?

'Ottilie,' he said, anger colouring his face. 'WHAT ARE YOU DOING IN MY HOLLOW?!' Spit flew from his mouth as he bellowed, outrage jiggling his jowls.

Ottilie nearly laughed. Not, *where have you been for the last two years?* She was painted with cuts and bruises.

Yet he did not ask, *are you hurt?* He was shocked, she supposed. She could give him that consideration.

What did she even want from him? Some acknowledgment of their blood tie? No, she didn't need that. She knew what she needed. She needed to know why her world had been turned upside down.

'Why?' she said, her throat so dry she could barely form the word.

'Why, what?' said the keeper, struggling to scramble out of bed.

Ottilie pointed the poker in his direction, warning him not to move.

'Why did you put Gully's name on the pickings list?'

He gaped at her. 'I … they pay me to watch for the ones with the best potential!' His face turned sour. 'That's how I keep this place running. How I keep them well fed.'

'*Well fed?*' she repeated in disbelief. Memories surfaced of dried brakkernuts and riverweed broth, and her eyes settled on his three chins. 'He was too young.'

'They don't mind that, as long as they meet the requirements,' said the keeper, hurriedly. 'He was always a runt, but he had energy and nerve. Those qualities were top of the list.'

Ottilie thought of Gully stuck by the sunnytree, Whistler rising from the tomb, and hot tears spilled down her cheeks. She blinked and saw their empty hollow on the morning he had disappeared. Her voice cracked as she said, 'How could you do it to Freddie?' She wanted to say *and me*, but couldn't get it out.

The keeper snorted. 'She barely even noticed.'

Tears dripped off her chin. 'You're lying!'

Ottilie sucked in a breath and pressed the poker against his belly. He snarled and shoved it away. She spun it in her hand and jabbed at his throat, stopping it an inch from his skin.

Purple blotches stained his cheeks as he sneered, 'You want to know why, you little bog rat! Because everyone *knew*, everyone knew *you* were mine. And he was someone else's. She was supposed to be loyal to me. Your runt brother was a walking insult. I'd have just as readily put your name down to get you out of my sight, but the pickers were never in the market for girls.'

Ned stepped to Ottilie's side.

'You're disgusting,' she spat, gripping the poker so hard her fingers turned white.

In that moment Ottilie knew, without a doubt, that she never wanted to set eyes on him again. This man wasn't family. This man was nothing.

Dropping the poker with a thump, she turned her back on the keeper.

They had to get back to the sunnytree, had to find out what had happened to Gully and everyone else. She didn't know what Ned had made of the conversation in the keeper's hollow, but he didn't ask her any questions as she led the way.

Dashing down those tunnels, past the old hollows, Ottilie felt that she was treading in two different worlds – one foot in each. She saw the place of her childhood, where she and Gully had played and hid and shivered in the dank dark. It almost felt as if a small part of her had never left; as if she'd left a piece of herself behind and finally clicked it back into place. But she also felt like an outsider, a visitor, someone who did not belong. It was dizzying and confusing, and all too much.

She felt the need to run, to create distance between herself and this strange, stagnant piece of her past. But then she saw them sitting outside her old hollow: Mr Parch, snoozing, his eyes wide open, and Old Moss, reading *Our Walkable World*.

A wave of warmth swept in, soothing every ache. She ran for them, skidding on the damp stone. Tears spilling down her cheeks, Ottilie dived on Old Moss, who barely had a moment to recognise her.

'Argh – oh – *Ottilie*!' cried Moss, squeezing her tight. She kicked at Mr Parch. 'Wake up!' snapped Moss. 'Rouse, you beak-faced corpse!'

Mr Parch blinked his eyes closed and then open again. 'Ottilie!' He began a slow, scrambling struggle to sit up. Finally managing it, he wound shaking limbs through their tangled hug. 'We so hoped you would come tonight!' he said, gripping her shoulders as if he still didn't believe she was there.

'What do you mean? How did you know ...'

Both Moss and Mr Parch were beaming at her, flashing the few teeth they had left.

Mr Parch pointed a hooked finger towards her old hollow.

Ottilie didn't know what she expected to find. She stood up on shaking legs, pushed open the door, and saw Gully asleep on his bed.

29

Slumber

She clutched at the door, feeling as if she had just stepped onto solid land after years at sea. It took her a moment to see straight. Finally, she took in the rest of the hollow. With a wave of relief she saw Skip fast asleep on her old mattress. Freddie's was empty. Before Ottilie had a chance to take him in, Leo struggled from his seat on the floor to wrap Ottilie and Ned in a bone-crushing hug. The movements roused Skip, who sat bolt upright, rubbed her eyes and beamed.

Gully didn't move.

'*Gully?*'

Skip grinned. 'He's fine.'

Ottilie exhaled. Gully always could sleep through anything. 'Where's Maeve? Is she … is she …'

'Maeve's out looking for you,' said Leo, with a look that clearly said, *calm down*.

'Tell me what happened.' Her head snapped back and forth between them. 'How are you all here? What happened when Whistler came out?'

Skip waved her hand. 'No, tell us what happened down there.' Her eyes darted to the doorway and she lowered her voice. 'Where's the sleepless witch?'

Ottilie didn't know where to begin.

Ned got in first, his voice thin and croaky. 'There was no witch, just a pipe in the coffin. Then Whistler dried to drown us.'

Leo looked confused. With a cough of laughter, he said, 'A smoking pipe?'

Ned shook his head. 'Musical.'

'No sleepless witch?' said Skip. 'You mean there isn't one … anywhere?'

'Don't know,' said Ned.

'But how did you get out?' said Leo, glancing between them.

'Dark tunnel. Glowing fungi,' said Ottilie, holding the lumi out for them to see.

Skip's eyes lit up. 'Wow!' She snatched it out of Ottilie's hand. 'Is that *lumi*? It's worth a fortune!'

Ottilie's weary arm dropped to her side. 'Tell us what happened to you?'

Leo frowned. 'We were hiding in the ditch. I was watching, ready to signal like we planned. But she must have known we were there, because the moment she appeared … I don't even know what happened.'

'The ground tried to eat us,' offered Skip, still gazing at the lumi.

'We couldn't move,' said Leo. His neck tensed, and Ottilie could tell he was reliving it. 'The roots made a gag so we couldn't call out to warn you.' He met her gaze, offering an unspoken apology.

Ottilie blinked and shook her head – it was the most she could muster in that moment.

'Then after she … took you down,' he continued, 'Maeve found us. She said Whistler spotted her and knocked her out of the air. She was unconscious for a while. By the time she woke up, it had all already happened. She thinks it's all her fault – that she gave us away when Whistler caught her.'

'It's not,' said Ottilie sharply, but she didn't elaborate. It was her fault, not Maeve's. She would tell them about the necklace another time, when she had enough strength to bear the blame. 'What happened then?'

'Maeve made the roots let us go.' Leo gripped Skip's shoulder. 'But Skip was injured.'

Ottilie's eyes snapped to Skip, who stopped prodding at the lumi and pulled back her hair to reveal a nasty cut across the side of her forehead that went down to the top of her cheekbone. 'I got cut on a rock when the roots dragged me down,' Skip explained.

'It was bleeding so much,' said Leo. 'Maeve thought she might be able to close it, but we needed to go somewhere safe where Whistler wouldn't interrupt her.'

Ottilie had a closer look at the jagged wound.

'It was messy and slow, but she got there in the end,' said Leo.

'She thinks it'll scar, but I don't really mind.' Skip grinned.

Ottilie gazed at Gully, still sleeping through all of this. She looked up to find Leo looking uneasy.

'He wanted to go down after you,' said Leo carefully. 'But Skip needed help and we needed to hide. We convinced him to show us the way here, but once we got here, he wanted to go back for you. Maeve was working on Skip and those roots mangled my bad leg again, so I could barely walk. We couldn't let him go alone. I knew you'd kill me if we did. So, Maeve …'

Ottilie remembered the way Whistler had made Ned sleep. She blanched. 'She put a spell on him?'

'Not *really*,' said Skip. 'She said there was a spell, but she didn't know how to do it.' She started speaking very quickly. 'She was scared of getting it wrong and making him sleep forever, so she found some sickles –'

'Sickles are poison!' said Ottilie. She had learned from a very young age never to touch the pale, crescent-shaped flowers that floated like ghostly boats in the swamp waters.

'Maeve used the petal powder to make him sleep,' said Skip, still speaking very fast. 'It worked great,' she added.

'I can see that!' said Ottilie, trying very hard to stay calm. 'But when is he going to wake up?'

'She said by morning,' said Leo, stepping away from her as if he feared violence.

'You better hope he wakes up by morning!' said Ottilie, panic gripping her again.

Ned put his arm around her, which didn't help her nerves.

'He will – she promised,' said Skip, the beginnings of a smile creeping onto her face.

'Wait, where's Nox?' said Ottilie. Had Whistler done something to them too?

'Nox and Maestro are hiding in the forest. We didn't want to scare everyone here,' said Skip.

'In Longwood?' said Ottilie. Her old fears resurfaced, but she shoved them back down. The wingerslinks braved the Narroway. They could handle Longwood.

'Hang on just a minute,' said Leo, stepping towards them. Ottilie noticed his limp. 'What's *this*?' He waggled his hand between Ottilie and Ned.

Ned quickly dropped his arm from around her shoulders and Ottilie awkwardly slid away from him.

Leo leaned in towards Ottilie and muttered, 'I'll have no-one messing with my fledge.'

Ottilie rolled her eyes and shoved him away.

Ned laughed. 'She's not your fledge.'

Leo gave him a look of mock distrust and said, 'She's not yours, either.'

'I'm not anybody's anything,' said Ottilie, feeling deeply uncomfortable with all the attention. 'We need to figure out what to do.'

They were stuck. Gully wouldn't wake until morning and Maeve was still out looking for them. While the others took the opportunity to rest, Ottilie crept out to sit with Old Moss and Mr Parch.

She told them everything, every little part of her story, and they filled her in on the slightly less exciting goings on of the Swamp Hollows. Finally, because she had gone too long without asking, Ottilie said, 'Where is she?'

Old Moss took her there, teetering back and forth, her walking stick clunking on the stone. When they came to the mouldy old curtain, Moss rapped her stick against the wall.

'Gurt!' she hollered.

'Whozat?' came a sniffly reply.

'Get out here,' said Moss.

Gurt eased the curtain aside as if it were delicate silk, and poked his waxy face through the gap. 'Well, hello there, little Ott! What brings you to Castle Gurt?'

Did time not move in this place? It was as if it were the same day Gully had gone missing – as if they'd all been asleep since she left.

'Take off,' snapped Moss.

'What's that, Moss? Take off what?' He dropped the curtain and started tapping his head as if looking for a hat to remove – then tugging at his shirt, revealing sharp ribs and pocked skin.

'Off with you, you crusty leech!' said Moss, brandishing her walking stick.

'This is my property,' he said, swinging his arms about proudly. 'You can't make me leave.'

Moss prodded him with the walking stick.

'Argh!' He jumped back.

She poked at him again and again until, grumbling, he scampered off down the tunnel, Moss hobbling just slightly behind.

Ottilie stepped into the hollow. Even after the rotting stench of the withering sickness, the smell of old bramblywine still turned her stomach. Freddie was in the corner, sleeping, just where Ottilie had left her nearly two years ago. Ottilie stood frozen, unsure if she wanted to rouse her. Finally, she moved over to the pile of old blankets and curled into her mother's bones.

❧ 30 ❧

Parting Gifts

Perhaps Old Moss had scared Gurt off, because he did not return to his hollow that night. Even in her sleep, Freddie's breaths were short and shallow. It was as if she never exhaled, just sucked little gasps of air into a void.

Ottilie didn't know what to expect when Freddie woke. Sometimes, first thing in the morning, Freddie was her old self. But it was rare and, as Ottilie lay beside her, she realised she couldn't risk the heartache. Not now, not after learning about the keeper. Not with Whistler on the verge of attack, and Scoot nearing the end. So, knowing that she might well regret it, Ottilie slunk from Gurt's hollow and back to her own.

Every one of them was asleep. Ottilie didn't want to wake them. She needed air.

She was just about to pull the door shut when a shadow bobbed and feathers whooshed. She nearly jumped out of her skin as a black owl swept across the hollow to land on her shoulder. The weight was like a reassuring hand and, surprising herself, she smiled.

Stepping carefully over Mr Parch's legs, she wandered through the winding tunnels and out into the damp air. Dawn was approaching. Through gaps in the trees a faint silver sheen brightened the sky, and the shallow swamp pools seemed to push towards it.

Maeve swept off Ottilie's shoulder and turned back into herself just before her feet sank into the mud.

'You're getting so good at that.'

Maeve didn't smile. Her eyes were hooded. 'They told me about the sleepless witch,' she said. 'It wasn't there? Just a pipe?'

Ottilie nodded and remembered what Leo had said about Maeve blaming herself. 'Thank you for what you did. You saved all of them. It wasn't your fault – it was mine.'

It was always easy confessing things to Maeve – so much easier than telling anyone else. Ottilie held out the bone necklace. 'Whistler knew I was there because of this. She was probably watching for you. You got caught because of me – we all did.'

Maeve fixed her eyes on the necklace and simply said, 'It doesn't matter.'

But Ottilie knew it did. She'd been a careless fool and she could have got them all killed. 'If you hadn't got them out I don't know what she would have done to them.' Her throat pressed in and her words were little more than a string of gasps.

Maeve offered her no comfort. Instead, her eyes swept from tree to tree as if she suspected Whistler was hiding behind one. 'She didn't come looking for us.'

'She has more important things to do.' Ottilie didn't dare imagine what those things could be. She dragged her focus to the present. Action – planning – it was the only thing that calmed her. 'Would you go back ahead of us? Go and talk to Alba – see if she can find out what that pipe might be for, and tell her to keep looking into Seika Devil-Slayer. Whistler said her coven put the coffin in that tomb – she might have something to do with the pipe.'

Maeve blinked. She too seemed calmed by the idea of doing something useful. 'I will – I'll go now.'

Ottilie jumped from thought to thought, trying to find anything else they could do. 'If you can figure out a way, try to warn Captain Lyre that Whistler's got what she's been waiting for, and that it's all about to start again … without telling him,' she sighed, 'anything that will get you into trouble.'

Maeve merely turned, shifted, and soared into the dawn.

With some reluctance, Ottilie returned to the hollow. She wanted to say her goodbyes before everyone rose, but she needed something first. She crept over to Ned. His jacket had fallen open as he slept, and his inner pocket was glowing slightly. Careful not to wake him, she plucked out the lumi and tucked it quickly away so the light wouldn't wake anyone.

For just a second, she hesitated. Lumi was worth a fortune. Was she robbing him? She was considering slipping it back when Ned's hand brushed hers. She nearly jumped. The light from the torch outside was dim, but she could see that his eyes were open. Well, he didn't seem to be stopping her. She lifted her finger to her lips and left the hollow.

Shutting the door behind her, Ottilie roused Old Moss and Mr Parch. Last time she'd left Swamp Hollows, she didn't get a goodbye. No matter how painful, she would have one this time.

Moss forbade her from going back to the Narroway, but Mr Parch just hugged her firmly and said, 'Good luck.'

When she held out the lumi, she thought Old Moss's eyes were going to pop out of her head.

'*Ottilie*,' said Mr Parch. 'Do you know what you have there?'

'Yes.' She pressed it into his twiggy hands. 'It's yours.'

He tried to give it back. 'Oh no no no, we couldn't. We can't!'

'I want you to have it,' said Ottilie. The lumi would earn enough to keep them fed for a long time to come. And best of all, she told them where to find more. With the amount in that tunnel, they could buy themselves a home and leave the Swamp Hollows for good.

'You just need someone trustworthy to get it for you.' She wished she had time to collect it for them herself. 'And make sure *he* doesn't find out.' She gritted her teeth, loath to even speak the keeper's name.

'We'll share it,' said Mr Parch. 'We'll find a way to get it and we'll share it with everyone here.'

'Do whatever you want with it,' she said. 'But … just … if you do leave, will you take her with you?'

Mr Parch's eyes crinkled. 'Of course, Ottilie. Of course we will. But … we can only ask. She has to decide to leave.'

Ottilie knew it was true – and she did not know if Freddie would leave.

'And this.' She held out the bone necklace. 'If you ever see a dredretch, one of you put this on and stay close to the other. It'll keep you safe while you get as far away as you can. But only ever wear it if dredretches are near. And you have to remember to breathe.'

She had thought it through. It was safe for them to keep it. Whistler would have no interest in them, and it could mean life or death if the dredretches breached the Narroway. She only wished she could give them her ring, too, but she was still no use without it.

Behind her, the door creaked open and someone leapt at her, strangling her with a hug.

'I wanted to go back for you!' Gully said. 'They wouldn't let me!'

'I know,' she said. 'It's all right. I'm here.'

31

Captain's Orders

Injured and exhausted, they could not risk flying inland over the Narroway. They took to the coast again, camping on a beach just across the border. As they set off the next morning, Ottilie felt an eager ache. Was it Fiory she was yearning for? The fort and the grounds? Or was it simply the return to normalcy? But of course, whatever peace might be found there, she knew it could not last much longer. Whistler might have attacked already – she could well have used the pipe for whatever dark purpose it was intended. The king could be dead, Fiory a ruin.

As they passed through the southern peaks, everything looked ordinary. The mountains were steady and silent as ever, and Fiory was still standing, still guarded, just the way they'd left it.

The lower grounds were ahead. Ottilie could see the pale wingerslink sanctuary curving around the edge of a field. She could imagine Bill inside, combing Glory's fur, or bribing Malleus with eel so he could file his claws. But she knew that wasn't what she would find. These were not ordinary days. Bill would not be humming and prying splinters out of paws. He would be rocking back and forth, his webbed feet buried in the straw, sorting through the past to help fix the future.

The wall watchers must have sent early word of their approach, because the moment they touched down two of Ottilie's least favourite people marched towards them – Wranglers Kinney and Furdles, with matching looks of cruel triumph on their faces.

Furdles had shackles hanging from his belt and Kinney was holding his whip, which he made a show of stroking as they were escorted up from the lower grounds. *Something to make him feel powerful,* Ottilie thought.

Ottilie and her friends walked to the tune of Furdles' gleeful murmurings and Kinney's sporadic spitting on the ground. No-one checked them over or ordered them to the infirmary. Not even Leo, who was limping and had to lean on Ned to make it all the way up the cliff stairs.

As they trudged inside, Ottilie wondered where they were being taken. To Conductor Edderfed? To the king? She knew she should be more nervous, but, after everything, a scolding seemed almost trivial.

They rounded a corner and Captain Lyre's door flew open. His face was heavier and harsher than Ottilie remembered. He looked like a statue of himself, sturdy and austere, with hard lines carved deep, trapping shadow.

'I'll see them,' he said. His eyes scanned them from head to toe, concern, anger and fear switching with each blink.

'We're taking them to Yaist,' said Wrangler Furdles, grabbing the back of Skip's shirt as if daring Captain Lyre to try to take her. 'He said he'd deal with them until the conductor gets here!'

Captain Lyre's nostrils flared. His eyes fixed on Skip, who was struggling to pull herself free. A muscle ticked in his jaw. 'I'll see them.' His voice was dangerously calm.

With much grumbling and muttering, Kinney and Furdles allowed them to enter Captain Lyre's chambers.

'Out,' said Captain Lyre quietly.

Furdles swore under his breath and shuffled out. Kinney lingered in the doorway, stroking his whip.

Captain Lyre stared him down and finally, with a nasty smirk, Kinney left.

The door snapped shut and Captain Lyre turned so slowly Ottilie was sure he was trying to settle his temper. 'Where did you go?' His voice was too quiet.

Ottilie felt like a little girl again. There was something utterly terrifying about being disciplined by someone who was usually friendly.

Skip stepped forward, unfazed. 'We went to stop Whistler from freeing a sleepless witch.'

Captain Lyre's eyes lingered on the jagged cut on her face, and his anger seemed to deepen. To Ottilie's surprise, he did not press for details or suggest it was a tall tale. Instead, he said, 'And you didn't think the directorate needed to know about that?'

'We can't tell you anything without risking being locked up or carted off to the Laklands,' snapped Skip. She seemed taller all of a sudden. Ottilie glanced down to check she wasn't standing on her toes.

Skip was right. How would they have explained that Ned was having dreams because Whistler had marked him with magic burns – and that he was leading her to the sleepless witch's iron coffin – and that they only knew about it because they had a secret goedl friend who had set himself up as the wingerslink's carer, and become best friends with Maeve, who was a fiorn?

'Do you have any idea of the danger you have put yourselves in?' said Captain Lyre, his eyes flicking between Ottilie and Skip.

Ottilie opened her mouth, but he cut across her. 'I'm sending you back.'

'Back?' Ottilie repeated.

'To the Usklers. You're out. All of you.'

She couldn't believe what she was hearing. It was a joke … a mistake … surely?

Leo hobbled forwards. 'You can't!'

'I *can*,' said Captain Lyre, thumping his cane. 'Conductor Edderfed is at Arko, and the directorate has the authority to dismiss you in his absence.'

'We've broken rules. We're untrustworthy!' said Ottilie, remembering what had been said at her own trial. 'The Hunt won't release untrustworthy people back into the Usklers!'

'Would you rather I sent you to the Laklands?' said Captain Lyre, jabbing his cane westward.

'You have to vote,' said Ned. His voice was raspy. It sounded as if thick frost coated his insides. 'In the absence of the conductor, the entire directorate and a member of the select elite has to agree.'

'Oh, they will agree,' said Captain Lyre. 'Any excuse to get Ottilie out – and they'll agree on the Usklers instead of the Laklands because two champions are involved.'

Ottilie knew what he wasn't saying. If it was just the girls, they'd be off to the Laklands in a heartbeat. She had a sudden image of her and Skip living wild in a cave, a blackened, festering world around them, beating back dredretches day after day. They wouldn't last long.

She blinked and refocused. Morning light was pouring through the window, flecks of dust drifting like glittering snow. It was surreal, having this conversation here, in this bright room that smelled of wildflowers, with an old duck painting by the door.

'You leave tomorrow morning,' said Captain Lyre, moving behind his desk.

Ottilie felt as if her stomach had dropped out of her body. They really were being sent away. They were *out*. Even Leo and Gully and Ned. After everything, all she had accomplished, everything they had discovered, it was over?

'YOU CAN'T DO THIS!' Leo bellowed, limping forward.

'I CANNOT PROTECT YOU WITH HIM HERE!' Captain Lyre thundered back, gripping his desk with white fingers, and Ottilie wondered if she'd misheard him. *Him?* Who could he mean? The king?

The door flew open and they seemed to jump as one. Ramona stood in the entrance, meeting Captain Lyre's eyes for just a moment before quickly pressing the door shut behind her.

'Where have you been?' she demanded, looking between them.

'He's trying to send us away!' said Leo, ignoring her question.

Ramona looked at Captain Lyre, her eyes searching. 'You're *what*? You can't.'

Captain Lyre looked like he was about to explode. 'That is my decision!'

'Wolt!'

He flinched.

Wolt? Captain Lyre's first name was Wolt? Ottilie thought there was something familiar about it.

Ramona tore her eyes from Captain Lyre. 'Go down to the infirmary and get yourselves checked over,' she snapped. They didn't need telling twice. Ottilie met her eye as she passed, and Ramona gave her a look that quite clearly said, *I'll deal with it.*

– 32 –

The Singing Duck

The infirmary was exactly where Ottilie wanted to be. Not because she was bruised and shivery and scraped, but because she hadn't seen Scoot in three days. As the group was tended to by the patchies, she slid behind the partitions into Scoot's corner. What she saw stopped her heart. Everything was white. All but a speck on his chest, no bigger than a thumbprint.

The walls seemed to curl over like barrelling waves. Tears welled. She tipped her head, pressing the room back into shape.

They had to fix him. They had to do it *now*. A fierce purpose took hold of her. Careful not to knock his head, Ottilie crawled onto his bed and scrambled out the window.

She felt as if she was breaking some rule, doing something wrong – but really, for the first time in nearly two years, there was nowhere she was supposed to be. No hunt or patrol. No wall watch or training. All the same, she feared running into some figure of authority and being locked in a room or hustled into a wagon heading for the Usklers.

Like a fugitive, she crept past Montie's kitchen. Montie and some kitchenhands were occupied with lunch preparation, but there was no sign of Alba, so Ottilie headed for the root cellar.

At the sight of her, Alba leapt up. 'I didn't know you were back! Maeve said you were coming ... wow, you look terrible. Are you hurt?'

Penguin was curled up on an empty sack in the corner. Raising a sleepy head, his ears pricked and he scampered over and sniffed frantically at her filthy clothes.

Ottilie pushed the door open and gave him a nudge. 'He's in the infirmary.' She knew the words made no sense to him, but he bolted past her all the same.

'Have you found anything to help Scoot? Can we make it slow down at least?' Her words tumbled out hard and heavy, rolling in all directions. 'There has to be something we can – how long has he been this bad?'

Alba's eyes drooped. 'It's been happening in big bursts. I haven't found anything.' She glanced sideways at her books, as if willing Ottilie to see how much she had read, how hard she was trying.

It finally caught up with Ottilie – the terrible truth. It clung to her, threatening to sink into her skin.

There was no fixing Scoot.

She felt her back curve. Was she bent double? Was she on the floor? Her eyes were closed. She forced them open and hot tears spilled. She was tired, she realised, completely exhausted.

'Come with me.' Alba ushered her to follow. She slipped under the lowest shelf – the entrance to the tunnels. 'I have to show you something. Maeve is there now …'

Maeve. Ottilie had forgotten about her. Scoot had taken over her thoughts – how could he not?

'Is Maeve in trouble?' She slid under the shelf, following Alba. Her pulse beat hard into the ground, as if calling for help – trying to signal something greater, some force woven into the fabric of the world.

Alba moved out of the way so Ottilie could drop into the tunnel. 'Maeve left and came back looking like a bird, so no-one saw her go. Mum told everyone that she had a fever and we were looking after her in our room.'

Ottilie nearly choked on her relief. Her feet thumped onto stone.

Alba pulled a vial of glow sticks from her pocket. 'But she told me about the pipe, and we've found out some things! I've left her in there, working through it all. I finally found an account of the sleepless witch in Whistler's old books. It's like a diary entry from one of the members of the coven who imprisoned it in the iron coffin.' Alba turned and walked backwards as she explained.

'It was Seika Sol's coven. They, Seika among them, used the water from the healing spring to ... *cure* it. Or at least that was their plan – to turn it back into a human. They got the witch into the coffin and lowered it into the well.'

Seika among them ...

A memory broke – in Ned's dream, Ottilie had seen the coven trying to imprison the sleepless witch. One member of the coven had been a girl, perhaps sixteen years old. Tall and very familiar. It must have been Seika Sol! She was said to be still a girl when she felled the fendevil. Ottilie blinked. Without knowing it at the time, she had actually seen the ancient princess – actually laid eyes on her face.

'But it must have been beyond healing, because the water reduced the witch to bones.' Alba ducked in a low section of the tunnel without even looking where she was going. 'And that was the end of the healing spring. After that it just dried up.'

So that was it – that was why the healing spring was gone. Seika and her coven had tried to undo the sleepless ritual with the healing waters.

Here breathing bones lie. Breathing bones really meant *living* bones. The sleepless witch's spirit was locked inside, conscious forever and unable to act. Ottilie shivered. What a terrible fate – the ultimate punishment. But where were the bones? Why was there only a pipe in the coffin? And what did Whistler want with it?

'So, the *pipe*,' said Alba, turning to face the front again as she navigated a tricky section of the tunnel. 'I've been searching and searching, and there's nothing in the books. But after Preddy and Skip found that old rhyme near the haunted stables, I started looking for more, and I found this!'

They climbed through a narrow gap into a wide dead-end. Alba held the glow sticks aloft, revealing markings on the wall. Witch script. Ottilie caught the symbols shifting into the familiar alphabet, but there were great chunks missing – scrapes and scratches marring the meaning. She held out her hand to Alba, silently requesting the glow sticks.

'You don't need that.' Maeve stepped out of the shadows.

Ottilie twitched. She hadn't even noticed her there.

'I've been piecing it together,' said Maeve. 'I already showed Alba some, but now I've got it all. I can show you the whole story.'

Maeve pressed her fingertips to the wall and a faint glow swelled. She held out her hand to Alba, who held hers out to Ottilie.

Light enveloped them.

It was like slipping into a story. Ottilie remembered the old days, when Freddie was absent and Mr Parch told tales to put them to sleep. She remembered closing her eyes and drifting into a new place. His words made pictures and sounds and smells. Sometimes fragments returned to her, as familiar as her own experiences.

Whether her eyes were open or shut she did not know, but Ottilie watched it all unfold. The sleepless witch, once the thirteenth member of Seika's coven, was hunted by the remaining twelve, bound by their collective power and subdued with fire and iron chains.

She saw pieces from Ned's dream, including the sentencing: 'Your soul will live on, locked inside your immortal bones: but this will be your prison – buried, eternally alone.'

She saw the chains break and the creature step out of the flames. The youngest of the coven, Seika, raised her hands. The others followed and, just as Alba had said, the creature was forced into the coffin and the coffin lowered into the well.

They waited, then heaved it out and thumped it onto the stone. Seika opened the lid and boiling water spilled out – hissing and spiralling upwards as steam. And there were the bones, white as puppy teeth – all that was left of that terrible creature.

The story shifted. Time had passed. Ottilie saw the fendevil, like a great wingless firedrake, swamp grey, with blue flame flickering from gaps in its scales. It wreaked havoc. She watched entire villages being set alight and people dropping dead from the dredretch sickness. Survivors came to the canyon caves begging for help, and Seika and the witches worked on a solution.

They transformed the bones into a pipe, binding it with bronze threads.

Ottilie gasped. The sleepless witch's spirit was trapped in the pipe. It had been in the coffin all along, in its final form. And now Whistler had it …

When it was done, Seika took the pipe and tracked down the fendevil. She blew into it, and a song played – an unworldly, thrumming call. The fendevil followed as if in a trance.

Evil sings to them …

It was both an instrument wrought of a terrible wrong and a cage for the creature who had enacted it. No wonder dredretches followed its call.

They tracked familiar territory. A blanket of misery moss spread across a riverbank, peaking-pines beyond and mountains behind. Seika Sol lowered the pipe and ran the last few strides to the edge of the Dawn Cliffs. She threw her arms wide, gold-brown hair streaming, as she plummeted towards the pooling river that was swollen from recent rain.

The fendevil barrelled after her and tumbled over the edge.

Seika shifted mid-fall. A duck beat its wings, clumsily skimming the surface. The fendevil was swallowed by the water. A writhing mass, it bobbed to the surface and was sucked back down. Snatched by the current, it was dragged along the river, between towering cliffs, and out into the sea.

Ottilie knew this was where it had truly met its end.

Maeve pulled back from the wall. Light flared, and the world dissolved.

← 33 →

Sleepless

They stood in silence.

Maeve's eyes were flitting from side to side. Finally, she said, 'This is just one version of the story. They chose it because it made them happy. No-one saw her jump, so no-one knows for sure if she really did turn into a duck and fly away. Seika Sol was never seen again after the clifftop. Some think she sacrificed herself for the Usklers – jumped with the fendevil, to be sure it followed. Others believe she transformed into a duck and decided to live the rest of her days peacefully, as a bird.'

Ottilie hoped the second version was true.

'Her coven found the pipe washed up on the river-bank,' said Maeve. 'They took it out of the Narroway and sealed it in the tomb near the Brakkerswamp.'

'How do you know all that?' said Alba. It hadn't been part of the story they had just witnessed.

Maeve's fingertips crawled over the wall. 'There are whispers trapped in there. Memories and thoughts … sort of like loose threads … they must have got woven in when they made the markings.'

Where her fingers trailed, a faint glow followed. 'I can see flashes and hear snatches. I bet this is what it's like inside Bill's head.' She squeezed her eyes shut and blew out a breath. 'Makes you dizzy.'

Ottilie's eyes swept the dark stone and flicked down to her boots. They had still not dried since Whistler flooded the tomb. She pictured it: the coffin. The pipe. All the hints made sense now. The witches had left clues about how to access the breathing bones – the pipe that could control dredretches – in case it was needed in the future. They'd left diary entries, painted stories across walls, made up rhymes and passed them along – some all but forgotten, but others, like the lightning song, still chanted by children all over the Usklers. They worked a loophole into the tomb's sealing spell. What had Maeve called it? *A weak point before the turn of the age.*

Whistler had used the information. She had utilised that loophole and taken the pipe for herself. 'What does

Whistler want with it?' said Ottilie. 'She can already control dredretches.'

Alba frowned. 'The only thing that makes sense is … well, Whistler never had a child …' She looked to Ottilie for confirmation.

Ottilie nodded and tried not to think about the terrible fate of Maia, who Whistler had loved as her own.

'So the sleepless ritual,' said Alba. 'It's not something she could ever do.'

'Or *would* ever do,' said Ottilie. It felt strange to defend Whistler but, oddly enough, she just knew it was true.

'But … here's the thing. The sleepless witch isn't dead. It still lives in the bones – in the pipe. It's eternal and conscious and *alive*. So maybe Whistler thinks she can enact the sleepless ritual using the bones of a sleepless witch. All I can guess is that she wants to use it to make herself invulnerable.'

Ottilie wrapped her arms around her ribs and stared at the wall – at Seika's story. She waited for her courage to kick in, but just felt sad and tired and afraid.

34

The Fall

A cold weight settled, like a wet blanket she couldn't shrug off. Ottilie wanted nothing more than to curl up in her bed and sleep for days. But she knew sleep was beyond her. She didn't know where to go or what to do. Whistler had the pipe and they didn't know where to find her. Ottilie couldn't bear to look at Scoot, knowing there was no way to help him. She didn't want to go anywhere she might encounter Captain Lyre, because for all she knew he would order her to pack up and leave the Narroway immediately. She had no shifts to distract her. She did not even know if she was still a huntsman.

These might be Scoot's final hours, and she was avoiding him. Finally, after wandering aimlessly around the largest pond, dodging the aggressive advance of the red goose, Ottilie found herself heading for the lower grounds to see Bill.

She had thought herself beyond hope, her spirit too damp and dark to manage a spark – but here it was. Somewhere in that strange head of his, Bill had to know something about stopping the spread of heartstone.

The wingerslink sanctuary was in chaos. The air hummed with distressed grunts, and everywhere she looked there were flicking tails and bared teeth. Ottilie clenched her shaky fingers into a fist, eyes searching. Were there dredretches near?

She found Bill in a dark corner at the end of the row of pens. He was a tangle of limbs, coiled up with his arms over his face, only mutters and murmurs escaping.

She approached cautiously. 'Bill?'

He mumbled something that sounded like *yabby-crab*.

She knelt beside him and laid a hand on his sleek, furred arm.

His eyes flew open. 'Midges!'

Ottilie jerked backwards in surprise, losing her balance and tipping sideways. 'Midges?' she asked, gathering herself.

'*Midges*?'

'You said it.'

'No, I didn't.' He looked down at his arm as if the memory might be marked there.

'Bill, I promise you. I touched your arm and you said *midges*.'

He narrowed his eyes. 'You're having dreams.'

Ottilie pinched herself. 'I'm awake – were *you* maybe having dreams, Bill?'

Bill looked very confused. '*I* was having dreams?' He blinked. '*I* was having dreams!'

Ottilie sighed with relief. 'Is everything all right? What were you dreaming about? Midges?' She tried to think of what a midge was. Some kind of insect?

Bill's hands shot to his horns. 'Bridges!' he burst out.

She knew instantly what he was talking about. Whistler's heartstone bridges – the ones Bill had said she planned to build so that dredretches could spread across the entire Usklers.

Bill's eyes clouded over. 'I just saw. Someone, another one of me – *like me*,' he corrected, 'we saw – they've been building bridges imbedded with bits of white stone, over the narrow gaps – linking the islands.'

259

A map formed in her head: Crown Canal, dividing east and west, and Pero's Passage cutting off the north. She could almost perfectly remember the angles and curves, the places where the islands cut in and reached out, shoulders leaning, fingers stretching towards each other.

'Who's building them?' she said. 'Why is no-one stopping them?'

'From Shortwood,' said Bill.

'You mean Longwood?'

He nodded.

'The Laklanders from Longwood are building heartstone bridges for Whistler?' said Ottilie, piecing it together.

'They've already done it … built them,' he said.

She felt like she was falling from a great height. They were already built. 'While the king's away,' she muttered to herself. 'And his whole army. She sent people out to build them while everyone's attention's been fixed on the Narroway.'

Bill covered his eyes and nodded. 'And now they're coming here, too – to attack from the east.'

'But there can't be many of them?' said Ottilie, seeking any scrap of comfort. It was true. There could not be many Longwood Laklanders out there. Nothing to rival the king's army and the entire Narroway Hunt, surely.

Bill slid his hands to his horns, eyes darting from side to side as if reading a book. 'After a big fire they got chased out.'

The fire Gracie's parents had set in Scarpy Village, burning Montie's house. The villagers had chased them out of Longwood and they'd scattered.

'Whistler found them,' said Bill. 'The ones that escaped the war and the slave traders. She told them they could avenge the Laklands. Some of them want it – vengeance. They've been gathering for years, seeking out the mistreated.'

Of course. Whistler had had thirty years to gather followers. She hadn't just been recruiting bone singers and raising dredretches. She'd collected people from all across the Usklers to fight with her. To destroy the Sol line, the Crown and everything her family had built.

A wingerslink in a nearby pen beat her tail against the wall, making Bill and Ottilie jump.

She squeezed his arm. 'But the king's whole army is camped in Longwood. They won't get past them,' she said, not daring to imagine how many followers Whistler really had.

'They're not trying to get past them,' said Bill, staring into her eyes.

Ottilie bit hard into her lip. Of course not. Whistler didn't need numbers in the Narroway. She had her monsters. She just wanted to get rid of the king's army.

'They'll sneak in when no-one's expecting,' said Bill, his eyes still darting back and forth. 'They know the forest.'

He was right. Ottilie jumped to her feet. She had to warn someone – right now. And there was only one adult in the Narroway she trusted.

———➤———

Ottilie found Ramona in the stables, but just as she reached her …

'You're back!' cried Preddy, glancing warily at the group of mounts he had just ridden in with.

The mounts stared at Ottilie's wild hair, ragged uniform and soggy boots with interest. Preddy turned a bit pink and dismounted. Leaving Warship untethered, he hurried over.

'Did you get Ned? Is everyone all right?' He lowered his voice. 'Where's Whistler?'

Ottilie gripped his arm. 'Everyone's fine. I'll tell you soon. First …'

She turned to Ramona, who was watching her intently. Ottilie could tell she was about to tell her to eat or sleep or wash, but Ottilie didn't have time for it. Without letting her get a word in, she hastily told Ramona about Whistler's followers.

She only said two words in response. 'You're sure?'

Ottilie wished she wasn't sure, but she didn't think Bill could have it wrong. Breathless, she simply nodded, and Ramona went straight to Captain Lyre.

Ottilie turned back to Preddy. He looked pale and drawn, and in that instant she remembered why she had gone to see Bill in the first place. For Scoot. She had meant to ask if he could remember anything, anything at all, that could stop the heartstone spreading.

Preddy frowned. 'Ottilie? What's wrong?'

There was no time to lose. She had lost too much already. She grabbed Preddy's arm and they headed straight back to the lower grounds.

Ottilie's mind rolled and tossed like a stormy sea. She thought of the pipe Whistler was using for who knew what. She thought of Maia, who was buried beneath the philowood tree, and the evil that had poisoned the Narroway. She thought of the healing spring, dried up, their only hope gone. Then she thought of Seika Sol, who had lured the fendevil over the cliff and into the Sol River – and it hit her.

Water picked up memory. It just had to be caught in the right spot. Evil had poisoned the land, but good could heal it. Seika Sol's selfless heroic deed. The river named for it.

The pool beneath the waterfall …

Ottilie gasped and stopped still, clutching the gate of a wingerslink's pen.

'*What?*' said Preddy. He looked as if one more piece of bad news would knock him out.

But she didn't have bad news. 'I think I know how to save Scoot!'

They hurtled past Bill, and Ottilie tossed him a comb. 'Brush Maestro,' she said. 'It'll calm you down.'

As she and Preddy saddled Nox, Ottilie explained her plan.

Nox snarled, not at all happy at the prospect of another journey. She did her best to shake off the saddle, but Ottilie was having none of it. She snarled right back and ordered Nox into the field. Nox scratched at the floor and flicked her tail. Ottilie shoved her with her shoulder and, with a booming roar of outrage, the wingerslink leapt into the early afternoon sun.

Ottilie snatched a jar of dry glow sticks from a shelf and tipped them onto the floor before climbing down the ladder. Then, jar in hand and Preddy behind her, they soared out over the boundary wall in the direction of the Sol River.

She could see it ahead. The river slid over sharp stones like a sheet of silk on a breeze. The waterfall was gentle today. A sunlit veil. Ottilie pictured Seika Sol leaping. She saw the fendevil, its scales glittering with petals of blue flame, its massive claws crunching on the rocky bank. She saw it barrelling over the edge with a volcanic roar.

Ottilie saw two moments at once, like pages pressed together and held to the light. Seika, still a girl, swallowed by the river; and Seika shifting into a duck an inch above the water, beating her wings and flying out to sea, following the dark shadow caught in the current. Whichever story was true, whatever had really happened, Seika Sol was a hero and this water would heal Scoot. She had to believe it.

Blinking back to the present, Ottilie swung over the side of the saddle. Getting drenched up to her waist, she held out the empty jar, filled it to the brim and pressed the cork in tight.

This had to work. It was the only thing that *could* work. Ottilie hoped one jarful was enough. There was no time for caution or planning. They would have to approach the king directly and ask for his help. Scoot was one of his people. Of course he would save him. Why would he not?

Murphy Graves was guarding the king's door. His bright green eyes were sleepy and his smile slow to form. He looked terribly bored. 'I'm not supposed to let anyone through,' he said apologetically.

'Pretend Preddy hit you,' said Ottilie. She didn't have time for this.

Both boys looked at her as if she had lost her mind. '*What?*' they said together.

'You don't want to get in trouble. So, fall to the ground, make a noise and say Preddy hit you. The king will only be angrier if you say it was me.'

Murphy blinked, made a lame '*arghhahh*' noise, and fell to the ground.

Without a second thought, Ottilie lifted the latch and marched, uninvited, into the king's chambers.

35

The Crown

Varrio Sol was lounging in a chair by the window. Ottilie ran a thumb over her dagger. She wanted to throw it at the wall behind him – shock him into reality. Girls and boys were out hunting. His soldiers were camped in that horrible forest preparing for war, no doubt planning and strategising. Whistler was on the verge of attack, and yet here he sat.

Ottilie thought he looked a little dishevelled. His olive skin had paled to a sickly greenish colour and she could spot the tension in his jaw and fingers. Despite this, he painted a lazy expression on his face and greeted the intruders with a wolfish smile. 'Not even a knock?

What do they teach you boys out here?' His eyes fell on Ottilie, but he didn't correct himself. '*Savages*, the lot of you. No better than those things you hunt.'

'We need your help!' she burst out.

Preddy tugged her into a bow, but she jerked back up. They didn't have time for bowing. Scoot could be gone any second.

'I live to serve,' drawled the king. His gaze shifted to Preddy. 'Have we met?'

'I — I don't believe so.'

'Name?'

'Noel Preddy.'

His eyes sharpened. 'Son of Jollion Preddy?'

'Yes,' said Preddy. His eyelids flickered.

'*My, my, my*, his own brother,' clucked the king. 'If I remember correctly, your eldest brother, Fonter, makes my North Wikric list in exchange for the Crown turning a blind eye to your father's dealings.'

Ottilie was horrified. Why had the king revealed such a thing? *The Crown turns a blind eye* ... He clearly thought them so insignificant that he didn't mind revealing his own misdeeds — seeing Preddy's face fall was worth it.

Preddy had turned white. Just as the keeper had sold Gully to the pickers, so had Preddy's brother. Ottilie wanted to comfort him, tell him she knew just how he felt, but it wasn't the moment.

'We need your help,' she repeated and, before the king could change the subject again, she said, 'Whistler turned our friend to stone, but we have a way to cure him.' She stepped closer, her voice pleading. 'Someone of her bloodline has to pour this water over him. We don't have much time!'

The king's eyes fell on the jar of water and his nostrils flared. 'You burst into my chambers and demand that I engage in witchcraft!'

'It's not witchcraft,' said Preddy, his voice shaking.

'It's healing,' added Ottilie, trying with all her might to keep it from sounding like a rebuke.

'Why should I do this?' The king ran his fingers down his grey beard.

Ottilie was outraged. Why had he not just leapt to their aid? Why would he not want to help?

'Because you have the chance to save someone's life,' she said carefully. She was terrified of saying the wrong thing, using the wrong tone of voice, tipping the scale in the wrong direction.

'I save lives every day,' said the king. 'Everyone in the Usklers is living and breathing because of me.'

'*What?*' said Ottilie.

'I. Am. The. *King*. You foolish little girl!'

She gaped.

He gestured to the window. 'I've kept the beasts out of my lands.'

'*We've* kept them out of your lands. You've done *nothing*.'

The king didn't react. Her words slid over him without causing a pinch of guilt. 'I am sorry about your friend,' he said icily. 'But I do not condone the use of witches' evil.' His smile turned vicious. 'And you, *girl*. You come here trying to tempt me into the dark.' He paused, his eyes fixed on hers. 'I'll have your neck for it.'

Preddy lunged across the room and shoved the king against the wall. 'You will fix our friend!' His forearm was against the king's throat.

'You'll have to make a puppet of my corpse, boy,' snarled the king. He shoved Preddy off and reached for the bell chain.

Alarms sounded all around, followed by thundering footsteps. The door flew open and Murphy Graves stood there, cutlass raised, clearly unsure what to do.

A few moments later, at least ten huntsmen burst in behind him, looking frantically for a dredretch. But all they found was Murphy, Ottilie, Preddy and the king, staring at one another in breathless silence. Preddy was shaking with rage.

'Take them to the burrows!' demanded the king.

Igor Thrike grabbed Ottilie from behind. But Murphy stepped forward and said, 'Why?'

The king's eyes bulged. 'Because I order it. I am your king and commander. Do as I say!'

No-one moved. Ottilie even felt Igor Thrike's grip on her loosen.

'Do you know the punishment for disobeying your king?'

The boys looked back and forth. They didn't. The king *wasn't* their commander. They took their orders from the directorate, through the wranglers, all of whom would have locked themselves away the moment the alarms sounded. All except …

Wrangler Morse thundered into the room. 'What's going on in here?' he demanded.

'Two of your huntsmen just attacked me, and I have ordered them to be locked away, yet here we stand,' said the king, gathering his composure.

Wrangler Morse looked at Preddy and Ottilie. 'Right,' he said, clearing his throat. 'What are we waiting for, boys? The king commands it.'

Ottilie's heart sank. Wrangler Morse was not on their side. He grabbed hold of Preddy himself and Igor dragged Ottilie after him.

They had barely made it to the stairwell when Morse whispered, 'Off with you, Thrike.'

'What?' said Igor.

'I said, *off with you*!' And he looked so terrifying that Igor let out a squeak, released Ottilie and hurried away.

'Tell me, quick,' said Wrangler Morse, bending down to hear.

And so Ottilie told him everything important, everything she could think of.

'The Sol bloodline, you say?' said Wrangler Morse, tugging on his red, braided beard.

'Yes,' said Ottilie. 'But it's only the king here.'

Morse shook his head. After a moment, he seemed to come to some momentous decision. 'No, you're wrong there. We have to find Wolter.'

'Wolter?' said Preddy. '*Wolter Sol*?'

Little bells chimed in her memory. Leo had told her Wolter Sol was the king's younger cousin, second in line to the throne. But there was something else. Ramona had once called someone Wolt right in front of her.

— 36 —

Her Bloodline

Captain Lyre had always been able to get away with almost anything. She should have known he was special – protected. What had Ottilie overheard him say to the king? That he had been trying to give the boys some semblance of a life? She remembered what Whistler had said about trying to stay on the king's good side so she wouldn't be parted from the princess she loved as a daughter. Captain Lyre bent the rules only just enough that he was allowed to remain in the Narroway, watching over the boys that the king had condemned to a life of danger and violence.

'Come on,' said Wrangler Morse.

They hurried to Captain Lyre's chambers, but found them empty. Ottilie's heart battered her ribs.

Preddy gripped the doorframe. 'Ramona!'

Of course! Ottilie had sent Ramona to tell Captain Lyre about Whistler's followers in Longwood. She would know where he was.

They had just stepped back into the corridor when Wrangler Voilies came trotting towards them, Igor Thrike at his side. Purple blotches flared on Voilies' cheeks. 'What is going on, Reuben? Igor says these two were ordered to the burrows.'

Wrangler Morse nudged Ottilie. '*Go.*'

As she and Preddy darted around Wrangler Morse, Ottilie heard Voilies shriek, 'Now wait just – *you two* – come back immediately!' But they were already bolting for the stables. They found Ramona filling the water trough in Billow's stall.

'Where's Captain Lyre?' Preddy burst out.

'Wha–'

'We know he's Wolter Sol,' said Ottilie. 'We need someone of the Sol bloodline to cure Scoot, *right now*!'

Ramona slopped water all down her front. 'You … you what?'

'Healing water!' said Ottilie breathlessly, shaking the jar in her white-knuckled hand. 'Has to be poured by a Sol. We need Captain Lyre!'

Ramona's face fell. 'He's gone to Arko.'

'How long ago?' Ottilie refused to give up. 'Can we go after him?' But Alba said the white was happening in bursts. If Scoot had another burst ... It could have happened already, with all this running back and forth.

Ramona was shaking her head. She bit her lip, then said, 'We don't need to go after him.'

'What are you talking about?' said Ottilie.

'Let's go to the infirmary. I'll explain on the way,' she said, leading them out.

They hurried across the grounds.

'Sol daughters,' said Ramona, 'have a habit of having accidents, going missing, or dying of mystery illnesses.'

'They think women of the Sol bloodline are a sort of curse,' said Ottilie. 'Whistler told me.'

Ramona nodded. 'Varrio Sol lost his first daughter, Maia, to a fever. That was the story everyone was told. Years later, when I got a job at the palace, I became friends with Wolter, who told me he suspected Varrio had actually been involved in her death ... Anyway, Wolt would visit All Kings' Hill every few months and report to him about the Narroway Hunt. But I didn't know about that for a long time.'

Ramona lengthened her strides. 'In the beginning, he didn't have a proper position with the Hunt. The king was always too cowardly to come anywhere near the dredretches. So he sent Wolt, his young cousin, in his place. He used the name Captain Lyre so that people wouldn't alter their behaviour. Only the three conductors and his close friends know the truth.

'He and I became very close, and his stays at the palace grew longer and longer. The king noticed and, when Wolt discovered that the rule of innocence was a lie, the king threatened my life to force him to keep the secret.'

'But what's this got to do with anything?' said Preddy.

'Wolt had other reasons for extending his stays,' Ramona continued, as if there had been no interruption. 'The king's second daughter was born, and Wolt confided in me about his fears for the girl. I offered to watch over her, pretending she was showing an extraordinary interest in horses even as a toddler.

'The king accepted it. He didn't want to be anywhere near her. When she was in his presence, he was so increasingly hostile that we knew he would do something to *remove* her before long. She was barely three years old. We decided the only way to protect the young princess was to stage an accident. I pretended she'd been caught under the hooves of a panicked horse and took the blame.' She gestured to her eyepatch.

'Wolt whisked her as far away as he could. He was due back in the west anyway, so he took her to an orphanage in Wikric Town along the way. We planned to keep her there until she was old enough to go where the king would never dare to tread – the Narroway.

'It didn't go as planned – she ran away from the orphanage,' said Ramona. 'But Wolt tracked her down in the slum tunnels eventually, and offered her a job as a sculkie.'

Ottilie's head spun and she nearly tripped over her own feet. She knew the rest of the story! She had never known it was Captain Lyre who offered the job, but she did know a sculkie who had run away from a children's home and lived in the Wikric slum tunnels.

'After that,' said Ramona, 'Wolt took a position as a permanent director at the fort that hired her, so he could watch over her. I don't think it was pure luck that the king sent me here too. I think he wanted me here as a reminder to behave. But that worked out perfectly for us, because I could look out for her too. I offered her riding lessons and watched her grow up ...'

'*Skip*,' said Ottilie.

'Skip?' said Preddy.

Ramona nodded. 'Isla Sol.'

— 37 —

Pay For What You've Done

Skip was the king's daughter. It was dizzying and mystifying and a little bit sickening. What would Skip think? That horrible man was her father. He thought she was dead – wanted her dead. She wasn't an orphan from the slum tunnels. She was an outcast, a princess in hiding, even from herself.

Ottilie shook her head, trying to clear it. They were going to save Scoot. It was all that mattered right now. All she could focus on.

They burst into the infirmary to find the partitions pulled back. Skip and Leo were there, sparkling clean and covered in bandages. Gully and Ned were not. They must have been sent back to their bedchambers.

There was a strange air in the room. Something was wrong. The patchies were hovering back. The other beds were empty. Skip had tears running down her face. Ottilie's chest tightened as she hurried across the room. She tipped her head, terrified of what she might see.

The patch over Scoot's heart was white.

'*No*,' said Preddy.

Ottilie would not, could not, accept it. It didn't feel real. It wasn't real. There could still be time. A scrap of him might remain. She shoved the jar of water into Skip's hand. 'Pour it,' she said. It was all she could manage.

'What? Why?' Tears dripped off Skip's chin.

'Please, Isla, just pour it over him,' said Preddy.

Skip's hand shook as she tipped the water over the perfect white statue.

Ottilie held her breath. The water scattered into rivulets, streaming off the stone and soaking the sheet. She watched it seep, waiting for magic. But it already felt wrong, like jumping off the ground and hoping to fly. It was too ordinary. Just water on fabric. A spilled drink. Washing left out in the rain.

It hadn't worked.

It was their last chance and it hadn't worked. Maybe they were too late, or maybe she had been wrong about the healing spring. Maybe the good deed had been done too long ago, or maybe they'd gone to the wrong spot. Maybe the water was just water.

Ottilie's legs buckled and she found herself on the ground, leaning against the bed. Preddy slid down beside her, sheet-white and shaking.

'Get up,' said Leo.

'Shut up, Leo,' Ottilie snapped.

'No. Ott, get up!'

There was something in the tone of his voice – something that made her jump to her feet. Ottilie looked at Scoot and coughed out a strange sort of squeak.

It was like ice melting.

It thawed from his heart outwards, creeping and seeping until he was him again, wearing the same clothing he'd had on all those months ago, still blood-stained and battle-worn, still torn from claws and teeth.

No-one wanted to touch him. They all stepped back.

Scoot took a huge, gasping breath.

Feeling dazed, Ottilie tried to grab onto Preddy, but he crossed behind her, over to Skip, and kissed the very top of her head.

Leo made an amused grunt and Ottilie laughed shakily, completely overwhelmed with joy.

'What's so funny?' said a croaky voice.

Ottilie whipped around. Scoot's eyes were open and he'd propped himself up on his elbows. She flew to his side, settling a hair's breadth away, still scared to touch him.

His eyes roved over her matted hair, mud-spattered clothes and innumerable scrapes and bruises. His gaze flicked from Leo's bandages to Ramona's smile and finally settled on Preddy, who was scarlet in the face as he stepped awkwardly away from Skip.

Scoot cracked a sleepy smile and said, 'What have I missed?'

No-one said a word. Ottilie didn't even know where to begin.

Finally, Skip broke the silence. 'I'm really sorry, Scoot,' she said. '*Very* glad you're not a statue anymore. But before we get into that, can someone please explain what I just did?'

The room was quiet. Skip held out the jar and jiggled it. 'What was that stuff?'

A single precious drop fell to the floor. They all watched it land, unable to explain.

Ottilie looked back up at Skip, and her breath caught. She knew now why Seika Sol had looked so familiar. The youngest of the twelve witches in that circle looked just like Skip. How had she not put it together before? Varrio, too — there had been something familiar about his eyes, the only gentle feature of his wolfish face. Skip's father's face.

'I'm magic, right?' said Skip. 'I'm a witch? How did you all know before me? Where's Maeve? I have questions.'

Ramona stepped forward. 'Let's go for a walk.'

Still holding the empty jar, Skip glanced between Ottilie and Preddy with suspicion, and finally followed Ramona out the door. Leo made to go with them, but Ottilie yanked him back.

'I want to know,' he protested.

Ottilie waited for them to leave before saying, 'Skip's the king's daughter. Ramona and Captain Lyre faked her death.'

'And Captain Lyre is actually Wolter Sol, the king's cousin,' added Preddy in a whisper.

'And that water was from where Seika Sol led the fendevil over the Dawn Cliffs nine hundred years ago,' said Ottilie. 'It's got healing magic.'

Leo looked as though his head was about to explode. '*Skip* is Isla Sol? The princess who got trampled by a horse?'

'Only she didn't,' said Preddy.

'She's the heir to the throne,' said Ottilie.

Leo was shaking his head. 'She's not. It goes to the closest male relative. There's never been an Usklerian queen.'

'Try telling Skip that,' said Preddy with a smile.

'*Scuse me*,' said Scoot.

They all turned to him.

'Umm …' He waved his arms. '*What?*'

They told him everything as best they could – everything that had happened since the battle at Richter – and when they were done, silence fell again.

Scoot took a deep breath. 'Can everyone stop staring at me with watery eyes!'

Leo snorted, but Preddy and Ottilie kept staring.

'I think I need some air,' said Scoot.

They helped him from his bed. He was stiff, he said, but otherwise fine. 'Just feels like I overslept. Or underslept. I dunno. Those things always feel the same.'

His knees and ankles kept giving way, so Ottilie and Preddy, so different in height, became lopsided crutches for him. 'That's better,' he said, as they stepped out into the lavender field. 'I hate that place.'

Skip and Ramona must have spread the word about Scoot's recovery, because Ned and Gully came hurrying over, followed soon after by Alba and Montie. Even Maeve, who had never got on well with Scoot, joined them in owl form – landing on Gully's shoulder, to his utter delight.

They wandered the fields, warmed by laughter and sunshine. But in a beat, everything changed.

Scoot stiffened.

'What's wrong?' Ottilie's words came out slurred. She looked around, her vision fogging.

Montie swayed. Preddy grabbed her arm to steady her. Alba fell to her knees and Scoot tripped down beside her. Leo lunged, but he was too late to catch him. Alba flopped over and her eyes slid shut.

The world spun. Ottilie saw other people falling in the distance. Had they all been poisoned? But Scoot had just woken up. He hadn't eaten anything. Neither had she, come to think of it.

Preddy lowered Montie to the ground. Ottilie stumbled, and Ned caught her. She was on the edge of an abyss. Her body was shutting down as a blanket of darkness settled over the world.

'She's breathing.' Leo sounded very far away.

'It's like they're sleeping,' said Gully.

Ottilie blinked.

'The rings,' she heard Ned say. 'The people wearing rings are falling asleep.'

Ottilie forced her eyes open. She was on the ground. Beside her, she could vaguely make out Scoot struggling to stay upright.

'Ottilie?' It was Gully's voice in her ear. 'I'm going to take it off. You ready?'

She tried to nod, but couldn't manage it. Slowly Gully removed the ring from her thumb.

The slumber whooshed out of her. She blinked and could see again. A vague sickness crept in. There were no dredretches near, but, without her ring, their massive presence in the Narroway was enough to weaken her. She could ward it off when they were at a distance. She was capable of at least that.

Alba was near. Ottilie tried to shake her awake, but she wouldn't budge. 'Sorry, Alba,' she muttered, and quickly slipped her ring off. But it was no good – she slept on.

Preddy tried Montie's, but the same thing happened. They wouldn't wake.

'Once it gets you, you can't wake up!' said Ottilie. 'Quick, get Scoot's!'

Scoot's eyelids were sliding open and slipping shut, over and over. He was fighting it hard. Leo got his ring off just in time, and Scoot sat up with a start. '*Whoa*!' he said, clutching his head. 'Twice in one day.'

'What's happening?' Gully stood up to look around.

Maeve flew behind a lavender bush and then leapt out as herself, whipping off her ring and looking around nervously to see if anyone had noticed the transformation. But no-one was paying them any attention. Anyone who wasn't on the ground was pacing frantically, or trying to wake the sleepers.

'That'll be all the fledges out,' said Leo, looking back towards the main building.

'And at least a third of the second tiers,' said Gully.

'And all the wranglers,' said Ottilie, but even as she said it she realised ... 'And the king's entire army!'

'And every guard on the border to the Usklers,' said Ned.

A wave of panic rushed in. 'Whistler's followers will cut through them while they sleep,' said Ottilie.

'Maybe they'll just pass through,' said Gully. 'To join Whistler.'

But Ottilie knew better. Bill had said their plan was to attack the king's army, not pass by them.

'We have to stop her,' said Ottilie, her stomach turning.

'Ottilie!' Bill came hurrying over, not bothering to hide. There was a little red bird clinging to one of his horns. Bill looked terrified beyond words. He fixed his eyes on Maeve. They must have been talking inside their heads. Maeve's eyes stretched wide.

'Look,' she said, grabbing Ottilie's hand and reaching for Bill's.

Ottilie felt someone take her other hand, but she wasn't sure who, because she had swooped up into the air. Flying high above Richter, through skies of clearest blue, she had, quite literally, a bird's eye view of the western border wall – the one that divided the Narroway from the Laklands.

At first, she thought it was a row of pale grey flags. But as she circled lower she could see at least twenty bone singers along the parapets, their robes whipping in the wind, eyes glowing.

Gracie Moravec was standing a little way back from the wall, astride the white wyler. Beyond, Ottilie got her first glimpse of the Laklands. It was green for a stretch, then brown, then a deadly wilting black as far as the eye could see. From that blackness, a mass of dredretches rolled like a wave, surging towards the Narroway — towards the gates that were wide open at the base of the border wall.

38

Deserters

The bells called them to gather, but they couldn't just leave Montie and Alba lying in the open. Leo and Preddy ran off to the Moon Court for explanation or instruction, while Ottilie, Gully, Ned and Scoot carried Alba and Montie into the infirmary.

'How did she do it?' Ottilie asked Scoot, as they lugged Alba through the double doors.

'I don't know,' he said. 'If she could do this all along, why didn't she make everyone sleep at Richter? It would have helped her win.'

'She obviously couldn't do it until now.' Ottilie's voice was strained — she'd barely had a moment to recover from the long flight, and everything that preceded it, and Alba was remarkably heavy for someone so small. 'It must have had something to do with that pipe.'

Scoot screwed up his face. 'The pipe made of witch bones?'

Ottilie nodded, still thinking. 'We have to get to Whistler and find a way to force her to wake everyone up, *now*, before they get slaughtered in their sleep.'

Bill was walking alongside them with his arms outstretched. At Ottilie's words, he made a breathy muttering noise that sounded like, *oh no*.

'But how are we going to get out there?' Scoot nodded down at the ring they had put back on Alba's thumb. 'We can't ward, Ottilie. Or can you now?'

She swallowed and shook her head. She and Scoot had always been the worst at warding. 'We'll just have to try,' she said as they heaved Alba onto the bed.

Skip burst into the infirmary. 'What's happening?'

Ottilie and Scoot whirled around.

'Why aren't you sleeping?' said Scoot.

Ottilie stared at the ring on Skip's thumb.

'It's daytime,' she said, approaching him slowly. She tipped her head towards Ottilie and whispered, 'Did he come back a bit funny?'

Ottilie managed a grunt of laughter. 'All the people wearing rings are falling asleep,' she explained, shaking out her arms. 'Except you, apparently. Didn't you see? Ramona wears one, doesn't she?'

Skip looked horrified, and then a little sheepish. 'I don't know where she is. I stormed off after she told me she staged a horse trampling when I was a toddler.'

'Fair enough,' said Scoot.

'*Blood*,' muttered Bill.

Scoot looked disturbed. 'Um, what, Bill?'

Maeve answered. 'Sorry. He got that from me.'

'You're having secret conversations in your head?' said Scoot. 'Creepy,' he muttered.

'What about blood?' said Ottilie.

'Whistler made everyone sleep,' said Maeve. 'Maybe she kept the people with Sol blood protected from the spell.'

'Why?' said Gully, removing the pillow from under Montie's head – he had never considered them comfortable.

'Maybe she couldn't help it,' said Ned. 'Because she cast the spell, so her blood is protected?'

Maeve nodded. 'Could be.'

But Ottilie had already thought of a darker reason. 'Maybe she wanted to keep the king awake – I have a feeling she doesn't want him to sleep through this.' Whatever Whistler had been planning all this time, it was about to begin.

The Hunt's scouts reported that the dredretches were gathering in two distinct groups. One was headed to Arko and the other to Fiory. Ottilie knew there was already a horde heading to Richter from the Laklands.

She didn't know how much control Whistler and her bone singers would have over the Lakland dredretches, but, with Bill and Maeve's help, she'd already seen them passing the border. They were moving across a coastal stretch that they usually avoided, led by those bound to the bone singers. It didn't bode well.

The huntsmen were preparing to defend the fort, but Ottilie had other plans. She and her friends gathered in the wingerslink sanctuary for their own meeting. Bill sat with his eyes closed, keeping in touch with the birds.

'Once we find out where Whistler is,' said Ottilie, 'me and Leo and Maeve will go –'

Skip kicked her heel into the barrel of eels beneath her. 'Why you three?' she demanded.

'Yeah,' added Scoot, from the floor by her feet.

'Because we're the ones who can fly,' said Leo impatiently. 'The rest of you won't be able to get out without someone stopping you.'

'We've been through this before – Maestro can take three people!' said Skip, kicking the barrel again.

'He's not a boat!' snapped Leo. 'If we're going to be beating off dredretches and dodging Whistler we can't just load him up like a cargo ship!'

'We don't have time for this,' said Ottilie. 'We have to go. Bill, any sign of her yet?'

Bill lifted up one elbow like a chicken wing.

'Does that mean no?' said Scoot.

Ottilie looked at Maeve, who shook her head.

'You promised,' said Gully quietly. 'You said you wouldn't leave me behind again.'

Ottilie was about to argue, but he was right. She had promised, and anyway, he was in just as much danger at Fiory as he would be with her. At least this way they could look out for each other.

'Fine,' she said. 'Gully comes with us.'

They all turned to Leo. 'Don't look at me,' he said. 'I'm not taking anyone.'

'The Withering Wood!' Maeve burst out.

Bill's eyes were open. He nodded solemnly.

'The magpie's seen Whistler –'

'At the big dead tree that looks like a spider,' Bill finished for her.

Scoot looked back and forth between them. 'So, are you just one person now?'

'She's not a person,' said Bill, crossing his eyes.

'Yes, yes, she's a bird,' said Scoot. 'I remember.'

Ottilie jumped up. 'Let's go,' she said to Leo.

'We'll meet you there,' said Skip.

Leo raised his eyebrows. 'What?'

'Am I speaking in Triptiq?'

Leo responded in a language that Ottilie didn't understand. Skip looked flummoxed.

Preddy cleared his throat and explained, 'He said, "No, *I* speak Triptiq."'

Skip was clearly trying not to smile. 'I *said*, we'll meet you there! You're not the boss of me, Leo. We'll find a way out.'

'We can try the bone singers,' said Ned. 'At least one of them has to know a secret entry point to the fort – that's how Gracie got the wylers in, remember?'

'They won't tell you anything,' said Ottilie. 'I've tried talking to Bonnie before.'

'Anyway, they're probably asleep,' said Scoot.

Ned shook his head. 'Bone singers can all ward – they don't wear rings. And I bet they'll speak up if we tell them an army of dredretches is headed here.'

Ottilie moved over to Nox's pen, and Ned followed her and Gully inside. She changed Nox's saddle from the single to the double, and moved towards the ladder down to the field. Through the wide open doors, she could see the others gathering below.

'Be careful out there,' said Ned, to both of them.

Ottilie glanced at her thumb. Her ring was in her pocket. She was going to have to ward. She already felt sick at the thought of it.

'You can do it,' he said, just to her.

They stared at each other for a moment. Ned looked unable to make up his mind about something. Ottilie's heart started beating very fast. She hadn't seen this coming. She didn't even understand where it came from.

She was caught between stepping towards Ned and turning away. The result was an awkward trip forward, and Ned stepped in to meet her. Ottilie found her feet, and without another thought she rose up onto her toes and kissed him.

It was like slipping beneath water. Safety and peril in the same instant. Slow but fleeting.

They parted in unison. Ned's eyes were smiling. Ottilie couldn't think. She sensed Gully looking between them and turned to him. Grinning, he said, 'What is happening right now?'

'Why does everyone keep doing that today!' said Leo from the field below. Ottilie was relieved to hear Scoot's responding laugh.

It took a fair bit of concentration to get down the ladder. She was giddy, weightless. Although meeting Ned's eye was terrifying, she was completely incapable of looking away. She couldn't quite feel it, but her feet hit the ground, and Ned and Gully followed after.

Ottilie hugged Scoot. 'You better still be breathing when this is over.' She gripped his upper arms, pressing her fingers into his flesh – a reminder that he was warm and walking.

'Promise,' he said.

Ottilie looked around. 'Where's Bill?'

Maeve climbed down the ladder from Maestro's empty pen. 'He's still in there. He's talking to the birds.' It was better that way. Bill had never been good at partings.

She squared her shoulders and looked up at the boundary walls. To anyone watching, it would look like they were fleeing – deserting Fiory in its hour of need. Gripping Nox's saddle, she mustered her courage. She pulled herself up and Gully followed behind her, quickly buckling in his legs. Ottilie nodded to Leo and together Nox and Maestro leapt into the air.

— 39 —

The Witch in the Wood

As they flew out over the trees, Ottilie did her best not to think about warding. She couldn't deny that the sick feeling and heavy-headedness were increasing.

A lone vorrigle beat its featherless wings, rising up from a webwood grove. Ottilie's head thumped, her stomach churning.

Leo shot it down and looked over at her. 'You can do better than that!' he barked, but she knew there was real concern behind it.

She looked back at Maeve, following behind. Should she have let Leo and Maeve handle this alone? Maybe she was just a burden. She might get them all killed … and now she'd dragged Gully into it, too.

In the midst of her worry, something occurred to her. Ottilie turned and called over the wind. 'Leo –' It came out with such purpose, but she wasn't sure how to say what she wanted to – how to get it across to him. Finally, she chose the only words that made sense to her. 'You're my brother.'

Leo scanned her face as if seeking signs the sickness had turned her mind. 'You know something I don't?'

She was determined that he hear it. 'You're a brother to me.'

'All right, Ott, calm down.'

'I mean it, Leo!'

To her surprise, Leo's face clouded. 'Stop it,' he snapped.

'Stop what?'

'Saying goodbye! You can ward. Just pull yourself together and believe it!' He glared at her. 'And I do – you too – I mean – me … you know what I mean!'

Gully shot down a flare that was circling below. The lizard-like beast splintered in a shower of sparks, shards of scale and bone scattering across the canopy. 'You two should really start paying attention!' he said, looking around for the others – flares almost always travelled in threes.

Ottilie felt a smile creep onto her face. The flare hadn't affected her. She didn't feel sick. She hadn't even noticed it.

'He's right, you just have to believe you can do it,' said Gully, in her ear. 'That's the trick. There has to be no doubt in your mind that you won't get sick – don't even think about it.'

'I don't know if I can do *no doubt*,' said Ottilie, her confidence already fading. No wonder Gully was so good at warding. He was the sort of kid who wanted to climb a tree in a thunderstorm. He didn't think things through. But she had to master it – there was no choice. If she couldn't ward, she would tumble off Nox into the blackened forest they had just begun to cover. She might not be good at dealing with doubt, but she was good at being strong-willed and determined. That had to help, surely?

The second and third flares were nowhere to be seen, which wasn't particularly comforting. In fact, they didn't encounter any more dredretches at all. Ottilie thought she knew why. There were no dredretches in the area because they were on their way to Fiory.

They had left Montie and Alba in the infirmary. Perhaps they should have put them somewhere more secure. And what of Bill? He wasn't human, so the dredretches shouldn't be interested in him. But a bloodbeast could be. She only hoped his hiding skills had improved.

Ottilie fixed her mind to the present as they approached the heart of the Withering Wood. There was no point in trying to sneak up on Whistler. After all, they had come to speak with her. It was eerie, this peaceful approach. Ottilie drew an arrow as Nox circled lower, but no attack came.

A figure became visible between the deadened branches: Whistler, all alone, watching them drift in, as softly and silently as smugglers mooring at midnight.

Nox and Maestro touched down by the philowood tree.

Whistler met Ottilie's eye, a look of surprised amusement on her face. 'I don't remember inviting you.' She glanced upwards, as if trying to remember something. 'Shouldn't you be flavouring a batch of tomb soup?'

'We got out,' said Ottilie, gripping her bow and arrow tighter.

'Bravo,' said Whistler. 'But shuffle off, would you? I've got an appointment.'

Ottilie risked taking her eyes off Whistler to scan the area. An appointment? With who? The king? But he was locked safely in Fiory.

That was when she spotted it. Set inside an old stump, a small copper cauldron was gently simmering, with faint spirals of violet steam trailing in the wrong direction – down rather than up.

Whistler liked answering questions. It seemed the safest way to begin.

'How did you make everyone sleep?' said Ottilie. She sensed movement behind Nox, and glanced back to see Maeve landing in a tree high above.

'Neat little trick, wasn't it?' said Whistler, leaning back against a branch of the philowood tree. 'You remember the pipe? Ordinary folk couldn't wield something so evil without a bit of protection.' She seemed to force a smile, and Ottilie wondered why. Even now, after everything Whistler had done, Ottilie couldn't believe that she truly looked down on people for not being able to enact evil. She was sure that smile was to cover something else. Something deep down … Could it be regret? *Everyone wants to be good, don't they?* Maeve had said that. It seemed Whistler had chosen a dark path and walked so far down it that she couldn't find the way back.

Whistler's eyes met hers. For a moment, Ottilie worried that she could read her thoughts – that she'd angered her. But she simply continued, 'Clever Seika had the pipe bound with the metal from a warding ring she'd forged herself – a device her coven had been experimenting with to protect people from the fendevil. It was the only way she could use the pipe without getting sick.'

Ottilie felt the weight of her own ring in her pocket.

'Afterwards, the witches made hundreds and hund-reds of rings, using the same protective charm,' said

Whistler, quite conversationally. 'They made as many as they could, wanting to safeguard as many people as possible if another fendevil ever emerged.

'The rings are all connected,' she went on. 'Kin, if you will. Made from the same metal, charmed by the same witches. That's how I was able to send my message to those who had displeased me. Change one, change them all – or most of them.' Her mouth twitched into a smile. 'I'm sure you noticed, I left you off that list. I'd have changed it after the business in the tomb, but I've been rather busy … and of course I thought I'd already dealt with you.'

It made sense now that the rings had been marked with a line from the lightning song. More clues from those ancient witches about the whereabouts of the pipe.

'Why does everyone think you made the rings if you didn't?' said Leo.

She smiled a cat's smile. 'White lie. I needed to make myself invaluable to the Hunt, so they would keep me around and let me do as I pleased.

'It's still thanks to me that they have them. The rings were hidden in the canyon caves – buried deep during the witch purge. I sought them out – studied the ancient texts and deciphered the clues. It was no easy task. Besides, they would never have used the rings if they knew they were made by witches.'

'How did you convince them you were just a mystic?' said Ottilie. 'Everyone knows mystics can't really do anything. How could they believe those rings weren't from witch magic?'

'It's amazing what people will believe when it's convenient for them,' said Whistler, her eyes falling on Leo.

'What has this got to do with making everyone sleep?' said Leo.

'Long story short: the rings are all linked, and the very first one was embedded in the pipe, in order to cancel out the toxicity of the sleepless witch's bones. That way, a good person could wield the pipe without getting poisoned,' said Whistler.

'So you made them sleep using the pipe?' said Ottilie.

'Clever, wasn't it?' said Whistler. 'Turns out it's not just the dredretches you can control with this thing.' She pulled the pipe from her pocket and clutched it in her sleeve. 'Bit of a design flaw, really.'

'Why make everyone sleep, then?' said Leo. 'Why didn't you just kill them all and be done with it?'

'My, my, such a violent mind for one so young!' She slowed her speech, as if she thought him dim-witted. 'The rings are linked by a *protective* charm, you half-grown thug. I can't do any harm with it.'

Leo seemed to have heard enough. Aiming an arrow, he said, 'Wake them up.'

Whistler didn't respond. There was a rustling all around. Ottilie's skin prickled. She would not get sick. She would not!

Maeve swooped lower, her eyes set ahead.

In a moment, Ottilie saw what the owl's eyes had caught first. Through the wilted trees, wylers prowled; a mass of fiery fur. Just behind them, Gracie was riding the white wyler, leading a lumbering shape with a rope.

← 40 →

The Afterlife

'Ah, Varrio,' said Whistler. 'Thank you for joining us.'

Ottilie breathed through her nausea and fixed her gaze on the king.

With bound hands, Varrio Sol stumbled through the muck. His skin was greener than before, and his eyes so wide his entire face seemed warped. He looked like a man just woken from a nightmare, not quite sure how to reach reality.

Ottilie forced her focus back to the pipe. If they could just get it away from Whistler, perhaps Maeve would be able to use it to wake everyone up.

Whistler looked at Gracie. 'Did he give you any trouble?'

Gracie cocked her head and made an impossible sound, like a calm shriek.

Ottilie's throat pulled tight. When was the last time she had heard Gracie speak? Was she even capable of it anymore? Whistler was a fiorn who could shift between her witch and winged forms. But whatever this binding was, whatever had been done to the bone singers, it was different. Had they known, when they chose to join Whistler – when they chose to be bound to bloodbeasts – had they known what they would become?

'Fennix,' snarled the king. 'Have this creature release me!' His eyes flicked to Gracie and away again, as if he couldn't bear to look at her.

Whistler waved her sleeve. 'Of course.'

Gracie's smile sent chills down Ottilie's spine. It was not an expression of mirth or joy. A human smile was beyond her now. As if the muscles still knew what to do, but the feeling behind it was gone. Just a creature baring its teeth.

Ottilie could see the king's hands shaking as Gracie gently unbound his wrists. Whistler had him now. While the dredretches tore down the Usklers' only defence against them, she was going to settle her score.

Whistler's eyes flashed not with magic, but deep human rage. 'Do you know what I'm standing on, Varrio?' She did not wait for an answer. 'I'm standing on Maia.'

The king blanched. 'What are you talking about?' he hissed.

'Forgotten her so soon?' said Whistler.

Ottilie felt the air liven, curling around her and invading her insides with the scent of the Withering Wood. She coughed and, behind her, Gully gagged, but Whistler did not seem to notice.

'Of course, you were busy,' she said. 'I heard you had the second one trampled by a horse ... smart to go for something so different to the first.'

She didn't know. Whistler didn't know that the king's second daughter still lived, that she'd met her. What she longed for had been under her nose all this time. She'd looked for the wrong thing.

When she'd first joined the Hunt, Ottilie had lied about who she was. Her deception had caught Whistler's attention. So had Maeve's isolation and power. Gracie's cruelty. Despite everything, despite believing herself a champion of the mistreated, the unwanted, Whistler had overlooked Skip.

'That was an accident,' said the king. 'Beyond my control.' He lurched, as if about to be sick. 'As was Maia's illness,' he managed to splutter.

The moment he spoke her name, the deadened leaves began to rustle and a hot wind whipped up.

'Get on with it!' croaked the king, clutching at his throat. 'You brought me out here to kill me. So *do it*.'

Whistler winked at Gracie, who whipped out her knives, spun them in her palms and lunged at the king.

Varrio squealed and fell to his knees. 'No, please! *Spare me.* I'LL DO ANYTHING!'

'There's my coward,' said Whistler. 'Don't worry, Varrio. I'm not going to kill you. Quite the opposite.'

His eyes fell on the cauldron, and for a moment the cheery bubbling was all Ottilie could hear.

'I thought about how to punish you for a very long time,' said Whistler. 'At first I thought death a good option ... especially if you ended up down there.' She dug her heel into the festering soil. 'Facing eternal torment.' She clicked her tongue. 'But that's the trouble. We can't be sure about what comes next. No-one really knows what happens after death ... where we go. It could be nothing at all – oblivion – far too good for you. But then I thought, *eternal torment* sounds quite good, doesn't it?'

With a pop and a snap, Maeve was a girl again, standing between Nox and Maestro. Ottilie tried to catch her eye. Why had she changed?

Whistler didn't acknowledge the disturbance. She merely gazed fondly at Gracie's wylers, then waved a sleeve over the bubbling cauldron. 'I can't reliably send you to a world of endless pain and violence, but after seeing the hell my devil of a father wreaked upon the Laklands ... I realised I could bring it to *you.*'

Ottilie was stunned. This was not at all what they had expected. Whistler wasn't going to make herself sleepless – she was going to do it to the king!

'And here's the best part,' said Whistler, pointing the pipe at the cauldron. 'It's a second-hand sleeplessness – a slightly watered-down version.' A gleeful smile stretched across her face. 'You'll live forever, but you won't be unbreakable. You'll break. I'll break you myself. You'll mend over and over ...'

Varrio's face was twitching with fear. He spat on the ground. 'You're *old*, witch! You won't live forever.'

'Do you know how I extended my life?' said Whistler. There was a crack and flash as Whistler whipped into the winged beast and, in a blink, shifted back. 'Dredretches don't die of old age. I'll live until I choose to end it with a bit of salt-forged steel, but *you* ... I'll make sure I do something really special with you before I go. I haven't worked it out yet ... but I've got an eternity to come up with that plan.'

The potion flickered to a bright, shining white.

'Look at that,' said Whistler. 'Tea's ready.' She hovered the pipe above the bubbling potion.

Ottilie's heart hammered. She couldn't let her drop it in. What if it was the only way to wake everyone up? She felt Maeve looking at her. Her bright eyes flitted from Ottilie to the king, and Ottilie understood. She drew back her bow string, not aiming at Whistler, but at the king. 'Wake them up,' she said.

Whistler didn't even bother to look at her.

Leo drew an arrow as well, and behind her, Ottilie felt Gully do the same. Maeve stood unarmed but frozen with focus, staring at the king.

'Ottilie, don't be slow,' said Whistler, finally turning to face her. 'How many times have I stopped your arrows?'

Gully changed his aim to Gracie, and Leo to Whistler herself.

'You can't stop all of them at once,' said Ottilie, not sure that was actually true.

But Whistler hesitated. She took them all in, her eyes settling on Maeve. Three arrows and a witch against her – it was a gamble. Ottilie had to believe she would not risk losing the king. Whistler had not waited all this time to have her revenge snatched from her at the final second.

'Wake them up,' said Ottilie, pulling back further on her string.

Whistler smiled and raised the pipe to her lips.

Ottilie tensed as a strange song surfaced. Like the call of something ancient far below, slithering through cracks in the world. Was this it? Was she waking them?

No. It was too easy.

Ottilie sensed them before they came, but the sickness was bearable. The song seemed to sharpen as, slowly, the dark shadows of dredretches pressed in from all sides. They were calmer than Ottilie had ever seen them, drifting as if in a dream.

'That's not what she asked,' said Leo through gritted teeth, his arrow still pointed at Whistler.

'It doesn't matter how many you call,' said Ottilie, her eyes fixed on the king. She could feel the sickness beginning to sink in. 'I'm a good shot.'

Whistler didn't respond. Ottilie's eyes flicked to her and she saw Whistler's thoughts flying about. She was weighing the risk.

Finally, Whistler's face hardened and she blew into the pipe once more. A high-pitched whistle pierced the air. Ottilie twitched and yearned to cover her ears, but kept her arrow pointed at the king.

The song seemed to cut out mid-note, and Ottilie felt a strange scraping and grinding in her teeth.

'They're awake,' said Whistler, coldly.

Ottilie would not celebrate, not yet. There was only one way to test it. She nudged Gully's foot and felt him shift his aim to the king.

She took her ring out of her pocket and, with a slight hesitation, slipped it onto her thumb. The relief was immediate. With the burden of warding lifted, Ottilie sighed, and remained entirely awake.

Whistler flipped back her sleeve, revealing her damaged hand. With a twirl of her wrist, the threads of Seika's ring pulled off the pipe like a pinched spider's web. Whistler flicked out her fingers and the shiny strands sprang from her skin like water. Then, causing a tiny splash, she dropped the pipe into the cauldron.

Ottilie was lost now. What was the right thing to do? Should they try to escape? Go back to help at Fiory?

The potion turned jet black. There was a sound like lightning striking rock as the cylinder of bone was broken apart. Great spirals of thick smoke billowed from the cauldron. Whistler waved her hand over it. A glass vial appeared from beneath her sleeve and filled slowly to the brim with shimmering black.

Ottilie stared. There it was: the remains of the sleepless witch. Transfigured again. No longer breathing bones, but liquid – a perennial punishment for the king.

Whistler seemed finished with conversation. She had no more mysteries, no more speeches. She stoppered the vial and smiled a triumphant smile. Looking at Ottilie one last time, her eyes flashed black.

Growls rolled in, shrieks cut the air, and from all around the dredretches attacked.

← 41 →

The Final Flight

A jivvie dived at Ottilie. She shot it down in an instant. Gully was struggling with something behind her. She turned to see him undoing the last buckle and leaping off Nox.

'What are you doing?'

'I'm better down here.'

'No, there are too many!'

There was no time to argue. Ottilie fired arrow after arrow and gripped hard as Nox ducked and weaved, swiping scales and cleaving bone. More and more dredretches were prowling out of the festering forest. Gracie was beside the king. Her proximity must have been protecting him, the same way Ottilie had shielded Leo against the squails.

Whistler was by the philowood tree, watching the king's face as he stood frozen, terror twisting his features. This might be the first time Varrio Sol had seen what his huntsmen were truly up against.

Ottilie didn't know how they were going to get out of this. It would take a miracle. The winged dredretches circled above, blocking their escape. Maeve shifted and soared up to meet them, but she was only one owl.

All around, the wilted trees were crawling with fanged pobes, yickers, cleavers, even knopoes. Beneath it all, Whistler was holding the vial.

'This is your future, Varrio!' she called above the clamour. 'What do you think of it?'

Maeve tore a jivvie to tatters, the struggle drawing her closer to Gracie. Gracie looked up with interest. Her mouth twitched as she twirled her knife and flung it right at Maeve.

Ottilie froze as Maeve tilted, the blade shaving the very tip of a feather.

Gracie Moravec was truly gone. She had never, not once in all this time, attacked Maeve. But now, it seemed that final scrap of humanity had been sucked into the dark.

Maeve let out a pained shriek and Ottilie knew it was not because she had been physically hurt.

The mass of monsters thickened and Ottilie could not see Gracie or the king through the swarm of claws and wings. She was down to her very last arrow. Tucking it into Nox's saddle, she whipped her cutlass from her back.

A wyler snatched at her ankle and Gully sent it flying. 'Gully!' she cried. 'Get back up!'

But there was no way to escape. All they could do was fight. Ottilie just wanted him back in the saddle so they could be near each other when it ended.

The winged canopy drooped lower. They were going to be torn apart from all sides. Ottilie's fear threatened to overwhelm her, like chains snaking across her body, tugging her inward and down.

There was a great screech from above. Her head snapped up and, through a curtain of scales, shadow and wings, Ottilie saw the birds. They barrelled through the darkness, sending the dredretches flying in all directions. Hundreds of them – eagles, kites, owls of all kinds … every fierce bird she could think of – wove this way and that, cutting through the swarm, diving to pierce the dredretches' eyes, snatching ripperspitters, morgies and shanks and tearing them apart with their talons.

Ottilie's heart leapt. '*Bill*,' she said. Bill had sent in the birds.

Whistler shrieked with rage and Ottilie felt the change in the atmosphere. A jolt disrupting her pulse.

The darkness flashed, signalling her transformation, but in those seconds before it happened, Bill, bent at an impossible angle, leaned out from a branch of the philowood tree and snatched the vial right out of Whistler's hand.

The winged beast screeched with such thunderous wrath that Ottilie felt it in her bones. Whistler beat her wings, reducing the surrounding branches to dangling ends. She rose above Bill.

A morgie leapt at Ottilie from below. Somewhere, she heard hooves thundering. Ottilie struck out with her cutlass. Whistler's talons were inches from Bill. The morgie fell. She didn't have time to reach her last arrow.

'Bill!' she cried out.

It couldn't happen. She couldn't lose him.

A spear shot through the air, tearing a hole right through Whistler's wing. She staggered, crushing a dozen dredretches in her path.

Ottilie's head whipped back. Astride a black horse, Ned galloped across and held out his arm to Gully. Gully climbed up behind him just as Echo and Warship tore into the clearing. Preddy and Skip had arrived.

'Where's Scoot?' Ottilie stood up in the saddle to look.

'He stayed back to help,' said Ned. 'The dredretches are attacking Fiory.'

With an ear-splitting shriek, Whistler righted herself and faced Bill once more.

Ottilie needed to draw her away – there was only one way to do it. 'Bill!' she hollered, holding out her hands.

From his perch on the branch, Bill threw her the vial. Whistler followed the motion with her hooked beak. Ottilie dug in her heels and, through the break made by the birds, Nox shot into the air.

Maestro followed, with Whistler after him, her wingbeat uneven.

Ottilie had never flown so fast in her life. She wanted Whistler far away from everyone she loved. She didn't even know where she was going until the edge of the Dawn Cliffs loomed. Whistler was gaining on them, her wing already starting to heal.

Maestro had overtaken Nox. Whistler was just behind her. Maestro circled back and Leo aimed arrow after arrow, but Whistler swayed and spiralled, dodging every one.

Ottilie still only had one arrow.

With a screech, Whistler shot at Nox. Nox rolled in the air, but there would be no escaping it. Leo tried to stop her. He fired more arrows and was so occupied with aiming that he didn't react quickly enough when Whistler changed direction and shot at Maestro instead.

Maestro lurched backwards and Whistler caught his wing with her claws. Blood sprayed and Ottilie cried out in horror as he tumbled down. The buckles around Leo's bad leg were the only thing keeping him in the saddle.

Maestro's roar of pain tore her heart in two. He couldn't right himself. He couldn't fly. Whistler dived, her talons tearing across his throat.

'No!' Leo cried.

Bright blood drenched Maestro's fur. He flailed and plummeted. One wing torn and bent, he rocked in the air and did all he could to slow his fall.

Whistler wasn't finished with him. She dived again, speeding towards the injured wingerslink.

There was so much blood. So much damage. Ottilie would not let Whistler touch him again! Gritting her teeth, she aimed her last arrow.

She couldn't think, couldn't see. If she missed, it was the end.

She wasn't even sure of releasing the arrow, but her fingers were free of it. She pulled her focus back and watched it fly true.

It felt like a story. She imagined words weaving the world. The river catching the light, like a serpent made of stars. The deathly quiet. The hunter's arrow piercing the winged beast's heart.

Whistler screeched. She twisted, plummeting down. She seemed bigger, more solid, all edges – jagged and sharp. She had never looked more wrong, more out of place. It was like a mighty piece of mountain falling from the sky.

She plunged into the Sol River. Water sprayed like shattered glass.

Ottilie felt all the air rush from her lungs. She nearly choked, or vomited, or was it a sob? She slumped forward as if whatever had been holding her up, keeping her functioning, was no longer there.

What had she done?

Was it over? Was everyone safe? It was so quick. Such a small thing – just an arrow and a target. Just another dredretch down – only it wasn't just another dredretch.

It was momentous. There should have been thunder, a whirlwind, the sky spitting light. But it was just the afternoon: calm weather, sharp sun, a lazy river … Ottilie in the air, out of arrows, tired and muddy but uninjured … Someone was injured … worse than injured …

Maestro was sprawled on the riverbank, Leo still lashed to the saddle.

She couldn't think straight. She guided Nox in beside him and held her breath as Nox sniffed at his wound. Maestro managed a broken growl. Red blood trailed down his beautiful silvery wings, pooling on the misery moss.

'Leo?' She leapt from Nox's back.

Leo was panting, struggling with the straps. With shaking hands, Ottilie helped him get free. He looked dazed. She didn't know if it was from the fall. If he was injured, he didn't say. Tears spilling, he limped around to face Maestro.

'He's breathing,' he said.

'Will he … is he …?'

'He's breathing.' It seemed to be all Leo could say. He pressed his hands against the gashes in Maestro's neck. Maestro dug his claws into the dirt, but didn't make a sound.

He should have growled. Why didn't he growl?

Something else drew her attention. Fearing the worst, Ottilie hurried to the edge of the water. There was a disturbance beneath the surface. Her muscles seemed to heat and reawaken. She clenched and unclenched her fist.

Whistler's great dark shape had disappeared. The water was swirling and, finally, with a shower like shooting stars, an enormous silver eagle soared out of the water and into the sky.

Healing water …

There was no dredretch left in her. This must have been Whistler's true shape, and Ottilie could not help but think her glorious.

The silver bird was losing height, dipping back and forth in the air. Ottilie didn't want to watch another winged thing go down, but there was nothing to be done. It landed a little way down the river on the opposite bank.

Ottilie peered over the softly flowing water at the silver bird mirroring Maestro. A strange rippling passed over it. Its feathers were falling out, its form thinning. It was ageing. Whistler's life was catching up with her. Finally, the movement calmed.

The silver eagle lay by the water's edge and never moved again.

42

Wreckage

Ottilie didn't know what to feel. Triumph? Sorrow? It all seemed wrong.

This should have been the end of the war. It seemed absurd that it was not. But the demise of the witch was not a magical lever that would set the world right.

Maestro was fading. The dredretches were attacking Fiory. It would take a great deal more than Whistler's death to fix what had been done. Ottilie remembered the patch of sickness by the slaver caves where the dredretches had risen on their own, and the thousands of monsters that the bone singers had led in from the Laklands.

Whistler had said the Usklers had rotted through. In her mind, there was no saving it. It was why she could do such terrible things. Perhaps this was why vengeance was all that mattered to her by the end. She had nothing to protect, nothing to fight for. But Ottilie saw things differently.

There was always something to fight for.

She turned back to Maestro. His head was tilted sideways, resting on the ground. He wasn't moving. Leo was by his side, still pressing his shaking hands to the wounds, blood seeping between his fingers.

He couldn't die. She wouldn't let him. She looked at the river. 'Leo.'

He turned to her, tears mingling with sweat and dredretch blood.

'It wasn't a spell that did it – so I think the water can heal him.'

Leo didn't seem able to speak. His face crumpled and he nodded, giving her leave to try.

Ottilie cupped her hands and tried to carry the water to Maestro, but what didn't drain out did little other than rinse off a layer of blood. He was too injured. The cuts were too deep. Still, she tried again and again.

A sob escaped.

Leo grabbed her wrist. 'Stop,' he croaked.

She shook her head, throat too swollen to speak.

Maestro shuddered and let out a long breath. They both froze, terrified that this was the end.

Still holding her wrist, Leo struggled to his feet. 'He needs to go all the way in.'

Ottilie turned back to the river. 'But ...'

Leo bent down, pressing his hand to the fur on Maestro's face. 'Get up,' he whispered. 'Maestro, get up. Get up!'

Maestro shifted his head. Leo ran a hand along his leg. 'Get up.'

Maestro's shoulders stirred. He was trying. He flipped a paw, pad down.

'You can do it,' said Ottilie.

He rolled his weight and shuddered again. With a huff, he seemed to press further into the ground.

Nox slunk forwards, her ears pressed back. Maestro managed a soft rumble, warning her not to come closer, but Nox ignored it. Shoving past Leo, she clamped her jaws on the scruff of his neck and strained, trying to pull him upright.

Ottilie held her breath. Leo grabbed her shoulder, as if losing his balance.

Maestro shifted his legs and with an agonised snarl he fought to his feet.

If she wasn't holding Leo up, Ottilie might have fallen to her knees.

Maestro was too tall; Nox had to release him. She withdrew, head low, staring intently. Maestro's jaw hung loose, his fangs dripping with blood. Leo approached with outstretched hands. Maestro sniffed in his direction and tucked in his good wing, his injured one hanging out at an odd angle.

Leo backed slowly towards the riverbank. He stepped into the water and it rushed over his boots, but he kept his balance, backing further and further, whistling for Maestro to come.

The wingerslink looked like he wanted to tear Leo's head off, but, slowly, shaking with every step, he followed. Finally, chest-deep, Leo had to hold onto the hulking wingerslink to keep his footing in the current. He coaxed Maestro to lower himself, and gently began pouring water over his injured neck and wing.

Maestro shuddered and growled as dark steam spiralled from the wounds. It was working! He stepped deeper, almost completely submerged.

Ottilie felt the promise of a smile as Meastro leapt to the shallows and shook himself out. Water sprayed like rubies and diamonds and Leo, glowing with relief, laughed out loud and pressed his face into Maestro's fur.

Nox and Maestro soared over the wetlands at the base of Fiory's hill. There were no stingers. No olligogs. The krippygrass stood still, the puddles perfect blue mirrors. Pure and undisturbed but for the echoes of horror that tumbled down the slope.

Ottilie tore her eyes from the ground, following the line of trees up to the fort on the hill. Even at a distance it was clear – the dredretches had breached the boundary walls.

As they approached, Ottilie could make out Montie on the parapets with a group of liberated bone singers. They were dropping chunks of rock from the broken wall onto monsters emerging from the wilderness.

Leo and Ottilie split apart, the battle calling them in different directions. He had given her half of his remaining stock of arrows, but it wasn't enough. Ottilie was down to one again as she landed, using it to shoot a wyler that was creeping up behind Captain Lyre.

His thin blade glinted in the glaring afternoon sun and his blue coat was spattered with black blood. It flared out as he spun and shot her a grim smile. Unable to return it, Ottilie jumped down from Nox's back and hurried straight for the weapons stored in a bunker behind him.

'I'll guard for you,' he said as Ottilie threw open the hatch and jumped inside.

'I thought you were at Arko?' she called to him.

'I was on my way. But then the wagoner and one of my guards fell asleep.'

Of course, she thought, as she stuffed her quiver with arrows. Captain Lyre was a Sol – he would have been immune.

'I knew something big must be happening, so I left the other guards to watch over them, took one of their horses and came straight back to Fiory. Almost as soon as I got here, everyone was waking up.'

'We made Whistler wake them.' She climbed out of the bunker. 'She's dead,' she added with a frown. It felt so strange to say. Whistler, who was behind all this violence, was gone, but the damage was too deep for her absence to mend.

Captain Lyre blinked at the news. 'What of Varrio?'

'I don't know.'

Ottilie turned to see Ramona galloping past on Billow. A shank somersaulted by, its narrow body curled into a wheel, spines poised to spear skin. Alba jumped out from around the corner. She tripped up the shank and pinned it with a knife.

Ottilie strapped on her weapons and scanned the upper grounds for any sign of the rest of her friends. She didn't have long to look. A pack of lycoats prowled across the grass, their shell-like armour catching the light. Ottilie readied her arrows but needn't have bothered. Nox pounced, sending three flying with one swipe of her claws, and from behind the pack, Scoot and Gully advanced, seeking out the monsters' weak spots with an accuracy that awed her.

Behind Ottilie, Captain Lyre battled an oxie as if he were in a fencing match – glowing antlers against gleaming blade. Nox was occupied in the air with a trick of flares and Ottilie fought her way eastward on the ground with Gully and Scoot.

She found Skip with Fawn and the rest of the Devil-Slayers, fighting their way up the hill towards the training yards. Skip twirled her spear, knocking back a scorver. Toxic gloop sprayed from greyish skin as its barbed back pierced the mud. Four rows of teeth were visible in its lolling mouth, and those yellow fangs fell like melting icicles as the scorver split into shadow and bone.

There was a great bellow from behind. Hot air whipped Ottilie's hair and the hill seemed to tremble as a barrogaul thumped to the ground like a boulder. Tucking in its scaly wings, it bared its sabre-fangs and lunged. Ottilie had to dive and roll down the slope. Steadying her fall, she choked on her fear as the barrogaul braced, humpback rising, black fur prickling, and fixed its bloody eyes on Gully.

Gully sliced a yicker clean in half and raised his cutlass to face the barrogaul towering above. Ottilie struggled to her feet and fired an arrow up the hill.

It pierced the beast's neck, but was little more than a splinter. She nocked another arrow, but it was going to be too late.

Its muscles rolled. It was about to spring. Gully's eyes widened. There was no time for escape.

But then the beast shuddered, and out boomed a broken roar as its back leg collapsed. Murphy Graves ducked out from behind it, spinning knives in his palms. Ottilie drew another arrow and fired, piercing its blood-red eye.

Murphy shot her a half smile, tucked one knife away, and gripped Gully's arm. 'Close one.'

'Thank you,' said Gully, as the barrogaul came apart at his feet.

There was barely time for a breath.

Penguin bolted past with three other shepherds and Ottilie spotted Ned over by Floodwood, a pack of wylers backing him towards the trees.

She whipped out her cutlass and looked around in horror. Where was Gracie? She must be near. Sure enough, the white wyler prowled out from between the trees, Gracie just behind.

Ned was trapped between the pack and the bloodbeast.

Ottilie's heart was in her throat. She, Gully, Murphy and Scoot bolted towards Ned as the pack moved in, black fangs bared.

The white wyler bent to spring, but just as it pounced a great pale shape shot out of the sky. Maestro dipped low. Ned grabbed Leo's outstretched arm and swung up behind him.

Ottilie clutched her side, winded with relief.

She, Gully, Murphy and Scoot met the pack of wylers, with Skip and the Devil-Slayers just a beat behind. For once, the wylers were outnumbered. They were falling one by one. Ottilie swung her cutlass, a wyler thumped to the ground, and she looked up to see Scoot running at Gracie.

Baring her teeth, Gracie drew two familiar knives: one that Leo had given her, and one she'd taken from Scoot's guardian, Bayo Amadory.

Ottilie couldn't tear her eyes away. Scoot swung his cutlass, clashing with her knives. The clatter of blades cut through the wylers' yowls.

Scoot was staggering, exhausted, but fighting hard. He jumped backwards and swung low, catching Gracie off-guard just long enough to knock Bayo's knife from her hand. He let out a triumphant, 'HA!'

Gracie's eyes flashed, first merely with rage, and then brighter, burning beyond red to Whistler's impossible black light.

She stepped back from Scoot. He looked confused.

Ottilie saw it coming before he did. 'SCOOT!'

The white wyler pounced.

Ottilie's heart stopped.

Scoot ducked low, and Hero leapt over his head. The leopard shepherd knocked the white wyler out of the air, pinned it to the ground, and tore into its throat with a guttural growl.

Gracie shrieked and stumbled. Nothing touched her. She just went down – like a child tripping in the mud.

She and the white wyler didn't crumble like the other dredretches. Gracie hit the ground in one piece, and her skin seemed to burn and then blacken like a log in a dying fire.

43

The Song

The wylers scattered, no longer a united force, and the Devil-Slayers picked them off one by one. Ned and Leo were on the ground, retrieving arrows from piles of bone. Scoot was gripping his ribs, his strength nearly spent. Beyond them, Murphy and a group of huntsmen were beating back a horde of horrahogs.

Ottilie didn't know what they were going to do. The dredretches were relentless. There was no-one left to control them, to pull them out if their numbers were depleting. They would simply attack and attack until the end. But there were too many of them. The huntsmen couldn't win.

'Ottilie!'

She turned. It was Alba, calling from further into Floodwood. She beckoned Ottilie over. Ned followed and Leo and Skip hurried after him.

Maeve was waiting for them beneath the twisted trunk of a viperspine tree.

The moment she set eyes upon Maeve, Ottilie's hand flew to her mouth. '*Bill?*' she hissed through her fingers. There hadn't been a second to think, and she realised she didn't know what had happened to him.

Maeve offered a small smile and pointed upwards. Bill was in the branches, clinging on for dear life. 'He's a bit distressed,' she said. 'He didn't take well to riding on the back of Skip's horse.'

'She rides *fast*,' said Bill.

Ottilie watched him twisting his hands around a scaly branch, and released the breath she hadn't realised she was holding.

'I've had an idea,' said Alba urgently. 'Do you still have that vial?'

Ottilie nodded. She had completely forgotten that she had that horrible potion with her. She'd been carrying the sleepless witch around in her pocket.

'Is anybody good at carving?' said Alba. 'Wood,' she added, in response to their confused silence.

'I am,' said Ned. 'But what … is now really the time?'

'I need you to make something that makes a sound,' said Alba. 'Just a whistle is fine. Quick as you can.'

Ottilie caught a glint of amusement in his tired eyes. 'All right,' he said. And, asking no questions, he cut a fat twig off the nearest branch, removed the smallest knife strapped to his forearm, and got to work.

'So ... what's happening?' said Ottilie, sliding down against the trunk of a tree. She regretted it as soon as she pressed her back to the bark. The full weight of her exhaustion settled upon her like layers of thick mud.

'We're making, sort of ... a new pipe,' said Alba. 'Maeve thinks she can use Whistler's potion to form ... or *remake* something to control the dredretches.'

Ottilie tried to smile. She was too tired to feel impressed. Her mind was slow, her focus slipping. It was a strange thing, sitting on the edge of a battle, watching Ned carve a whistle.

Skip cleared her throat, staring between the stationary figures. 'This is very clever and everything,' she said. 'But if I'm not needed ...' She waved vaguely back towards the action.

'What she said,' said Leo, reaching for his bow.

There was a ghastly shriek from the skies and an enormous shape passed overhead.

Leo ducked down next to Ned. 'Nice whittling, mate,' he said, gripping his arm. 'Might want to hurry up there.'

Ned's expression danced between irritation and amusement, but he stayed focused on his work and didn't respond. He rested the twig on a damp log and began knocking on the surface of the bark.

Leo and Skip left Floodwood, but Ottilie stayed – partly because she was so tired she wasn't sure she could move, but mostly because she knew exactly what to do with the whistle Ned was carving – and it had to be a flyer to do it.

Finally, Ned finished. It looked like a chipped twig, but he blew into the end and a shrill whistle sounded.

'Perfect,' said Maeve, taking it from him. She lay it flat on her palm. For a moment nothing happened, but with her exhale, the whistle lifted up to hover in mid-air. Maeve carefully unstoppered the vial and tipped the dark, shimmering contents over the wood. It was not quite liquid – more like vapour or smoke, but weighted.

Maeve's eyes flicked back and forth under her eyelids and her hands shook as dark tendrils curled around the twig, slithering through the gaps Ned had carved and settling into veins of deepest black.

With a shaky breath, Maeve opened her eyes and said, 'Do you have your ring?'

Ottilie slipped it from her thumb and passed it over. She remembered Whistler saying no-one could wield something so evil without protection.

Maeve held the ring in one hand and the pipe in the other, closing her eyes. Nothing happened.

There was yelling far off. A mord bellowed. Ottilie heard the crack and rumble of stone as another piece of the wall tumbled down. Her heart beat faster.

'Maeve?' she said, trying not to sound impatient.

'It's not working!' said Maeve, clenching her fist over Ottilie's ring.

Ottilie spotted glowing eyes in the forest behind them. She could hear growls and hissing and thundering hooves. Overhead, she caught the unforgettable shriek of a kappabak, like a thousand bats all screeching at once.

Ottilie got to her feet. She, Ned and Alba gripped their weapons.

Maeve closed her eyes again.

'Maeve, we have to get out of here!' said Ottilie.

Above them, Bill disappeared higher up the tree. Ottilie watched his webbed foot slip behind the fish-scale leaves, his pale fur catching the trapped light. She wondered if it would be the last she would ever see of him. Blinking, she banished the thought and reached for the whistle, but Maeve snatched it away.

'No-one should use it like this. I don't know what will happen,' she said, her eyes wild.

Ottilie understood, but there was nothing to be done. 'I'll wear my ring,' she said. 'It might help.'

'What are you talking about?' said Ned, looking between them.

But Ottilie didn't explain. There was no time to argue. Something jumped out of the undergrowth and Ned gripped his knife and dived.

Ottilie grabbed the whistle and, this time, Maeve didn't stop her.

Whistler had wanted to punish the king. Everyone else was just collateral damage. But the dredretches … Voilies had said it, when they were training for the fledgling trials: *it is their primary instinct to attempt to tear us apart*. Monsters from the underworld, called to the surface by acts of true evil. Their only purpose: to destroy, to rip out hearts.

It had to end.

Ottilie lifted her fingers to her lips and whistled loudly for Nox. Maeve stepped back, offering a blink that Ottilie knew meant, *good luck*. Alba's wide eyes had filled with tears. Ottilie hugged her and whispered, 'You're a genius,' before hurrying out of Floodwood.

The wingerslink appeared from beyond a turret and landed with a great spraying of mud. Ottilie leapt into the saddle, lifted the whistle to her lips and blew.

Pain flared, like ashes flicked in her face. It was wrong. She felt sick all the way to the tips of her fingers, which twitched on the whistle, aching to drop it.

The sound that came out was not the thin squeal Ned had made, but the otherworldly song of the dredretches. It wasn't loud, but it thrummed through her veins, filling her head and weaving in and out of a dance with her breath. Above the beat, air shrieked and scraped like claws on steel.

They flew south, across the lower grounds and over the boundary wall. Ottilie didn't need to look. She blew again and could feel them following. They were tethered to her by the song. She felt stretched and weighted, as if she might crack open and leak the sickness into the sky.

They passed between snowy peaks and veils of mountain mist stained blossom-pink. Nox settled on the edge of the cliffs looking out over the sea. The sun was sinking low in the west. Squinting against the golden spears, Ottilie blew again into the whistle. The pain worsened. She felt unsteady in the saddle, but held herself upright.

They were gathering around her. She could see their shadows out of the corner of her eye. Ottilie fixed her foggy gaze upon the sea, watching the water darken to midnight as dusk folded in.

She tore her eyes from the ocean and twisted to watch them come, like distorted shadows crawling, flying and slithering along the coast, across pebbled beaches and towards the edge of the cliff. They were as quick as ever, but absent somehow – lost in a dreamy trance.

She waited until the approaching numbers thinned to near nothing. She knew it could not be all of them. Some were slower, or perhaps too far away to hear the call. She shut her eyes and prayed that this would work. It had to work. She blew again, nudging Nox to leap.

Nox arced over the edge of the cliff, plummeting towards the crashing waves. It felt like freefalling. Ottilie clutched the saddle, clinging on for dear life. Air roared in her ears. Nox spread her wings wide and pulled out of the dive a whisker from the dark sea.

Ottilie gasped and flattened forwards as Nox shot upwards and curled in a vast circle to face the beasts behind. She stared at the clifftop, transfixed by the dark shapes tumbling over the edge.

Ottilie felt a tug and slipped into blackness. A strange knowing came over her. She had more control because the whistle was not limited by the protective charm. She could reach more of them – call them into the waves from far away.

She cast out her sight and saw them entering the ocean over the cliffs at Richter and Jungle Bay. Ottilie didn't know if she was witnessing or commanding, but felt sure it would come to pass.

She blew the whistle once more and this time felt a dreadful lightness. She seemed to disconnect from her own body, but she could still feel *them* … Step by step they entered the ocean: some slipping in from the beaches, some leaping from the cliffs. Few of the winged dredretches took flight. Most just dropped into the sea, lost in the call of the song.

A scattering of jagged shapes approached in the air, drifting in like visible nightmares. Nox circled and swept low, her claws dragging in the water, and behind, low over the salty sea, the dredretches began to flail. They tipped and dragged. The waves tossed and snatched, tearing them from the sky.

Twilight veiled the coastline, but Ottilie knew there were more to come. She lifted the whistle, but it was a struggle to hold it steady. The sickness had her.

Nox flew higher again, circling back towards land. Ottilie's head spun. Something seemed to close around her throat. Her shoulders shuddered and her neck bent under the weight of her skull. Her head lolled. She felt the whistle slip from her grip and plummet into the waves.

Nox growled. Ottilie heard it distantly, and somewhere deep down she knew it was because of her. The wingerslink lost height. Ottilie was slipping sideways. Nox was speeding towards land. There was still ocean below – she could feel its salty breath.

Ottilie tipped and tumbled down, sinking beneath the waves.

She couldn't see, couldn't breathe.
Something gripped her in its jaws.
A searing pain in her shoulder.
Everything was black.

44

To Sleep

The swamp creatures were busy. Ottilie watched them going about their business. Little brown crawlers with spines down their backs, grey paddlers with horns, and something bigger, quieter, slipping in and out of the lights down in the deep. She fixed her grip on the damp branch and leaned further, trying to make out its shape.

Rain was bucketing down. It was so loud and yet she was completely dry. The swamp waters were smooth, undisturbed but for the quiet ripples pushed by gentle feet. Ottilie stared down into the water. In the windows between algae she could usually see her reflection. But there was nothing.

She blinked. The swamp was gone. There was only darkness. Darkness and heavy rain.

'Ottilie?'

Someone was speaking from far away.

'I think she's waking up!' said a familiar voice.

Someone was gripping her arm.

Slowly, as if pushing through thinning fog, Ottilie could see his shape. Gully was at her side.

'Careful! Watch her shoulder!' said Leo's voice.

Her vision sharpened, her awareness with it. Her right shoulder ached as if she'd been run through with a spear. She felt over it with her opposite hand. The whole area was padded and bandaged.

Ottilie squinted at Leo. He was sitting in a chair on the other side of the bed.

'Nox,' said Leo, in explanation.

'She fished you out of the water,' said Gully.

'And nearly ate you by accident,' said Scoot, from across the room.

Ottilie blinked at him. They were in the infirmary.

'She just gripped a bit too hard with her teeth,' said Gully. He ran his hand up and down his own arm. 'They say it didn't mess anything up. It'll just take a while to heal.'

Ottilie rubbed her eyes. 'What happened?'

'You poisoned yourself with an evil whistle and fell into the sea,' said Scoot.

'That's right,' said Ottilie. Slowly, it was coming back to her. 'When … ?'

'A bit over a week ago,' said Gully. 'We didn't know if you were going to wake up.' She tried to sit up, but her shoulder protested. 'A week? What happened after? Are the dredret– is everyone …'

Leo shifted in his seat. 'We lost some people,' he said stiffly. 'But we're all …' He didn't seem able to finish the sentence. 'Someone should tell the others.' He jolted as if he had just thought of something. 'Gully, go get Ned! He'll be so mad he missed her waking up!'

Gully looked outraged. '*You* go and get Ned! I'm staying here.'

'I'll go tell everyone,' said Scoot, rolling his eyes.

He left the room and they sat in silence for a while. Ottilie's thoughts were sluggish. The shutters were closed above her head and the comforting rush of heavy rain threatened to lull her back to sleep. She didn't know what time of day it was. It could be the middle of the night. She found that she didn't care to ask. There were more pressing questions.

'What happened to the king?'

'He's gone,' said Leo. 'Not *gone* gone – just back to the Usklers.'

Ottilie tried again to pull herself up. Gully helped press her pillow back so that her head was nearly upright.

'They saved him in the Withering Wood,' said Gully. 'Maeve distracted Gracie and Preddy rode off with him.'

'So nothing's changed?' said Ottilie. She wasn't entirely sure what she meant by it.

'Oh no, a lot's changed,' said Leo. 'You do know you wiped out most of the dredretches, right? You remember that?'

Ottilie was about to answer when Ned and Penguin burst in, nearly bringing the partitions down with them. Ned was grinning from ear to ear. He lunged at the bed and Leo and Gully both cried, '*Careful!*' But he just bent down beside Gully, took her hand and said, 'Hello.'

Her fingers pressed into his, and she wondered if this would ever cease to take her breath away.

There were footsteps outside and Skip hurried in, followed closely by Preddy, Alba, Scoot and Maeve.

'You're back!' said Skip, leaping onto the end of her bed.

Alba looked a bit teary and Preddy was pale. Maeve's face was unreadable, but Ottilie could feel something in the air. Something like stepping from shade to sun on a frosty day. Relief and joy and just a hint of dread, as if clouds threatened to block out the sunlight again. Ottilie met her eye, silently saying that she felt the same.

She wished she wasn't the centre of everyone's attention. She looked between them all and realised with a swoop of dismay that someone was missing. 'Where's Bill?'

Maeve and Skip exchanged a look and Ottilie paled.

'He's fine,' said Ned, squeezing her hand. 'Don't worry. He's just –'

'Not here,' said Skip, screwing up her face.

'What do you mean? Why? Where is he?'

'It's Ramona's fault!' said Skip. 'She told Captain Lyre about him.'

'What?' said Ottilie. 'So they sent him away?'

'Well, sort of,' said Skip, very quickly. 'They had a long talk and Captain Lyre convinced him to sneak onto one of the king's carriages. He really wanted to stay and wait for you to wake up, but there wasn't enough time.'

'What? Why would he … ?'

Maeve stepped forward. 'Bill's going to spy for Captain Lyre. They didn't want to miss whatever happens when the king arrives back at All Kings' Hill – after all this, it's bound to be interesting.' Her eyes flicked around and she lowered her voice. 'They're – Captain Lyre and Ramona, and I'm guessing some others – they're planning to overthrow him. We're not supposed to know that, I don't think. But Bill told me, and they told Skip, obviously … because they want her to go east with them.'

Ottilie stared at Skip. 'You're leaving?'

Skip nodded.

'But ... so ... if they get rid of the king, then doesn't his first cousin step in?' She looked at Leo. 'Odilo Sol?'

'I think they want to stop that happening, too,' said Preddy, from behind Skip. 'They're planning to put Captain Lyre in as regent until she's older ... and ready.'

'She?' said Ottilie. Her eyes snapped to Skip. '*You*?'

'Let's not get ahead of ourselves,' said Skip. 'I said I'd go with them and they can teach me whatever they want, but we'll just see ...'

It was too much to wrap her mind around. Ottilie kept reliving the moment she had met her – Skip, surprising her in the springs and swinging a mop around, saying she wanted to hunt dredretches. Ottilie felt like her head was about to explode.

'But ... what's happening *here*? What about the rest of the dredretches? What's going on with the Hunt?'

'It's been a big week,' said Leo. 'There are some dredretches left. We don't know how many. But mostly in the Laklands, we think. There's still the Withering Wood and the patches of sickness, but we're not sure if dredretches can come through there without Whistler to call them out – like they can from that patch above the slaver caves.' His frown deepened. 'We're going to test what we can do with water from that spot below the Dawn Cliffs – see if it helps.

'And we think there are still some bone singers out there, so we're working on tracking them and their bloodbeasts down. The plan is to make the Narroway safe and then see what we can do about the Laklands.'

'The Hunt's changing,' said Skip. 'The king just left it in the hands of the directorate and ran as far east as he could. But Captain Lyre took control. It's the first part of his rebellion. He said that, as far as he's concerned, the Narroway's not under the king's rule. After everything that happened here, the king's not stupid enough to try to take it back – not right now, at least.'

Ottilie didn't know what to think. Penguin sniffed at her bedcovers, drawing her gaze. She stared down at Ned's arms, which were resting on the bed. His sleeves were rolled up and his star-shaped burns had finally begun to heal.

'Captain Lyre spent the whole week dismissing people,' said Ned. 'Edderfed is out. So are Yaist, Voilies, Kinney and Furdles … and that's just at Fiory. I don't know how many he threw out of Richter and Arko. Pretty big surprise to a lot of them that he's a Sol, but the confusion around that helped him take control. Plus, a lot of the adults aren't too keen on sticking around anyway – not after the dredretches attacked the stations. He's making Wrangler Morse the new Cardinal Conductor of Fiory.'

'And they've announced that the Hunt's voluntary,' said Scoot, with a grin. 'Anyone who wants to leave can go.'

'The pickings won't happen anymore,' said Ned. 'And eventually they're going to spread the word and let people come here to train. But they know recruiting is going to stir up trouble with the king, so they're going to wait a while.'

It was so much news, all at once. Ottilie felt dizzy. But she couldn't get past one thing. Looking at Skip, she said, 'I can't believe you're leaving.'

Skip cringed, and Ottilie got the sense she was missing something.

'It's not just Isla,' said Preddy. 'I'm joining them. I want to help.' He glanced at Alba.

Ottilie turned to her and said, 'Not you too?'

Alba nodded, her mouth drooping. 'I think I'll be of more use with them, and I want to help Skip.'

'But what about Montie?' said Ottilie.

'She's going to come too.'

Ottilie felt like her world was crashing down. Bill was already gone. Skip, Preddy, Alba and Montie were all going east to join the rebellion. She didn't know what to do. What did she even want? Her eyes flicked between them all, landing last on Leo. Could they all go? Bringing down Varrio Sol was a worthy cause.

Leo seemed to read her mind. He shook his head. She knew; of course he would not want to leave. He wanted to hunt dredretches. She didn't even need to ask Gully. Gully would want to stay too. But Scoot? Scoot had never seemed truly happy being part of the Hunt. She looked at him, raising her eyebrows in question.

'I'm staying. I want to clean up this mess,' he said, his jaw jutting out.

'Me too,' said Maeve. 'I think magic is needed here more than anywhere, and there's a lot of witch history in the Narroway – so much more to learn.'

Ottilie looked at Ned.

'I'm going home – once they can spare me,' he said.

Her face fell.

'Not for long,' he added. 'I want to see my aunt and my brother. But I'll come back.'

Ottilie felt pulled in every direction. She wanted to stay. She wanted to go east. She wanted to find Old Moss and Mr Parch. She even wanted to go and see Sunken Sweep – see anything, everything, fly Nox across the Usklers and see the land that they had saved. Further, even … Triptiquery and inland beyond, whatever was left of the Roving Empire. There was so much more out there.

But Gully was staying, so that was it, wasn't it? She would have to stay too. Or would she? She looked at him. He wasn't so small anymore. He was a champion of the Narroway Hunt. He could look after himself, and he wasn't alone. It wasn't just the two of them. Leo would be here, and Scoot and Maeve.

'You don't have to choose,' said Gully.

Ottilie fiddled absentmindedly with the bandages on her shoulder. Her stomach rumbled. She had not eaten in an entire week and was in no state to go anywhere or do anything.

For now, they were together. The rain grew louder and her weary head settled on a single thought: how miraculous it was to be safe and warm in bed.

She glanced at Gully, then let her eyes slide shut. It was true. She was free to go wherever she liked. Her world was so much bigger now. She could hunt dredretches, join a rebellion, explore as much as she wished.

She had wings.

THE END
of

THE
Narroway
TRILOGY

Acknowledgements

To everyone at Hardie Grant Egmont, I cannot thank you enough. Marisa, Penny and Emma, it has been an absolute pleasure working with you – thank you for everything. And a very big special thank you to Luna – I can't imagine how these books would have turned out without you! Thank you, too, to Haylee, Tye, Ella, and to everyone who helped Ottilie on her way.

Maike and Jess, this cover is breathtaking. I adore it. I am so grateful for your brilliant work across all three books.

Thank you to all the reviewers and bloggers who have been so kind, and to the librarians, teachers, booksellers and everyone who has talked about this series or passed it along.

A big thanks to Julia and Trish for becoming my unofficial distributors, and to the rest of my family for being so wonderfully supportive. I live for tales of 'uncley pride'.

To my sisters, I know I am a strange stony creature, undeserving of your warmth. Thank you for caring about this, and me, and everything.

Mum, thank you for doing all the things I tell you not to do – the compulsive buying, the chatting, the dropping into bookshops, libraries, and schools ... Dad, thank you for printing out covers and waiting patiently until you're allowed to read final drafts.

This series was a beast at times, but mid-battle a smile or a shoulder was always nearby. To my fantastic friends, I have no idea how I found you or why you stick around, I thank you all so very much.

Jack, thank you for spelling out titles on planes and forcing these books upon everyone you meet. I'm so grateful for your tireless encouragement. Carl, thank you for dealing with my doubts – you are so very good at letting in light. And Lu, you're the Bill to my Maeve and I could never have finished this thing without you.

About the Author

Originally from Taradale, Victoria, Rhiannon Williams is now a Sydney-based writer. She studied Creative Arts at university, has climbed Mt Kilimanjaro, and once accidentally set fire to her hair onstage. Her Ampersand Prize-winning debut novel, *Ottilie Colter and the Narroway Hunt*, was published in 2018 and has also been released in Germany and the Netherlands. In 2019 it was named a CBCA Notable Book, an Aurealis Awards finalist, and shortlisted for the Readings Children's Book Prize and the Speech Pathology Australia book awards.

IF YOU LOVED THE NARROWAY TRILOGY, CHECK OUT THE JANE DOE CHRONICLES BY JEREMY LACHLAN!

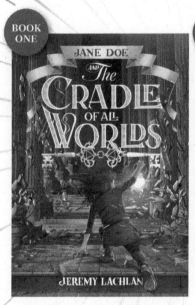

BOOK ONE

BOOK TWO

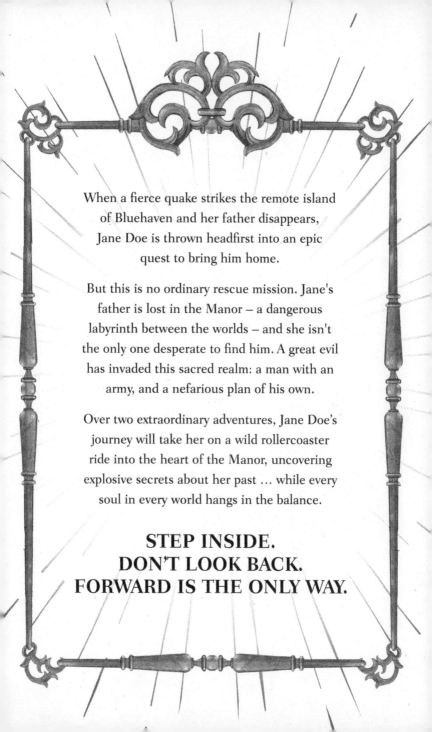

When a fierce quake strikes the remote island of Bluehaven and her father disappears, Jane Doe is thrown headfirst into an epic quest to bring him home.

But this is no ordinary rescue mission. Jane's father is lost in the Manor – a dangerous labyrinth between the worlds – and she isn't the only one desperate to find him. A great evil has invaded this sacred realm: a man with an army, and a nefarious plan of his own.

Over two extraordinary adventures, Jane Doe's journey will take her on a wild rollercoaster ride into the heart of the Manor, uncovering explosive secrets about her past … while every soul in every world hangs in the balance.

**STEP INSIDE.
DON'T LOOK BACK.
FORWARD IS THE ONLY WAY.**